DEVLIN

LIGHTHOUSE SECURITY INVESTIGATIONS
MONTANA

MARYANN JORDAN

Devlin (Lighthouse Security Investigations Montana) Copyright 2025

All rights reserved. No part of this book may be reproduced or transmitted in any form or by any means, electronic or mechanical, including photocopying, recording, or by any information storage and retrieval system without the written permission of the author, except where permitted by law.

If you are reading this book and did not purchase it, then you are reading an illegal pirated copy. If you would be concerned about working for no pay, then please respect the author's work! Make sure that you are only reading a copy that has been officially released by the author.

This book is a work of fiction. Names, characters, places, and incidents are either products of the author's imagination or are used fictitiously. Any resemblance to actual persons, living or dead, events, or locales is entirely coincidental.

Cover by: Graphics by Stacy

Cover photograph: Eric McKinney 612Covered Photography

ISBN ebook: 978-1-965847-14-5

ISBN print: 978-1-965847-15-2

❀ Formatted with Vellum

ABOUT THE AUTHOR

I am an avid reader of romance novels, often joking that I cut my teeth on historical romances. I have been reading and reviewing for years. In 2013, I finally gave in to the characters in my head, screaming for their story to be told. From these musings, my first novel, Emma's Home, The Fairfield Series, was born.

I was a high school counselor, having worked in education for thirty years. I live in Virginia, having also lived in four states and two foreign countries. I have been married to a wonderfully patient man for forty-three years. When writing, my dog or one of my cats can generally be found in the same room if not on my lap.

Please take the time to leave a review of this book. Feel free to contact me, especially if you enjoyed my book. I love to hear from readers!

Facebook

Join my Facebook group: Maryann Jordan's Protector Fans

Sign up for my emails by visiting my Website!

Website

Author's Note

Please remember that this is a work of fiction. I have lived in numerous states as well as overseas, but for the last thirty years have called Virginia my home. I often choose to use fictional city names with some geographical accuracies.

These fictionally named cities allow me to use my creativity and not feel constricted by attempting to accurately portray the areas.

It is my hope that my readers will allow me this creative license and understand my fictional world.

I also do quite a bit of research on my books and try to write on subjects with accuracy. There will always be points where creative license will be used in order to create scenes or plots.

All books have errors, no matter how many author, editors, proofers, and readers have looked at the manuscript. If the errors are minor and do not affect the story, please forgive and ignore. But, if you find errors that you deem necessary to report, please send me an email with your notations and do not try to report to Amazon.

Be kind to authors… we are human!
authormaryannjordan@gmail.com

1

UGANDA REFUGEE CAMP

Mia sat in the dimly lit office, the glow of her computer screen casting light across the cluttered desk. In the otherwise quiet night, the faint hum of the camp generator sounded out. She leaned back in her chair, her eyes burning from hours of poring over spreadsheets, trying to make sense of discrepancies in the food supply data. The last delivery for the evening had occurred, and most of her workers had left.

The sharp creak of the door hinge made her look up. Charlie, the ever-charming Australian, stood in the doorway, his golden hair catching the light, framing his tanned, surfer-boy face. His grin was as irreverent as ever. She could never decide if he was more rogue or rascal.

"I thought I saw your light on in here. What the hell are you doing? Everyone else is over in the dining hall. Someone got the satellite up so we can binge on TV series."

Mia allowed herself a small smile, the corners of her mouth tugging upward. Before she could respond, Charlie sauntered closer, his tone dropping into playful mischief.

"But if you're determined not to watch shows with us, you and I could head back to your place and binge on each other."

He leaned in, mockingly nibbling at her neck. Mia laughed and gave him a light shove. "Stop slobbering on me, Charlie!"

He straightened, feigning a wounded expression. "Mia, you're no fun."

Settling himself on the edge of her desk, Charlie glanced at the papers spread before her. "What are you doing, anyway?"

"Going through our food shipments for the past six months," she replied, her tone weary.

His eyebrows shot up. "Shit! Are we getting audited?"

"No, at least not more than the usual visits. It's just… things aren't adding up."

Charlie's expression softened, concern flickering in his blue eyes. "Girl, you know nothing ever adds up around here. You're lucky if the food arrives at all, let alone enough for everyone. The camp is huge. How can you possibly figure out where it's all going?"

Mia nodded, appreciating his concern but feeling the weight of responsibility. "I know. But I can't let something happen on my watch."

"You're amazing at what you do, Mia. The best food security officer I've worked with," he said sincerely. With a grin, he reached over and closed the file. "Now, come on. Be a good little girl and join us for some mindless shows."

Mia chuckled, shaking her head. "You go on. I'll join you as soon as I finish this."

Charlie stood, his grin morphing into a teasing smirk. "If you ever want to review anything privately or decide you can't stay away from me, you know where to find my room." He paused dramatically. "Oh! Maybe we should devise a secret knock so I know it's you."

Rolling her eyes, Mia leaned back in her chair. "How many secret knocks have you handed out to unsuspecting women determined to tame the outback Australian?"

"Damn, girl. You know me too well," he said with a mock sigh, spreading his hands in pretend defeat.

"Well enough to know I'm not coordinating anything with you in your bunk." She smirked.

"Your loss," he sang, tossing her a finger wave as he headed for the door. He turned and inclined his head toward her desk. "Seriously, Mia, put this to bed soon."

She nodded, then turned back to her screen as the door clicked shut behind him, her momentary amusement fading. Her brows knit as she traced the suspicious trail that hinted at missing food supplies. Someone, somewhere, was stealing from the camp.

Her stomach churned as her mind cycled through potential suspects: staff, volunteers, and even refugees coerced by external threats. The possibilities were endless. Usually, she'd bring concerns to Dr. München, the camp director. But this felt... bigger.

Mia shoved her chair back with a groan of frustration, standing abruptly. "Oh, fuck it. I need some air," she muttered. The night air greeted her as she stepped outside, a welcome reprieve from the stuffy office. The camp bustled with its usual evening rhythm. Children's laughter echoed faintly as they kicked a ball around in the dirt, their parents' voices calling them home for the night. The scent of roasted meat and spices wafted through the air, mingling with the aroma of the dusty roads and the outdoor firepits.

She leaned against the main building that housed the

camp's food intake. Her sense of responsibility was heavy, but it was also mixed with gratitude for being part of something so vital. The resilience of the refugees never ceased to humble her.

Hearing a noise, she greeted the roving guard with a nod and a warm smile. Stepping back inside, she bypassed the stairs to her office and walked into the large storage facility. Fewer workers were on the night shift, and she waved as she walked around. Inside, the lights overhead illuminated the neat rows of supplies. She moved methodically down the aisles, pulling back tarps and peering into wooden crates.

Staples like rice and beans formed the backbone of their rations. Camp members who cultivated small plots of land contributed vegetables to supplement these basics. Another section contained the perishable goods: root vegetables, eggs, and dried meats. She moved to the refrigerated containers, where precious stores of cheese and fresh produce were kept. Everything appeared as it should, matching her earlier inventory.

If someone is taking something, they're not doing it in broad daylight... too many eyes around. Her gaze drifted back toward the door, her mind lingering on the workers. She knew they were diligent, but desperation could make anyone vulnerable to corruption.

It's not from here. It must be at one of the smaller storage facilities, she concluded. Waving her hand to the others, her resolve hardened. Climbing into the Jeep she used, she decided to check the smaller storage sites dotted around the camp's villages.

The road ahead was lined with the simple homes of the camp's residents, made from corrugated metal, wood, mud, and thatched roofs. Families had already gathered inside for the night, though a few stragglers lingered. Men sat around campfires, their voices low and companionable. Mia waved as she passed, exchanging brief nods of acknowledgment.

The first village she visited was Bulit. Everything was quiet, with no sign of anything amiss. The village food distribution centers had a small number of night shift workers, all she recognized. She drove on to Mukando, then Kaoni, and Sweswe. Each village mirrored the last, settling in for the night with guards posted outside their storage facilities. They waved in recognition as she passed, their presence reassuring.

Her final stop was Kaborogota, the camp's northernmost village. By now, darkness had fully enveloped the area. The faint glow of the facility's exterior lights cast long shadows, creating an eerie stillness. Mia frowned as she approached, not seeing a roaming guard on duty.

Her unease deepened as she parked the Jeep and scanned her surroundings. The silence pressed against her, heavy and suffocating. A sudden noise to her left made her spin, her heart leaping into her throat. The young guard emerged from the shadows, his rifle slung casually over his shoulder as he fastened his belt.

Relief washed over her as she realized he must have been on a bathroom break. She chose not to comment, simply offering him a wave before restarting her engine. Driving back toward the heart of the camp, Mia chastised herself for venturing out alone. She'd always felt safe here, but the risks of inviting trouble, especially at night, were undeniable.

Once back in her office, she locked the door behind her and flipped on the light. Sitting at her desk, she powered up her computer, her earlier frustration now tempered by a renewed determination to uncover the truth. She opened her email and began typing a message to Margarethe

Gunther, her superior at the World Food Program. Margarethe would know what to do.

Once finished, she closed her laptop and glanced at the clock. The others would be far enough in their TV bingeing by now, and she had no desire to join them. The dusty path leading to her quarters stretched before her, lit by the faint glow of security lights. She strolled, the cool night air brushing against her skin.

Her room, a converted shipping container, was a stark reminder of the conditions in the camp. A single bed with a thin mattress was pushed into the back corner. Next to it was a nightstand with three drawers. A standing bureau was in the other corner, giving her a place to hang some clothes and store boots and underclothes in the bottom. A desk with a lamp and chair were just to the left of the doorway, her items stored in the various cubbies and drawers. A half bath with a sink and toilet was just to the right. She considered those a luxury, even if showers had to be taken at the staff bathrooms in a building nearby. She locked the door behind her and flipped the light switch, the fluorescent bulb buzzing faintly.

She changed into her pajamas and brushed her teeth. Looking into the mirror, she noted the faint lines around her eyes. Her body was leaner than ever with hard work and sometimes forgetting meals. Not wanting to continue to dissect her appearance, she flipped off the light and walked out of the bathroom.

Mia climbed into bed, pulled the mosquito netting around the bed, then slid under the covers. But sleep didn't come quickly. Her mind replayed the day's discoveries. And as usual, when she was worried about something, her thoughts then danced around memories she'd rather forget. When she finally drifted off, her dreams were fragmented, haunted by shadows of the past, long placed in the part of our soul where we stored what had hurt us the most.

Morning arrived too soon, and as she opened her eyes, exhaustion settled heavily in her chest. Today would bring answers or maybe just more questions. Either way, she had to be ready.

2

MONTANA

Devlin leaned back in his chair on the front porch, propping his feet on the wooden railing. The sprawling Montana mountains stretched across the horizon, bathed in hues of gold and crimson as the sun dipped lower. Sharing the tranquil view were two of his closest friends, Sisco Aguilar and Logan Bishop, men who had fought beside him during their SEAL days and were now coworkers in the private sector. Their relaxed postures mirrored his, boots resting on the rail, whiskey glasses in hand.

"Hey, San Fran," Devlin called out, a deep chuckle rumbling from his chest.

Sisco shook his head, rolling his eyes. "Honest to God, I have to say I'm probably one of the few former SEALs glad to give up their call sign when I became a civilian."

Logan glanced over with a crooked grin. "Who gave you that name?"

"Who do you think? That hard-ass commander at boot camp. He thought San Francisco was a fucking hoot."

Devlin smirked. "At least you were called Preacher."

Logan's grin widened as he looked toward Sisco, and they both said in unison, "But we both made a deal with the devil!"

Devlin shook his head, laughing. While on their team, Jim Devlin had been able to get just about anything they needed when they were on a mission—extra or better food, a specialized weapon, a vehicle repair, fixing the broken transmitter, or acquiring a state-of-the-art radio. Someone on the team once said that all it took was to make a deal with the devil, and Devlin could get it. Hence, his call sign was born, and he became known as Devil. "Preacher and Devil... what a team," he said, taking another sip. "You just have to know how to negotiate."

For a moment, the three men grew quiet. The lighthearted camaraderie gave way to the unspoken weight of shared memories. Devlin knew where their thoughts had drifted. For Logan and him, their final mission had been perilously close to their last in more ways than one.

"You know, Logan," Devlin said, breaking the silence. "I wouldn't be here if it wasn't for you."

Logan's gaze softened. "Neither of us would be here if it weren't for Sisco."

"Ain't it the truth," Devlin agreed, lifting his glass in acknowledgment. "But you're the one who came back for me. If you hadn't done that, Sisco wouldn't have had a body to work on."

He exhaled slowly, his thoughts pulling him back to that mission. The memory was vivid, burned into his mind like the scar on his chest. A stray bullet had found its mark, piercing just above the edge of his body armor. Dropping like a stone, he'd been sure his time was up. Blood poured from the wound, the pain searing and unrelenting.

While Devlin clutched his bloodied chest, Logan bent low and lifted his body over his shoulder. Logan was strong, but Devlin was built like an ox—tall, bulky, and muscular. Even in his pain, he knew he was a burden that might cost Logan his life by slowing him down. "Goddamn, you took a risk."

Logan's voice was quiet but firm. "I wasn't leaving you there."

"I could hear the blades of the bird and knew they were close."

"I was hanging out of the bird, ready to get you two when the fucking explosion hit," Sisco said, his voice hoarse.

Logan's knee had given out under the weight, sending both men crashing to the ground. They'd been close enough for Sisco to drag them into the helicopter, bloodied and battered. As the team medic, Sisco had worked desperately to stabilize Devlin. Most of the story was not remembered by him, only relived through Sisco and Logan's retelling of the harrowing helicopter flight to the nearest hospital.

The aftermath was brutal. Logan's knee was beyond repair, ending his SEAL career. Devlin's injuries had taken him out of the field. Sisco served another year before leaving the military, the three men scattering to separate civilian lives until fate and Logan's determination reunited them with an offer they couldn't refuse.

Logan had spent years in Montana, covertly working special ops while overtly rescuing stranded hikers and flying tourists in his helicopter. When Mace Hanover and Carson Dyer from Lighthouse Security Investigations approached him to open a Montana branch, he agreed, but only on the condition that he could recruit his own team.

Logan had tracked down Sisco in El Paso, working as a paramedic. Devlin was stunned when Logan's call revealed they were not only in the same state but close enough to meet. Devlin lived and worked on the Blackfeet Reservation, helping them acquire certain necessary materials while working with the Tribal Council. Without hesitation, he decided to join Logan's endeavor. Together, he and Sisco became the first employees of the Montana branch of Lighthouse Security Investigations, known as the Keepers.

"And now you all are dropping like flies, getting married and starting families," Devlin said with mock gruffness, though the warmth in his voice betrayed him. Logan's wife, Vivian, was a biologist he'd met during a mission in Alaska. Sisco had married Lenore, a teacher, and adopted her daughter, Evie.

"I heard you gave relationship advice to Landon and Noel," Sisco said, his eyes twinkling as he fought to keep from laughing.

"Hell, the awkward way they were trying and fucking failing at making conversation on the plane... I couldn't find my earbuds and knew if I had to listen to them during the whole flight, I'd throw myself out over the ocean!"

"So you can dish it out?" Logan laughed.

"Fuck yeah. I can give it, but I guess I'm shit at taking it."

Looking at his two friends as they shared whiskey with him, he saw they had a contented look about them, one he wasn't sure he would ever find. Another Keeper, Landon, had met his fiancée, Noel, on a mission that took him from Wyoming to the Caribbean. He snorted as he thought about the missions that ended in finding a spouse.

"A good woman makes all the difference, Devlin," Logan said.

Before Devlin could respond, Sisco added softly, "But then, you already know that."

The words hung in the air, heavy with unspoken meaning. Devlin's jaw tightened. His friends had been with him in the early days, having met the woman who had stolen his heart years earlier. They had also been with him during the days when he had blown the relationship out of hell. He'd had good intentions, but as they said, the road to hell was paved with good intentions.

He never meant for the evening to take a maudlin turn. Pushing back the memories, he grumbled, "Drink up, men. You've got wives and babes to get back to."

The others nodded as they tilted their heads and tossed back the whiskey. The sound of boots hitting the wooden deck resounded. They stood and walked into the kitchen. He watched as they walked to their vehicles, their headlights flooding the front of his house until they turned and headed down the road. Once their taillights were no longer visible, he went inside, secured his home, and poured another whiskey.

In truth, while he was finished going down memory lane with his friends, he was still consumed with thoughts of the past and not quite ready to let them go. He settled on his sofa but didn't turn on the television. The lamp cast a soft glow over the room, leaving much of the room in shadows, resembling his thoughts. Devlin sipped, letting the familiar peaty burn slide down his throat.

He leaned his head back against the sofa and inhaled deeply before letting out a soul-rumbling sigh. He was transported back to when he was sixteen years old. Already a big guy at six feet two inches, he played on the high school football team's offensive line. He wasn't a dumb jock—he put in time in the classroom as well as on the football field. But with his dark hair, which was just long enough to curl at the back and around his ears, and the muscles built on the weight machines and his parents' Kansas farm, it wasn't hard to see the admiring gazes from the teenage girls. They were interested in the brawn, not the brains.

He had almost lost his virginity to the seventeen-year-old head of the varsity cheerleaders. But he'd heard she was working through the first-string team, and he resented the idea of being another tinsel in her pom-pom. Of course, he'd taken a few ribbings from his friends, but when one dumbass accused him of being gay, his fist found its way against the guy's jaw. Devlin had an older cousin who had come out the year before, and he'd be damned if he was going to let somebody make a homophobic slur. It hadn't hurt his reputation—instead, it made him a bit of a legend. His parents kept him humble, but he knew he was a big man on campus, even at sixteen.

And all it took was a girl—a sweet, funny, passionately caring girl—to bring him to his knees.

The team was outside practicing on the football field when he heard a group shouting and chanting. Glancing over, he recognized one of the school's activist groups, often seen working on posters about saving whales, the Amazon rainforest, or the California redwoods. He rolled his eyes at first, amused by their zeal. But then, the principal and two police officers started striding toward them, stern determination etched into their faces.

Suddenly, one of the girls broke from the group and rushed onto the field. Before anyone could stop her, she wrapped a bicycle chain around the goalpost and locked herself to it. Devlin turned his full attention to her, his curiosity piqued. She held a sign aloft, protesting the cafeteria's use of styrofoam and plastic straws. Her voice was steady, and her chin lifted proudly in defiance. She wasn't screaming, but her presence demanded attention.

Laughter rippled through the players around him, but Devlin felt rooted to the spot. Pulled back in a long braid, her dark hair shimmered under the sun. Her slightly pointed ears and delicate features gave her an elfin appearance, like a character from *The Lord of the Rings*. Slender but curvy, she radiated a natural beauty that captivated him even from a distance.

As the principal and police approached her, Devlin's feet moved before his brain caught up. He closed the distance, stepping in front of her and placing himself between her and the authorities. His towering frame's shadow completely hid her safely behind him.

"Back off," he said quietly, his voice calm but firm. "She has a right to protest."

The principal's face turned an alarming shade of red as he sputtered, and the coach came barreling onto the field, yelling about his practice being interrupted and spouting threats about him being suspended from the next game. But Devlin didn't budge. He remained a solid wall of defense.

A light touch on his arm startled him. He glanced down to find her looking up at him, her eyes wide but steady.

"I don't want you to get in trouble," she whispered. Her fingers moved deftly as she unlocked the chain and let it fall to the ground. Then she turned, lifting her chin as she addressed the principal. "Our school isn't being environmentally proactive. I wanted to make a statement, and I think I have your attention now."

Her words were measured and resolute, but Devlin's gaze remained fixed on her. When she walked away with the principal, she glanced back over her shoulder, offering him a smile that shot straight through his chest. "Thank you," she mouthed.

The coach's barked orders barely registered as Devlin jogged to catch up with her. "I'm Jim," he said, touching her shoulder lightly. "Jim Devlin."

She smiled again, a blush rising to her cheeks. "It's nice to meet you, Jim. I'm Mia."

"Can I have your phone number? I want to make sure you get home safely and without further problems."

She peered deeply, then smiled and nodded. She rattled off her phone number before the principal ushered her away. Devlin memorized it instantly.

He watched her disappear into the school, his heart hammering in his chest. The coach's threats fell on deaf ears as he returned to practice with a goofy grin plastered across his face.

Devlin hadn't understood then what had struck him. But now, all these years later, he knew exactly what he'd had—and what he'd lost.

3

The tires of Devlin's SUV crunched over the gravel as he drove through the main gates of Lighthouse Security Investigations Montana. The early morning sun chased away the last whispers of night and the dreams that had lingered like ghosts in his mind. Shadows of the past always clung to him, but last night had been different. The memory had surfaced with startling clarity, leaving him to wake with an ache that settled deep in his chest, a reminder of wounds time couldn't fully heal.

He pulled into his usual spot outside the low, unassuming building that served as LSIMT's headquarters. The structure might have been modest, yet what went on inside was anything but. As he stepped out and approached the entrance, his shoulders straightened, and the heavy weight of the past began to lift. Work had a way of sharpening his focus and giving him purpose when the rest of his life sometimes felt unfulfilled.

Pushing through the doors, Devlin walked through the outer room. "Morning," he said, his voice warm as he smiled down at the petite woman maneuvering her wheelchair with practiced ease.

"Howdy, yourself, big guy." Mary Smithwick's sharp eyes sparkled with mischief as she rolled past, offering a wink that made him chuckle.

She was the backbone of the operation, a Keeper in every sense of the word. She managed the office like a general commanding troops, balancing the chaos with an uncanny ability to know exactly what everyone needed—even before they did. Fiercely efficient and endlessly compassionate, she'd become the heartbeat of LSIMT, and someone they all relied on.

Devlin moved deeper into the building, passing through the intricate security measures Logan had insisted on—the fingerprint pad, retina scan, and employee passcodes. Once inside, Devlin bypassed the equipment room, where Bert Tomlinson was tinkering with something. Usually, he'd stop to chat, but today was different. Logan had called for a morning meeting, hinting at a new mission, and Devlin wasn't about to be late.

"Morning, Bert," he called with a quick wave, striding past without breaking pace.

He reached the conference room, where a few Keepers were already gathered. The air hummed with camaraderie, and nods of acknowledgment passed between them. Devlin glanced around, once again struck by the caliber of the people Logan had assembled. His SEAL team had been elite, but this group was the best he'd ever worked with. Each brought a unique skill set forged through years of military service in special ops, honed by Logan's exacting standards.

Landon Sommers had transitioned from the military to the FBI, becoming a liaison with the West Coast branch of LSI. He then left the FBI and joined the Montana branch, wanting a new place to call home. Cole Iverson, their pilot, had come from the original LSI team in Maine. Frazier and Dalton Dolby, brothers who worked with seamless precision, had followed in their sibling's footsteps from LSIWC. Cory Brighton, a former Army Ranger sniper, sat quietly, his sharp eyes taking in everything. Casper—Aldo Casponi—moved with an eerie silence that had earned him his call sign, while Todd Blake brought a familial connection with siblings in Maine and on the West Coast. Timothy Clemons shared a similar tie through his brother-in-law. And then there was Sadie Hargrove, the tech genius who could unravel even the most complex digital puzzles, her skills honed during her time with military special ops.

The chatter tapered off as Logan entered the room, and all eyes naturally turned to him. Without a preamble, Logan began the meeting as he reviewed ongoing cases. One by one, the Keepers provided updates, each member contributing a piece to their ever-evolving work.

Devlin leaned back slightly, arms crossed as he listened. The sense of purpose in the room was almost tangible, a shared commitment that went beyond any one person. Moments like this reminded him why he'd joined LSI and why he stayed. Here, surrounded by these people, he felt fulfilled.

Logan leaned forward, his tone shifting to something more serious as he prepared to delve into the new mission. "A request came in from someone I met years ago while recuperating in Germany. At the time, she was visiting a close friend who was hospitalized. During those weeks, I learned she worked for the World Food Program—the WFP. It's the largest humanitarian organization in the world, providing food relief in emergencies and assistance wherever needed most. Specifically, she oversees food programs in refugee camps across Africa."

"Damn," Sadie said, her brows lifting. "That's a massive responsibility."

Logan nodded, a faint smile tugging at the corners of his mouth. "It is. Back then, I was still trying to figure out my next move. My SEAL career was over, and I had no clue what my future would look like." His expression softened, almost amused at the memory. "I think she saw an opportunity to recruit me. We spent a lot of time talking."

His shoulders lifted in a casual shrug, though the weight of that time lingered in his eyes. "Ultimately, I knew it wasn't my calling, but we stayed in touch. Usually, just a few emails a year to check in. Recently, her position was split because the workload was too much for one person. She's now responsible for refugee camps in Uganda, Sudan, and a few other places. When I got her message, it wasn't the usual friendly update—it was a request for help."

Devlin's interest was piqued, his mind already turning over the possibilities. He'd never met this woman, but the mere thought of someone dedicating their life to such work stirred something deep inside him. It reminded him of the time he'd spent on the Blackfeet Reservation and the respect he held for anyone called to serve. But that thought struck a nerve, sharp and sudden. An ache radiated from his chest, and instinctively, he lifted his fist, pressing it against his sternum as a memory surged to the surface, unbidden and raw.

"You good, man?" Sisco's voice cut through his haze, low and quiet.

"Yeah." Devlin forced the word out, his voice rough. "Just indigestion." He lowered his hand, shaking off the unease, and fixed his attention back on Logan.

Logan's gaze flicked toward him for a moment before continuing. "The email came from Margarethe Gunther, but I've also spoken with her superior at the WFP. They were notified by their food security officer at Bidi Bidi, one of the largest refugee camps in Uganda. It's suspected that food is being stolen."

Dalton leaned forward, his elbows resting on the table. "I don't want to sound insensitive, but isn't a certain amount of theft expected in those conditions?"

"I asked the same thing," Logan admitted. "But this isn't random pilfering. The thefts appear systematic. The food security officer brought it directly to Margarethe because they don't know who could be trusted in the camp. There's concern that the stolen food is being sold on the black market—and possibly funneled across the border to supply the Congolese military."

Frazier's voice was tight with concern. "Is the whistleblower in danger?"

"She didn't indicate they felt threatened." Logan's expression hardened. "I wasn't given their name. Margarethe is keeping it under wraps for now. Of course, any whistleblower in this situation could be at serious risk if discovered."

Devlin leaned forward, his voice steady. "What's the mission?"

Logan's gaze swept the room, his words measured. "I need a team of three to fly to Uganda. Margarethe will meet you in Germany. It's not unusual for her to visit the camp. She often conducts unscheduled audits, so her presence won't raise any alarms. She's used to traveling with WFP personnel—interns, security, and sometimes both. So the three of you going with her will look perfectly normal. She will only be able to stay a day or two, but it will be enough for her to check on things and to get you established there."

"Why us?" Todd asked, his tone curious but not defensive.

"Margarethe specifically requested someone outside the WFP," Logan said. "She knows what we do here and trusts this team to handle whatever comes up. She got permission from the United Nations High Commissioner for Refugees. Uganda is one of the most welcoming nations for refugees, but there are still risks. Margarethe wants someone to protect the whistleblower while you assist in investigating the thefts."

A silence fell over the room, the weight of the mission settling in. Devlin's mind churned as he considered the implications—not just the logistics of the task but the people it would impact. He didn't know what it was about this mission that tugged at him so fiercely, but he felt it, profound and undeniable.

Logan's sharp gaze settled on Devlin. "I thought of you first. Don't take offense, but with the deals you've made in the past, I know you've got the skills to dig into what might be happening."

Devlin chuckled, a wry grin tugging at his lips. "No offense taken. Bartering was always about getting what someone needed and never stealing. Dealmaking, if you want to call it that. But stealing from people desperate for food and possibly selling it on the black market? That's a whole different level of fucked up, and it needs to stop."

Logan nodded, his attention shifting across the room before landing on Cole. "I want you on this team. You will all fly military transport to Germany and then board a UN flight to Uganda, carrying food supplies."

Cole gave a quick dip of his head, his signature grin flashing as he turned to Devlin. "Got your back, man."

Logan's steady voice continued. "Todd, I'd like you to go as well."

Todd leaned over the table, his fist bumping Cole's and Devlin's with a grin. "You got it, boss."

"What kind of intel do I need to start pulling?" Sadie's voice cut through the room, her hands poised over her keyboard.

"Start with everything you can find on the World Food Program and Bidi Bidi in Uganda. Margarethe mentioned she'd send a map, but don't expect it to match anything official. The camp layout constantly shifts—new refugees come in, some leave, and the buildings serve multiple purposes. If they're overwhelmed, a classroom might double as a housing unit for new arrivals or as a temporary medical ward."

Logan's orders disbanded the meeting, and the team scattered to their respective tasks. Devlin stayed behind, grabbing the mission file Logan had handed him and heading to one of the smaller tables. Todd and Cole followed, their expressions solemn as they settled into seats nearby. At her workstation, Sadie was already deep into research, screens glowing with data.

Devlin flipped through the file, then looked at what Sadie was sending to their tablets. His brow furrowed in concentration. "The camp is a coordinated effort involving several organizations," he said, scanning the pages. "The United Nations High Commissioner for Refugees is the primary agency overseeing coordination and protection. The Red Cross is responsible for health, shelter, and emergency response. The WHO handles health interventions and disease prevention, and the WFP focuses on food security and nutrition programs. Then there are groups like Save the Children, Care International, and even the Peace Corps, all managing specific sectors."

Todd whistled low as he skimmed the data Sadie had uploaded to their tablets. "That's a hell of an operation. It's amazing they can all work together. But with so many players, it's no surprise that the WFP makes for a solid cover."

Devlin nodded, tapping a finger against the table. "Exactly. According to Margarethe's intel, the food security officer noticed enough inconsistencies to start digging. Evidence found made them feel justified in notifying someone they trusted—someone higher up in their organization, not necessarily someone at the camp."

Cole leaned back, his expression thoughtful. "Smart move. If the thefts are systematic, someone in the camp may be in on it. Going to someone outside the immediate chain of command was the safest option."

Devlin glanced up as a familiar presence approached. Mary rolled toward the table with her usual confident ease. Grinning, he tipped his head in her direction. "Let me guess—you've already got our itinerary worked out."

Mary smirked, holding up a folder as if it were a trophy. "You know it, big guy. Flights, logistics, and a whole lot of headaches, all wrapped up with a bow. Welcome to your next mission."

She nodded to the files she laid on the table. "The full itinerary is already on your phones. You're wheels up from Malmstrom Air Force Base tomorrow. Tonight, you head there together in one vehicle. Logan wants you to keep reviewing on the way. You'll have accommodations at the base, then fly out on military transport to Germany. From there, you'll fly private with Ms. Gunther to Uganda. You'll be able to take your equipment and weapons."

Todd raised a brow, his grin teasing. "Do I even want to know how long it will take us to get to Uganda?"

Mary met his grin with one of her own, leaning in conspiratorially. "I suggest you load your tablet with some good reads and have a killer playlist ready. Between flights, layovers, and logistics, you're looking at close to twenty-four hours." With a knowing smirk, she dipped her head and rolled out of the room, leaving the team feeling a mix of anticipation and tension.

Moments later, Bert strode into the room. "Once you've gone through the intel, meet me in the equipment room. We'll make sure you have everything you need."

Devlin, Cole, and Todd returned their focus to the files spread before them, diving into the detailed breakdown of the refugee camp's layout, operations, and the WFP's role within it. If they were going to blend in seamlessly with Margarethe, they needed to understand every layer of the camp's ecosystem.

"And the whistleblower?" Devlin asked, his gaze still fixed on the information as he sifted through the details.

Sadie looked up from her station, her fingers flying across her keyboard. "You'll meet them once you're on the ground and at the camp."

"So we're going in as security?" Cole inquired.

Sadie nodded, her tone brisk. "You'll be introduced as a security detail working with Margarethe Gunther on oversight of food management for the UNHCR." She glanced down, then added, "That's the United Nations High Commissioner for Refugees."

The Keepers spent hours dissecting every detail, building a mental map of the camp's dynamics, and preparing for what they might encounter.

"Food is sourced locally or internationally," Devlin noted, scanning the logistics breakdown. "It depends on cost, availability, and transport logistics. In Uganda, most food is moved by truck once it lands at the airport."

"And there's more than one refugee camp," Cole added, studying his tablet. "Someone from the WFP coordinates the shipments at the airport, but it's clear our whistle-blower only started seeing the thefts on their end."

"So the food is making it to Bidi Bidi," Todd clarified, leaning forward. "And then it's being stolen. Why not divert it earlier, straight from the source?"

"Pull up the map again," Devlin said to Sadie. He studied the highlighted location of the camp, his jaw tightening. "It's not the closest camp to the Congo border but the most secure. That's not just where a lot of the refugees are coming from—it's also where the Congolese military could be picking up stolen goods. Food. Weapons. Whatever they need."

Cole let out a low growl. "They're probably getting both from various sources."

Devlin nodded, pointing at the diagram of the camp. "Bidi Bidi has one central warehouse for food, but the camp is so massive it's divided into villages. Each village has its own smaller warehouse."

"Just one food security officer?" Todd asked.

"Yeah," Devlin confirmed. "They'd have a staff under them, but if they suspected someone on their own team, they wouldn't risk reporting it internally. Going to their superior at the WFP was the smart move."

"You'll certainly be watched by the security officer for the whole camp," Logan said as he walked closer.

By the time they'd combed through the files and spent hours in the equipment room with Bert, the team was prepped. This mission wasn't just about providing security; it was about uncovering a system of theft that affected hundreds of lives. The weight of that responsibility hung heavy but invigorating.

Later that evening, Devlin headed home to pack, his mind already ticking through the mission's moving parts. Unlike a standard security detail or installation plan, this assignment was investigative, and he felt the familiar itch of anticipation.

Once his bag was packed and his house secured, he stepped outside just as Cole's SUV pulled into the drive. Todd was already in the front seat, his grin visible through the windshield. Devlin climbed into the back, tossing his bag beside him. The ride to Malmstrom Air Force Base wouldn't take long, but the camaraderie in the vehicle made it feel like an extension of the mission itself.

Leaning back in his seat, Devlin let his thoughts wander as the Montana landscape blurred past the window. He'd worked missions all over the globe, and while Africa wasn't new to him, Uganda was. Closing his eyes, he let himself wonder what this mission would hold.

For now, he let the hum of the road lull him into a light rest, knowing full well that tomorrow, everything would change.

4

Mia rose with the first light, the faint glow seeping through the window in her room. She stretched briefly before heading to the staff communal showers, her well-worn flip-flops slapping against the packed dirt. The rhythmic murmurs of the Ugandan refugee camp were already stirring outside in a mix of soft voices, the clatter of makeshift pots, and the distant hum of early morning activity.

Grateful for the luxury of warm water, she adhered strictly to the five-minute limit. Even if it hadn't been a rule, Mia's conscience wouldn't allow indulgence. Water was precious here—a gift many refugees didn't have. As she briskly worked shampoo through her hair, she tried to recall the last time she'd indulged in a deep conditioning treatment. It felt like a distant memory in a life that seemed worlds away.

After stepping out of the narrow shower stall, she quickly wrapped herself in a plush towel, a gift from her parents. The fabric soaked up the droplets clinging to her skin before she bent to wind it around her hair. A smile curved her lips as she remembered her mother's insistence on a salon visit during her last trip home—the pure luxury of having her hair cut, treated with salon products, and blown out to a sheen. It had been cut to her shoulders then, but now it hung long, grazing her back. With no salon in sight, she relied on a friend's steady hands to snip at the fraying ends.

Mia dressed quickly, donning her usual uniform of khaki pants, a white T-shirt, and a long-sleeved khaki shirt left unbuttoned, the sleeves rolled up for practicality. The heat of the day would soon become oppressive, but she made an effort to protect her skin. She shoved her toiletries into a mesh bag and slung her wet towel over her arm, then slipped out of the women's bathroom.

Back in her small room, she hung the towel to dry on a bar hung on the outside of the wardrobe and placed the toiletry bag on the edge of the narrow sink. Catching her reflection in the mirror, she snorted softly. Makeup had become a relic of her past. Sunscreen was her only priority now. She reached for a tub of SPF moisturizer, spreading it over her face and neck with practiced efficiency before swiping on a layer of sun-protecting lip balm. The routine was efficient... she spent little time getting ready for a job that required long hours, hot conditions, and no one to impress other than the food she could deliver.

She sat on the edge of her cot to tug on socks and lace up her boots. A glance at the clock made her grin. Fifteen minutes flat from start to finish. "Always date-ready," she muttered to herself, a hint of sarcasm in her tone. Not that dating was on her agenda. The very thought drew a derisive chuckle, though a faint ache nestled in her chest.

It had been a long time since she'd wanted more than a quick horizontal dance between the sheets with anyone. And, in truth, that was fine with her. Or at least that was what she told herself whenever these unbidden thoughts popped up. Her line of work wasn't conducive to romance. Long hours, relentless travel, and the emotional toll of her duties left little room for love. She wasn't opposed to the idea, not in theory, but experience had taught her that love could be more painful than solitude. She hadn't looked for love in years and had no plans to break her streak. It was safer to keep her distance.

Locking her door, Mia stepped out into the already warming air. The ground was dry and dusty, the sun's rays beginning to heat the day. She approached the large, military-style tent that served as the staff's dining area. It wasn't located in a permanent building in case they needed to move it as the camp became more crowded and the needs changed.

Along the way, she greeted others with a smile and a nod, exchanging brief pleasantries as the camp came alive around her.

Inside the dining tent, the shade offered some respite. She grabbed a metal tray at the end of the line and filled it with her usual breakfast— a small bowl of oatmeal dusted with cinnamon, a slice of toast adorned with a modest smear of passion fruit jam, and a scrambled egg. At the end of the line, a steaming cup of coffee waited. Mia paused, inhaling the rich aroma and letting it ground her in the moment. For a few precious seconds, she savored it, allowing her mind to simply ease.

She was about to sit at the table holding some of her staff when she saw Charlie's hand gesture for her to sit with some of the other officers. They had a staff meeting after breakfast, but if Dr. Horace München had the heads of each department sit together at breakfast, she knew he must have additional news to impart. He liked to keep meetings quick and efficient, so he'd occasionally use breakfast as a way for them to start the day together while conveying some new business. She slid into an empty seat beside Charlie and smiled at the others around the table.

Along with the head of the camp was Ritah Nakawunde, the protection officer. Dr. Elaine Harker, the medical coordinator, sat beside Ravi Kumar, the WASH coordinator. The logistics and supply chain officer, Robert Ellyson, sat beside Percy Wilson, the education program coordinator, on the other side of the table. Elizabeth and Mark Carter, the economics recovery officers, were at the end, along with Moses Kamoga, the camp security officer. Charlie was the information reporting officer.

She sometimes found refugee camp titles confusing, but she'd easily adapted after eight years of working with them. Robert winked at her before glancing to the side to see what Elaine was discussing with Dr. München.

Mia turned her attention to breakfast, hoping the rock in her stomach would allow her to eat. Ever since she'd emailed Margarethe, she couldn't help but watch everyone around her. The stealing of food she'd discovered wasn't random or uncoordinated. She was sure it wasn't kids breaking in or an adult deciding one night they would see what they could get. She felt sure someone was coordinating a large enough theft that numerous people and at least one truck would be needed.

"How can you eat jam?" Charlie asked, sitting across from her with a grimace. "Vegemite is the only thing that should go on bread!"

"Only a true Aussie would say that." Percy shook his head. He turned to Mia. "Eat up, my dear. A delicious jam on toast is the perfect way to start the day here."

Charlie wadded his napkin and tossed it at Percy. Mia rolled her eyes at their antics, glad for the diversion.

Dr. München allowed them to eat breakfast, keeping

the conversation general before saying, "We have some visitors coming in."

His opening words snagged her attention. Not because they were unusual but because having visitors come into the camp was an almost daily occurrence. Journalists, volunteers, mission groups from all over the world, representatives from the various organizations that helped organize and fund the camps, and even the occasional celebrity who, whether led by a drive to do good deeds or needing publicity, would come by with their PR team.

Now curious, she gave Dr. München her full attention.

"We have two members of the World Health Organization who will be working with Dr. Harper. They're bringing vaccines and will use her staff and some refugee volunteers to help us start with the children first."

Elaine was smiling, and Mia was glad for the medication to arrive.

"There will be two mission groups arriving—one has fifteen people, the other has twenty-three. All adults. They will be checking in with Moses, and I understand that they will be helping in education, the clinic, and food distribution."

Dr. München had already informed her that some volunteers would be coming to help at the various villages for food distribution during mealtime and work with some of the families for food preparation. She had directed her staff to expect them.

He looked around the table and noted, "If you are finished eating, we have a few more items to go over, but we will do those in our staff conference room."

Swallowing the last bite of toast and finishing her coffee in a single, satisfying slurp, Mia handed her tray to one of the kitchen staff with a quick smile of thanks. The leaders moved together as a group, their footsteps kicking up small clouds of dust along the sunbaked path.

The main admin building was a modest two-story structure that stood as a center of activity amid the sprawling refugee camp. Its simple, utilitarian design housed several offices and a central conference room. While some lead officers claimed small offices within, Mia preferred her workspace near the large food storage facility. It was practical, close to her team, and allowed her to keep a watchful eye on operations. They settled into familiar positions around the long table.

"We have at least two oversight visits scheduled in the coming weeks," Dr. München began, his manner unflappable as usual.

Mia's pulse quickened. She couldn't help but wonder if her email to Margarethe had set these wheels in motion.

"The Red Cross will be visiting," Dr. München continued, "evaluating the nurses and doctors in the clinic. Elaine's team is already prepared."

"Oh, lucky you," Charlie quipped, his grin teasing.

Elaine gave a casual shrug. "It's to be expected. Nothing we aren't ready for."

Dr. München's gaze shifted down the table to Mia. "We also have someone coming from the World Food Program," he said. "Margarethe Gunther will be leading her team. She's familiar with our work here. Mia, I trust everything is in order?"

Mia nodded, her tone calm as she replied, "She's my supervisor in the WFP. I've worked with Margarethe before. This shouldn't be anything new."

"Good. I understand she'll be focusing on inventory and distribution."

"My staff will be ready," Mia assured him, keeping her expression neutral even as relief coursed through her.

Margarethe's brief email, a single word—"acknowledged"—now made sense. Her supervisor had opted to address the issue in person, bringing reinforcements. If Margarethe's team included investigators, Mia's hope for uncovering the thefts rose considerably.

As Dr. München delved into further details, Mia's attention wavered, her thoughts drifting to the people around the table. Each leader played a crucial role in the camp's delicate ecosystem, and under Dr. München's guidance, the camp operated with remarkable efficiency.

Elaine, the no-nonsense British physician, worked tirelessly to ensure the clinic ran smoothly. Ravi, the WASH coordinator from India, maintained the camp's water, sanitation, and hygiene systems, a vital shield against disease. Robert, the Canadian logistics officer, kept the supply chain humming, managing everything from food to emergency provisions with precision.

Percy, another Brit with a self-deprecating sense of humor, headed the refugee children's educational programs. Elizabeth and Mark oversaw agricultural and economic initiatives. Mia's team occasionally collaborated with theirs on farming projects. Moses, the camp's Ugandan security officer, was a towering figure both in stature and presence. His leadership kept order in an environment that could easily descend into chaos without firm but compassionate oversight.

Then there was Ritah, the protection officer and a close friend. Ritah's dedication to safeguarding vulnerable groups—women, children, and the elderly—was unparalleled. Her warmth and resilience inspired everyone around her.

And finally, Charlie, the irrepressible information officer. His knack for data collection and resource management made him invaluable. Mia had mentioned her concerns to him but no one else. In hindsight, even that felt risky.

She refocused as Dr. München wrapped up the meeting, his authoritative voice grounding her wandering thoughts. Margarethe's arrival loomed large in her mind, a mix of anticipation and uncertainty.

When the meeting concluded, the group dispersed, each leader heading toward their respective responsibilities. Stepping back into the relentless heat of the day, Mia felt the familiar press of time. The demands of the camp were unyielding, and the hours ahead would be as challenging as ever. Yet beneath the strain, a spark of determination pushed her forward.

Mia waved as Elaine headed into the medical building, then continued down the lane toward her office. Across the road stood the warehouse for other supplies, and she caught sight of Robert disappearing inside.

"What's on your agenda today?" Ravi asked, falling into step beside her.

"I thought I'd continue with inventory," Mia replied.

"Doesn't Farid handle most of the inventory?" he asked.

"I thought I'd give him a hand today," she said lightly, steering the conversation away from herself. "What about you?"

"I'm heading down to Sweswe. We're working on adding more sanitation facilities. It's the smallest village, but it's likely the next to see an influx of refugees."

Mia nodded, a shadow of understanding crossing her face. There were always more refugees. Yet no matter how thin their resources stretched, they would always find a way to welcome them.

"Good morning!"

Both she and Ravi turned as Doreen Ateenyi, Ravi's second-in-command, approached and then waved. The

Ugandan woman's bright smile was as radiant as the sun overhead. She held a master's degree in public health, and Mia knew it was only a matter of time before another camp sought her expertise.

Mia continued, entering her office to find her second-in-command, Farid Hussein, already at his desk. The South Sudanese refugee had worked tirelessly over the years, rising to a position of leadership through sheer determination and skill.

"What did the good Dr. München have to say today?" Farid asked as Mia dropped into her chair.

"We'll have some visitors," she replied. "Actually, several visitors. A mission group will be arriving, and some of them want to assist with food preparation and distribution."

"Do you know which village you'll assign them to?" Farid asked, his brow furrowed thoughtfully.

"I'm thinking Bulit or Mukondo," she said. "Mukondo might need more help, but if there's a large enough group, we could split them between the two."

Farid nodded. "Mukondo could use the extra hands. I'll make sure everything is ready."

Mia leaned back, grateful as always for Farid's insight. "That's not all. We'll also have an on-site inspection," she added, watching his expression carefully. "Margarethe Gunther from the WFP is coming."

Farid's face lit up with a broad grin. "Having her back in the camp will be a delight."

Mia couldn't help but smile. Margarethe could sometimes look like a battalion general, but she had a heart of gold and had been a source of kindness over the years with Mia. "You're right. It will be."

"Anyone else coming?" Farid asked.

"I'm not sure," Mia admitted. "Margarethe's bringing a

team, but she'll take care of them."

"Excellent," Farid said, standing. "Do you want me to handle inventory today?"

"Yes, focus on the main camp storeroom here. I'm planning to check the village warehouses."

"Do you want me to go with you?"

"No, thank you. You'll be busy here. Besides, it's good for me to make rounds and keep a clear picture of what we have on the ground."

Farid nodded, his confidence in her unshakable, before heading to the warehouse. Left alone, Mia closed her eyes briefly, her mind heavy with unanswered questions. She didn't want to believe anyone she worked with could be involved in the food thefts, but the logistics didn't add up. Refugees couldn't do it alone, especially if food was leaving the camp.

Inhaling deeply, she gathered the items she'd need for her inventory review, tucking them into a satchel slung across her body. Keys in hand, she stepped outside and headed to the Jeep. She would retrace much of where she went last week when she'd made the trip at night. But the camp felt very different in the light of day when the shadows were chased away by the sun.

5

The plane's engines hummed as they touched down in Germany, marking the first leg of their journey. Devlin and his team disembarked alongside a contingent of military personnel stationed at a nearby base. With quiet anticipation, they were escorted to the airport transport area. Waiting for them there was Margarethe Gunther.

Devlin had read Margarethe's background report from Sadie in preparation for the mission. Margarethe was a mid-fifties woman of medium height with a sturdy frame that spoke of resilience. Her steely gray hair was cut into a short, no-nonsense style that suggested practicality over vanity. But her eyes twinkled with an unexpected warmth, drawing him in as she greeted them. Her voice, soft and measured, carried a quiet authority.

"Welcome," she said with a smile that offset her businesslike demeanor. She ushered them into a meeting room tucked away in the airport. "We only have an hour before our plane to Uganda departs. It's a humanitarian flight, so we'll take supplies."

Inside, the room held a modest table laden with sandwiches and water. Devlin, Todd, and Cole didn't hesitate to partake, grateful for the meal after the long flight.

Margarethe settled into one of the chairs, her posture relaxed but alert. "All right, gentlemen," she began, her tone pragmatic. "We won't spend much time exchanging pleasantries since it's unnecessary for the mission. That said, I know your leader, and he assures me you're a highly skilled team, adept at military operations, with insight and investigative skills that will be invaluable to me. I trust his judgment."

Devlin leaned forward slightly, listening intently as she continued.

"Let me give you a rundown of the situation we're walking into. When we arrive at the camp, I've already informed the director that I'll be bringing a team for security purposes. We'll be auditing inventory and distribution procedures—something I've done many times before. It's a believable cover and won't raise suspicion. Due to other obligations, I can only stay a couple of days, but you'll be able to do what you need to do."

"Does the camp director know why we're really there?" Devlin asked, his voice steady.

Margarethe's expression was grim. "Yes, but just the basics. Theft isn't uncommon in refugee camps, though it's a tragedy wherever it happens. Sometimes locals break into storage units for food, which is usually isolated and dealt with quickly. But what's happening here... could be systematic, organized theft. There's the fear that the stolen food might be crossing the border into Congo and sold on the black market. If that's true, it's not just theft—it's exploitation of the desperate for profit. And if someone in a leadership position at the camp is involved..." Her frustration was evident.

Devlin nodded, his mind already turning over the

implications. "And the whistleblower? What do we know about them?"

Margarethe's expression softened slightly. "She's someone I've worked with for years. Intelligent, tenacious, and dedicated. She's put herself at risk to bring this to light."

Devlin smiled faintly, picturing someone with Margarethe's fortitude and resolve. "And her safety?" he pressed.

Margarethe's gaze hardened. "The camp should offer some protection. But if this operation is as extensive as I fear—if large sums of money are changing hands—there's no telling who might be involved. The danger is very real."

The weight of her words settled over the room, a somber reminder of what lay ahead. Devlin exchanged a glance with Todd and Cole, their silent understanding confirming their readiness.

"Wouldn't the thieves assume the food security officer discovered the discrepancy and raised the alarm?" Devlin asked, his brow furrowed in thought.

Margarethe shook her head, her calm demeanor underscoring her years of experience. "Not necessarily. If the stolen goods are being moved outside the camp, suspicions wouldn't immediately fall on anyone specific within. The organizer could be someone in the camp—or someone further down the chain on the black market."

The conversation was interrupted when their boarding was announced. They gathered their belongings and followed Margarethe to the plane. Owned by the World Food Program, it was designed for transporting personnel and supplies, and its utilitarian interior was stark but efficient.

Hours later, the plane touched down in Entebbe, Uganda. Warm air greeted them as they stepped onto the tarmac, the sun bright in the expansive sky. Around them, workers buzzed with efficiency, sweat dripping as they loaded supplies onto waiting trucks.

A young man approached them, his stride energetic and his grin infectious. "Margarethe!" he called, his exuberant voice carrying above the noise. She turned, her face lighting up as she embraced him warmly.

"Jonan!" Margarethe exclaimed, pulling back to gesture toward her companions. "These are the people traveling with me. Everyone, this is Jonan Muwange."

Jonan nodded in greeting, his posture both relaxed and confident. He led them to a van, and together, they loaded their luggage and equipment into the back. Margarethe claimed the passenger seat while Devlin, Cole, and Todd slid into the middle row.

As the van pulled away, Jonan glanced at them in the rearview mirror, his smile as bright as the Ugandan sun. "Is this your first time in Uganda?"

"For me, yes," Devlin replied, his voice steady.

"I've been here before, but only briefly," Cole added, his eyes scanning the streets outside. "I never left the airport."

"New for me, too," Todd said, his tone tinged with curiosity.

"You'll like it here," Jonan assured them. His smile widened, revealing straight white teeth. "It's a beautiful country."

Devlin watched the city as they drove. The streets were well-paved, and traffic was orderly. For a moment, it reminded him of a European city—clean, bustling, and efficient. But as they left the heart of Entebbe, the surroundings began to shift. Neighborhoods gave way to more rural areas, where the roads grew narrower and less marked. Traffic became chaotic with vehicles and pedestrians. Walkers darted between cars, and motorcyclists weaved through traffic with practiced ease and what Devlin assumed was a hefty dose of hope.

Jonan glanced over his shoulder. "Are you here to investigate something?"

The Keepers exchanged sharp glances, their silence speaking volumes. Margarethe, unfazed, nodded. "I need to conduct an inventory inspection and ensure everything is as it should be."

Jonan's brow quirked in understanding. "If you're here, I imagine it's not as it should be."

Margarethe smiled, turning in her seat to look at Devlin, Cole, and Todd. "Jonan isn't just a driver."

Jonan chuckled, meeting their curious gazes in the rearview mirror. "That's true," he said, his tone laced with humor. "I'm Ugandan. I served in the military for several years before leaving to pursue my education in health, welfare, and safety. Now, I work in the department of WHS and am contracted by the WFP for security."

Devlin nodded, impressed. Jonan wasn't just their guide —he was an ally who understood the terrain, the culture, and the stakes. But he couldn't help but feel a flicker of surprise at Margarethe's candor about Jonan's background. It wasn't that he doubted her judgment, but his years of service had taught him that trust could be as fragile as glass. Anyone could become a traitor under the right or even the wrong circumstances.

As they drew closer to the refugee camp, the road changed. Though still paved, it was riddled with potholes, making the van's progress slower and bumpier. Dust kicked up around them, catching the sunlight in golden swirls. Finally, they reached the main camp entrance, where Jonan eased the van to a stop.

Devlin took in the scene outside. Young men with rifles slung casually over their shoulders stood at the gate, their khaki uniforms clean but worn from use. Their gazes were sharp, their postures a mix of authority. Jonan and Margarethe produced their identification, and Margarethe handed over the Keepers' passports. The guards cross-checked the documents against a list, their movements methodical but unhurried. After a moment, the barrier lifted, and they were waved through.

The van rolled forward, and the road was now a mix of dirt and packed gravel. Devlin scanned the camp's surroundings, noting the variety of structures that lined the way. Some were humble mud-and-thatch huts, while others were patched together with corrugated metal and weathered wood. A few larger, sturdier buildings made of wood were scattered among them. Margarethe's voice broke the silence. "The area we just passed through serves as the reception zone. This is where buses bringing in new refugees arrive. Once the refugees are processed here, they're assigned to one of the villages."

"Are the villages still completely separate?" Todd asked, his curiosity evident. "We were given information but were told it was ever-changing."

"Yes," Margarethe replied. "Each village operates independently but interconnected through shared resources and infrastructure. Once you've had a chance to explore, the layout will make more sense."

"Do we start with the food warehouse?" Devlin asked, ready to get down to business.

Margarethe shook her head. "Not yet. First, we'll meet Dr. Horace München, the head of the camp. He oversees the entire operation, coordinates with international and government agencies, and liaises between them and the camp. He's also responsible for maintaining order across the villages."

"Sounds like a hell of a job," Cole muttered.

Margarethe chuckled, nodding in agreement. "It is. But it's essential to check in with him first. Everyone working in the camp reports to Dr. München when they arrive."

The van slowed to a stop outside a rudimentary two-story building. Its construction was basic but functional, with peeling paint and reinforced windows that hinted at both resourcefulness and the challenges of the environment.

Jonan stepped out first, his ever-present smile firmly in place. "I can take your belongings to the guesthouse," he offered. "Just leave them here."

"Thanks, but we'll keep them with us," Devlin replied firmly. They weren't about to part with their equipment or firearms.

Jonan nodded, unbothered, and stepped aside to let them unload their duffels. The Keepers followed Margarethe into the building, passing through a reception area where a young woman sat behind a counter. She greeted Margarethe warmly, and the two exchanged a few words before Margarethe led the group down a short hallway and up a narrow staircase.

"Moses!" Margarethe called as they reached the top.

Devlin's eyes landed on a towering man standing near the window. His build was imposing, and his presence commanding. He was dressed in full military gear, complete with body armor and a sidearm holstered at his hip. His expression was serious but relaxed as Margarethe approached.

She turned with practiced ease to make the introductions. "Moses, these are the men assisting me with an inventory in food storage. The WFP approved them as security. We're about to meet with Dr. München, and I'd be glad if you could join us."

"It would be my pleasure," Moses replied, his smile

directed at Margarethe. Though his demeanor appeared calm, his sharp eyes appraised the Keepers, lingering on each of them for a moment longer than necessary.

Margarethe led the way to an open door, pausing to knock on the frame before stepping inside. The room beyond was modest in size, made to feel even smaller as the group filed in. Devlin quickly took stock of the space. A cluttered desk, stacked high with folders and papers, sat at the center of the room. Behind it, maps of the camp lined the walls, dotted with pins and scribbled notes.

Dr. Horace München, tall and thin, stood as they entered. His gray hair was neatly combed, and his glasses perched precariously on the bridge of his nose. Despite his slightly wrinkled clothes, his presence exuded a quiet authority.

"Margarethe," he greeted warmly, rounding his desk with open arms. He embraced her briefly before pulling back. "It's always a pleasure to see you."

"And you as well, Horace," she replied with a smile. "Thank you for seeing us on short notice."

Dr. München's gaze shifted to the men behind her, curiosity sparking in his expression. "I understand you've brought security with you. Should I be worried?"

"We're making a food delivery and reviewing inventory," Margarethe explained smoothly. "Allow me to introduce Jim Devlin, Cole Iverson, and Todd Blake. They're private security, approved by the WFP, and will assist me during my stay. They are authorized to stay after I leave and will investigate any problems. You know how thorough the WFP can be."

Dr. München's serious expression softened into a welcoming smile. "Welcome to Uganda and Camp Bidi Bidi," he said, extending a hand.

"Dr. München." Devlin clasped the offered hand firmly.

"Thank you for having us. I usually just go by Devlin." Devlin shifted his attention to Moses, who stood silently at Margarethe's side.

Margarethe gestured toward the head of security. "I'm glad Moses is here. These men are armed, but it's purely procedural. Like Moses, they're former military and highly trained. I thought it best for you to meet so there's complete transparency."

Moses gave a small nod of approval. "I offer my own welcome to Uganda," he said, his voice deep and steady. "The camp runs efficiently, and I hope Margarethe will not need your assistance, but you are welcome here. With the influx of newcomers this week, my officers are stretched thin. If your presence helps ease the load, I'm all for it."

With that, Moses gave a curt nod and exited the room, his boots thudding against the wooden floor. Dr. München turned his attention back to Margarethe, offering logistical details. "Your accommodations are prepared," Margarethe said. "Once we've settled, I suggest heading directly to the warehouse. The food delivery you brought with you will need to be sorted and logged."

Another round of handshakes followed, and the group made their way out of the administration building.

Outside, the sun bore down relentlessly, the air thick and humid. Jonan waited by the van, his ever-present grin lighting up his face. As they approached, Margarethe turned to the Keepers. "The guesthouse accommodations are rudimentary," she said with a touch of humor. "But I'm sure you've seen worse."

Devlin chuckled, his easy demeanor belying his alertness. "I assure you, we'll be fine."

Margarethe smiled warmly and turned to Jonan. "If you could take my things to Elaine's quarters, I'll stay with her.

These gentlemen can handle their belongings—it's just a short walk to the guesthouse."

Jonan nodded, giving a small wave before climbing back into the van. The vehicle rumbled down the dusty road, kicking up a soft plume of red earth in its wake.

"Elaine is Dr. Elaine Parker, the head medical officer of the camp," Margarethe explained as they began walking. "She and I met twenty years ago, and we've been close friends ever since. Whenever I visit, she lets me stay in a small room that doubles as an office. It's cozy, with a little bed tucked in the corner. It's like being roommates again."

The Keepers fell into step behind her, their boots crunching softly against the packed earth. The road was bordered by grass and vibrant trees. Overhead, the blue sky stretched endlessly, dotted with cotton-white clouds that offered brief moments of shade from the relentless sun. A faint breeze stirred the air, carrying the mingled scents of earth, wood, and distant cooking fires.

They soon approached a modest one-story building made of weathered wood with a thatched roof. An awning stretched over the front porch, shading several chairs arranged around a firepit. Margarethe led them inside, guiding them through a narrow hallway to a room tucked into the back corner of the house. "Here we are," she said, motioning them in.

Devlin stepped through the doorway, quickly surveying the space. Four military-style beds lined the room, each accompanied by a narrow metal wardrobe. The room was sparse but functional, the kind of accommodations he'd seen countless times before in the military.

"You can store your things here," Margarethe said. "I'm going to get keys for your room."

As she disappeared down the hall, the Keepers tossed their duffels onto the beds, each claiming a cot. The mosquito netting was strung over each bed, pulled to the side during the daytime. They worked efficiently, stowing their belongings in the wardrobes and securing their equipment with the padlocks they'd brought. Devlin knew the locks wouldn't stop anyone determined to break in, but they might deter someone with idle curiosity.

The sun shone through the slats of shutters over a small window. An overhead fan rotated lazily, barely disturbing the heavy air.

Margarethe returned, a kerchief tied around her neck to catch the perspiration. She dabbed at her brow before handing each Keeper a key. "I don't expect you'll have trouble with security here," she said, her tone steady but cautious. "That said, these are uncertain times. Our visit may unsettle someone who has something to hide."

Devlin nodded. "We'll remain armed, like any other security personnel here."

"Understood," Margarethe replied, her expression resolute.

They stepped outside, the sun blazing as it descended toward the horizon. Along the lane, Ugandans and refugees moved about, some carrying baskets of supplies and others chatting in small groups. Most smiled and waved as they passed, their warmth and resilience striking Devlin. Despite the hardships, there was an almost tangible sense of hope here.

After a short walk, the road widened, revealing several large buildings on either side. Margarethe gestured toward one of them. "Food storage is over here. I see our truck has arrived. Let's head inside so you can meet the team."

They entered a reception area, where a woman sat behind a wooden counter. Her face lit up when she saw Margarethe, and her smile was warm and genuine. "Oh,

Ms. Gunther," she said in halting English. "It is so nice to see you again."

"It's lovely to be back," Margarethe replied. "Is our truck being unloaded?"

"Yes." The woman nodded. "Farid is in the back, ready for intake."

Margarethe turned to the Keepers, her eyes alight with purpose. "Let's get started."

Devlin exchanged a glance with Cole and Todd, each silently preparing for what lay ahead. This mission wasn't just about inventory but about peeling back layers to uncover a truth someone was desperate to hide.

Without hesitation, Margarethe led the Keepers through a side door into a sprawling storage facility. The air inside was cooler but carried the earthy scent of packed goods and wooden crates. Devlin's sharp gaze swept over the space, noting the organized rows of crates stacked with precision. Workers moved purposely among them, carrying, stacking, and inspecting items with practiced efficiency. From what he could see, a method and controlled rhythm kept the chaos at bay.

Near the center of the room, a man with dark hair and sun-kissed skin stood holding a clipboard. His sharp eyes scanned the workers. As he turned and saw Margarethe, his serious expression melted into a broad smile. He strode toward her with open arms, his joy palpable.

"Margarethe!" he exclaimed, his voice reaching them through the buzz of activity.

Margarethe engulfed him in a hug, her warmth unmistakable. Keeping an arm around him, she turned to the Keepers. "This is Devlin, Todd, and Cole." She gestured toward them. "And this is Farid Hussein. He's the second-in-command here, and this place wouldn't function without him."

Farid offered a firm handshake to each of them, his demeanor welcoming. He turned to Margarethe. "I know you are anxious to see her. She's on the other side," he said, shaking his head with a grin. "Let me get her!"

Margarethe didn't wait, following him as he navigated through the rows of crates toward the far side of the building. Devlin and the others trailed, weaving among the rows. As they approached, his eyes locked on a woman standing with her back to them. Her long, dark braid hung down her back, swaying slightly as she moved. She wore a simple white T-shirt tucked into khaki pants that fit her snugly, emphasizing a lithe, graceful frame.

Margarethe quickened her pace, and as she reached the woman, the two embraced heartily, their laughter cutting through the activity in the building. The woman turned partially, offering a glimpse of her profile, and Devlin felt an unexpected jolt. She was much younger than he'd imagined.

Margarethe waved them over, and Devlin followed, his steps slowing as they drew closer. The woman turned fully, her smile bright and welcoming as her gaze landed first on Cole, then shifted to Todd. But when her eyes reached Devlin, the air thickened, making breathing difficult.

They stared at each other, the space between them suddenly electric. Devlin's heartbeat thundered in his ears, drowning out the distant chatter and the scrape of crates being moved. His world narrowed to the impossible reality standing before him. The woman he had loved fiercely when they'd been together and still loved after he'd walked away was now standing before him, her gaze just as wide and disbelieving as his.

Margarethe's voice broke through the haze, though the words barely registered. "Devlin," she said, her tone cheerful. "Let me introduce our food security officer, Mia Duff."

Mia Duff. Her name echoed in his mind, loud and clear. It was as if time had rewound the years between them into nothingness. Her expression was unreadable, her lips slightly parted as though she, too, couldn't find the words.

Devlin didn't move, his body rigid and his chest tight. Questions swirled in his mind, unanswered and unanswerable at the moment. All he knew was that Mia Duff was here. And just like that, the mission took on a whole new weight.

6

Mia stared, unblinking, at the man before her—a tall mountain of a man with black hair and a heavy black beard. And blue eyes that were pinned on her. Her breath caught, and her mind struggled to process the sight of him. She stared at a vision she never thought she'd see again.

Jim Devlin stood in the dusty warehouse, his presence commanding, as though he belonged there despite the improbability of his being in Uganda. Every visit back to her parents in Kansas had been fraught with the risk of stumbling across memories she'd buried. The high school they'd shared, the spots where they'd laughed, argued, and fallen in love—ghosts of a past life she'd carefully avoided. She'd succeeded in never crossing paths with him or his family, always managing to stay out of reach. But now, there was no evading him. No running.

Her instincts urged her to look away, but her body refused. It wasn't that he'd changed so very much in the past decade, but he just seemed so much more... more everything. He seemed to fill the room, every inch of his tall, broad frame a tangible reminder of the boy he'd been and the man he'd become. His dark beard was full, his black hair trimmed shorter than he used to wear. But his deep, piercing blue eyes held her captive. Beneath perfectly arched brows, his eyes searched hers, their intensity undiminished by time.

The warehouse buzzed with activity, the clatter of crates and murmur of voices a distant hum as if she were underwater. Slowly, Margarethe's voice penetrated the fog, drawing Mia back to reality. She blinked, her chest tight, realizing that Jim wasn't a mirage. He was here and real.

Margarethe had called him Devlin. Not Jim. Why the formality? Then again, she knew nothing of his life now, not even what he called himself. For all she knew, he could be an entirely different person. Right now, she didn't want to think of Jim, the once love of her life. No... Devlin is fine. *Except I always thought that would be my last name.* She winced and tried to still her heart pounding in her chest.

Her gaze traced his face, lingering on the features she'd once memorized. Her shock and disbelief was mirrored in his expression. He took a step closer, and a vivid memory flooded her mind—him standing between her and a police officer after she'd chained her fifteen-year-old self to the goalpost in protest. The clarity of it stole her breath. They say your life flashes before your eyes in moments of crisis, but she'd never believed it until now. She wasn't dying, yet scene after scene from their shared history played out in her mind.

Then, like a slap, came the memory of their last encounter—his face etched with indifference, offering nothing but heartbreak. Her body jerked involuntarily as if recoiling from the thought. She tore her gaze away from him and turned to Margarethe, her focus sharpening as another man stepped closer.

"Are you okay, Mia?" Robert's voice was soft but insistent, his hand resting on her arm.

A low, guttural sound came from Devlin—a growl, almost imperceptible but unmistakably there.

"I'm fine," she managed, her voice steady despite the chaos within her.

Devlin's eyes locked on Robert, his jaw tightening. "And you are?" His tone was clipped, edged with something primal.

"I'm Robert Ellyson." Robert extended a hand, oblivious to the tension coiling around them.

Margarethe stepped into the fray, her voice brisk and professional. "Yes, Robert is our logistics and supply chain officer. He works closely with Mia on food distribution."

Another low growl rumbled in Devlin's chest as Margarethe introduced the others, her tone unbothered. Mia's mind raced, trying to understand his presence and connection to Margarethe. *Why was he here?*

Margarethe's voice broke through again. "Mia, are you sure you're all right?"

The question jolted her back to the moment. She shook her head quickly and forced a smile. Or at least, she hoped it was a smile—it felt more like a grimace. "Yes, I'm sorry. I wasn't expecting anyone with you."

Devlin's eyes never left her, the weight of his gaze pressing against her skin like a brand. Her pulse thrummed as the past collided with the present, leaving her unsure of how to breathe, let alone what to say. In the heat and chaos of the refugee camp, one thing became clear—she couldn't escape her past anymore.

"Since I'll be working with inventory today and tomorrow, I have these men with me as security. We are unloading the truck now, and I don't want to interrupt what you and Farid were doing," Margarethe said, her voice carrying easily over the bustling noise of the warehouse.

Mia was glad for the excuse to turn away, her mind still racing as she numbly followed Farid to the back of the truck. The air was thick with dust and heat, the sharp scent of diesel fuel hanging heavy. Farid leaned closer, his voice low and concerned as he repeated Margarethe's earlier question.

"Are you sure you're all right?"

"Yes, yes," she bit out, waving off his concern. It was on the tip of her tongue to explain that she'd known one of the men, but her past felt too personal to share, especially in the middle of a delivery. "I skipped lunch. That's probably why I feel a little strange. As soon as we finish this, I'll talk to Margarethe and have some tea."

Together, they monitored the unloading process. Mia was grateful for Farid, who shouldered most of the responsibilities for checking the food supplies from the WFP. But even as she worked, she couldn't shake the sensation of being watched. The prickling awareness on the back of her neck was impossible to ignore.

Her head turned with a will of its own, and her gaze sought him out. There he was, standing across from the warehouse, his hands on his hips. His body was angled toward the other men, but his head was twisted in her direction, his unwavering eyes locked onto her.

Her chest heaved with suppressed emotion. She wanted to scream, to throw her clipboard at him, to cry until the ache in her chest subsided. *How the hell can he still affect me like this after so long?* Her chest heaved, and she could tell he noticed even from the distance. That was one thing about Jim Devlin—he observed everything. He always had. When they were together, she'd reveled in how deeply he knew her. *Until he didn't.*

Hardening her heart, she willed her racing pulse to slow and lifted her chin defiantly. *He broke me once.* Turning back to the task at hand, she forced herself to focus, though her hands trembled slightly as she checked off items on the clipboard.

"You've already checked off those boxes," Farid said gently, glancing at her clipboard.

Mia blinked, realizing he was right. She'd been so distracted she hadn't even noticed. Looking up, she saw nothing but understanding in Farid's eyes. Though she'd never shared her personal life with him, he clearly sensed the tension emanating from her.

"We're almost done," she said, her voice strained. "Would you mind finishing up?"

"Of course not," he replied with quiet assurance.

Mia turned to leave, unsure where to go, when Farid placed a hand on her arm. She looked back at him, waiting.

"You were surprised by the visitors. Especially the one named Devil."

Her brow lifted, remembering his call sign. "Devil?"

"That is what it sounded like when Margarethe introduced us."

Mia scoffed, a bitter laugh escaping her lips. "Devil. That's apropos." She nodded, exhaling sharply. "And yes, seeing him was a surprise."

Farid smiled, his expression gentle. "Mal ya ca ma rot ke loŋ," he said in South Sudanese. "What is unexpected can be a blessing. That is what my mother used to tell me. Not all surprises are bad. Some may bring joy or opportunities."

Mia swallowed the lump in her throat, the desire to cry nearly overwhelming. "I'm not sure there's a blessing to be found in this."

Farid's smile deepened. "Then give yourself time to discover if there is some joy to be found."

She doubted there was, but she nodded quietly and turned away, steeling herself for whatever came next.

The intake was quickly finished, and Farid handled the paperwork. When all items were checked off, Mia scanned the warehouse, her gaze settling on her staff and the volunteers from the mission group diligently organizing the food supplies. From across the space, Margarethe waved her over. Mia sighed, knowing she couldn't put off the meeting any longer.

"Farid, stay and oversee everything here. I'll meet with Margarethe now."

"She may be your superior but also your friend," he said. "She will help."

Mia managed a sad smile and nodded. "Never doubt that you're also my friend."

Farid's smile broadened, and he bent slightly, dipping his head in acknowledgment. "Keec ci ok de luɔr ke mac. Friendship is like a tree that offers shade. Your friends will be your shade during this time."

Inhaling deeply, Mia closed her eyes, counted to ten, then released the air from her lungs. With her head held high, she walked past the rows of food crates, making her way to the quartet waiting for her. She kept her gaze on Margarethe but could feel the men's eyes on her as she approached. Her forced smile felt tight, her heart hammering as she avoided looking at Devlin's face. She didn't want to remember him from long ago as Jim, the man she loved. Nor did she want to see him as he was now. To guard her heart, she preferred to remember him as he'd been the last time she saw him—when he was a lying, cheating scum unworthy of her love.

Just as her thoughts spiraled into that *Devilish* hole,

Margarethe's commanding voice cut through. "Let's go to your office, Mia, so you can get me up to speed with everything that's going on. I know you didn't feel comfortable putting it in an email. Cole, Todd, and Devlin...it'll be a tight fit, but I think it's the best place for us to meet."

Mia inclined her head, her throat tight. "Okay." Her one-word response sounded ridiculous even to her ears, but being close to Devlin was the last thing she wanted. As she climbed the wooden steps to her small office overlooking the warehouse, she shook her head, dislodging thoughts of him. *I don't give a fuck what he calls himself. Maybe Farid was right. He is the devil.*

The small landing at the top of the stairs felt cramped, with barely enough space for the group. Mia unlocked the door and stepped into her office. She'd never thought much about the size of her workspace before. Meetings with staff usually took place in the warehouse, where they'd stand or perch on wooden crates arranged haphazardly. But now, with her office about to host this group, it seemed starkly barren.

An old wooden desk sat against the wall, accompanied by an equally weathered chair. A laptop rested on its surface next to a locked filing cabinet. The only personal touch was a framed collage of photographs hanging above the desk.

Her gaze lingered on the images—one of her family on bales of hay in front of their barn and another from her last visit home, surrounded by extended family. A more recent photo was of her brother and sister-in-law, along with cousins and their families. In the center stood Mia. She had once loved that photo, but now it struck her how solitary she appeared amid the crowd.

Other photos captured moments from her work in various camps. One, a favorite, showed her surrounded by refugees as they received their first food rations. Their expressions radiated gratitude, a humbling reminder of why she did what she did. She hadn't known the picture had been taken until someone presented it to her.

The clatter of boots on the wooden floor jolted her from her thoughts. Turning, she saw Devlin descending the stairs to retrieve the wooden folding chairs one of the workers had brought. He carried them back up, his movements deliberate. Mia glanced at the chairs and bit back a smirk. They looked too flimsy to hold his weight. If one collapsed and sent him sprawling on his ass, she wouldn't mind.

By the time the door was closed, she had insisted Margarethe take her chair, leaving Mia perched on the edge of her desk near the laptop. Devlin, Cole, and Todd formed a semicircle, and to her disappointment, each chair supported them without incident.

"Tell us what's happening," Margarethe prompted, her tone direct as always. "And elaborate, for the benefit of our security investigators."

Mia opened her laptop, navigating to the files she needed. She avoided looking at Devlin and focused on Margarethe as she began. "As you saw downstairs, all the food delivered to this camp comes through here. This is our central delivery and distribution center. While we can't always account for what happens before it arrives—whether it's flown in or transported from an outside agency—we inventory everything as it's unloaded. Discrepancies happen occasionally. Human error, or sometimes someone local helping themselves to a crate of tomatoes. Those we don't worry about chasing down."

She clicked on another file, continuing, "Once the food is secured here, our priority is maintaining the integrity of the distribution center to ensure the supplies reach the refugees in the villages."

"And each village has its own distribution warehouse," Margarethe added.

"Correct." Mia nodded. "My staff and I oversee the distributions from here to the five villages. I'm also ultimately responsible for ensuring those distributions make it to the refugees."

"That's a huge responsibility," Devlin said, his voice even but probing. "We've learned you have over a hundred thousand refugees."

Her jaw tightened as her gaze snapped to him. "Yes, it is a huge responsibility. And like all my responsibilities, I take it very seriously."

As soon as the words left her mouth, Mia recognized her tone was far from welcoming or encouraging. She closed her eyes for a second, reminding herself that, for whatever reason, he had come here to help. She wondered if he'd known she was at this camp, then recalled the shock on his face when his eyes landed on her. *No, he had no idea I was here.* She wasn't sure if that made her happy, sad, or downright pissed off.

"You were saying?" Margarethe prodded.

"Yes, yes," Mia said, dragging her thoughts back to the matter at hand. "I'm not at every intake or distribution, although I am probably present at over half of them. Farid is my second-in-command and has been at this camp for many years."

Cole asked, "When food leaves this distribution center here and goes to one of the villages, what is the process?"

She shifted slightly on her desk and turned her laptop around. "Our internet is not always reliable, so we usually have our spreadsheets to check off when crates are loaded from here. One of my staff or I will go to the village with the truck and note it as the food is transferred. The staff assigned to that village's food distribution center oversees the refugees in that area. When they get low on supplies and notify me, the process begins again."

"Are the food distribution centers guarded?"

"Yes and no." She shook her head, her shoulders slumping. "When no food distribution staff member is present, the centers are secured and locked. Moses provides security for each village, and his team makes rounds near the food distribution centers. It's not a perfect system, but aside from small thefts, we remain fairly secure."

She lifted her chin and slowly looked at Cole, then Todd, and finally, Devlin, meeting each man's gaze in turn. "I'm sure you must assume that the refugees are so desperate for food that they would take everything they could by any means possible. But you will find that most refugees are so grateful to be here because their lives were so poor where they came from that they work with us, not against us. I've seen families turn away some of their rations when they realized we were running short so there would be enough to go around. I've seen men go without so their wives and children could eat. I've seen families with meager portions share with newcomers just arriving. While there is evidence of small thefts—a bag of rice, a crate of fruit—these refugees also farm, grow what they can, and share or sell their produce."

The room fell silent as she finished, the weight of her words settling over them. She fought the urge to shift on the desk again, wishing now she'd asked for another chair to be brought in.

As though he could read her thoughts, Devlin stood. "Please, sit," he said softly, stepping away from the chair.

She battled the desire to bark at him, refusing any act of

generosity. But not wanting to raise questions among the others, she stood, shifted the chair next to her laptop, and sat down. Devlin leaned against the wall by the doorframe, casually crossing one booted foot over the other, his arms folded across his broad chest. For all outward appearances, he seemed calm, in control, and unbothered.

She wanted to slap him.

The intensity of the desire shocked her. She wasn't a violent person, yet she was surprised by how much she wanted to hurt him. Christ, even after a decade, just being in a room with him could make her lose herself.

She continued with another shake of her head to dislodge all stray thoughts. "The villages are set in a semicircle. There are five, the largest of which is Bulit, which holds about thirty thousand refugees. Then there is Kaborogatu with twenty-five thousand. The next ones farther along are Mukondo and Kaoni, at twenty thousand each. The smallest village is also the farthest from us. It's the one where some new refugees will be brought. Sweswe only has about twelve thousand refugees. It is also the village closest to our outer perimeter on the north."

She leaned over and jerked on a drawer, jiggling it until it opened. Pulling out a map, she spread it on the desktop. "While the camp is in constant flux, this shows how it is now."

"Is each village self-sufficient?" Devlin asked.

"Yes," she replied, casting a furtive glance his way before looking back down at the map as though it was the most interesting thing in the room. "Each village has its own food distribution center, supply distribution center, and director who reports straight to Dr. München. They have their own medical clinic and their own WASH representative." Her brow furrowed as she considered how much the three men understood about the camp. "WASH stands for water, sanitation, and hygiene. As you can imagine, without the work of these people, many of the refugees would die of disease."

She spared another glance toward Devlin, finding him nodding, his gaze still pinned on her.

Shaken slightly, she pushed forward. "I began to see discrepancies from Sweswe. My records of what they distributed and requested for months didn't match up. I noticed this last month. I brought it up with my staff, but none seemed to understand where the discrepancy was. When we looked, we found crates were missing. At first, I thought it was refugees stealing. Most of the refugees there came from the Congo and were in bad shape when they arrived. I also understand that many have had to steal, beg, and borrow anything they could to survive. I hoped the discrepancies would stop as soon as they realized there would be plenty of food, and we would all work together."

"They didn't," Margarethe said.

Mia shook her head as she lifted her hand to rub her temples, staving off the blossoming headache. "I reviewed several months' records and realized that the village was requesting more and distributing less than what would have been correct. Thinking my staff might have been overwhelmed, I shifted around a few people. But that didn't seem to make a difference. Because the thefts were not random, I then began to wonder if I didn't have a systemic problem on my hands. I also began to think that more than just a few refugees were stealing. It was too much at a time. It was too coordinated."

Cole nodded. "What made you think of the black market?"

She scoffed. "I live and work in an area surrounded by

countries with military regimes that are just as desperate for money and goods as the refugees are. The black market abounds. Food, clothes, medical supplies, office supplies, and weapons. A refugee camp can be the perfect place for these predators. They prey on the weak and take whatever they can."

"And you went to Margarethe because you weren't sure who to trust here."

Once again, Devlin spoke, and Mia felt forced to meet his gaze. His rich and steady voice seemed to wrap around her, pulling her attention even as she tried to resist.

"I don't deny that there could be refugees here who the Congolese placed specifically to steal what they can," she said, her tone sharp. "But it's so organized. And it makes me not trust anyone. Even the heads of the camp that I work with." She squeezed her eyes shut briefly, hating the bitterness that had crept into her heart.

"Mia."

The way he said her name softly sent a jolt through her. Her eyes snapped open, locking and then narrowing on his. Devlin leaned against the wall, arms still crossed, his posture seemingly relaxed, but his expression told a different story. Something flickered in his eyes—sadness? Regret? She couldn't tell, and it infuriated her.

Dragging her gaze away from him, she turned to Margarethe. "I went out one night last week, and when I came to the food distribution center at Kaborogota, I noticed I didn't see a security guard around. I parked down the lane and waited. He finally came around, so I left and came back here. It just made me realize we have no consistent way to ensure no one is stealing. And with trucks coming and going at all hours, the food can be vulnerable. I emailed you immediately. Unable to know who I might trust, I thought it best to go straight to my superior outside this camp."

"You should always take someone with you when you are out at night," Margarethe gently chastised.

The three men erupted simultaneously, their voices blending into chaos, but Devlin's broke through above the rest. "What the fuck, Mia? What the hell were you thinking?"

White-hot fury surged through her. She turned on him, her gaze burning. "How dare you question what I do in my job?" she bit out, her voice shaking with anger. Her fist pounded against her chest. "I understand the qualities of loyalty and protection, not just ensuring the nutritional needs of these people."

Margarethe raised a hand, her expression a mixture of concern and authority. "Enough," she said firmly. "You've given us plenty to start with, Mia. It's almost dinnertime. I'll take these files and look them over tonight. We'll regroup in the morning."

Dipping her head, Mia stood. "You may use my office as long as you like. I need to check on my staff." Her voice was calm, but her feet itched to carry her far away. Without waiting for acknowledgment, she nodded to the others before pushing past Devlin and heading out the door.

She battled the desire to race down the stairs but forced her feet to descend slowly, her movements deliberate. Spotting Farid across the warehouse, she crossed to him. "I need to check on the villages. Can you handle locking up after Margarethe and the others leave?"

"Of course."

Relief softened her features as she gave him a grateful nod. She stepped outside and climbed into her Jeep. When she started the engine, she looked over her shoulder. The three men were leaving the building, but she only felt Devlin's sharp, unyielding, piercing gaze through the growing dusk. She needed to put as much distance between her and him as she could. Her chest tightened, and she gripped the wheel tightly before driving away.

7

The moment Mia left the small office, a hollow ache settled in Devlin's chest. It was a void he hadn't felt in years but recognized instantly. Her absence had hit him harder than he could have imagined, leaving him grappling with the heartache he had buried long ago. But even amid the weight of that pain, a strange clarity came with seeing her again. It was a bittersweet relief, like taking his first breath after holding it underwater for too long.

Before he could follow her, the room's tension sharpened. Three sets of eyes fixed on him, unrelenting in their scrutiny.

Margarethe arched a brow, her no-nonsense demeanor cutting through the quiet. "Do you want to explain what just happened? I've known Mia a long time, and I've never seen her like that."

Devlin shifted uncomfortably, his gaze flicking between Margarethe and his two fellow Keepers, Cole and Todd. Their expressions revealed a mix of curiosity and concern, paired with the expectation that he'd handle this without derailing the mission. He recognized it because it was exactly how he'd look if the roles were reversed.

He scrubbed a hand over his face, releasing a heavy sigh that felt as though it had been lodged in his chest for years. When he finally looked back at Margarethe, her steady, expectant stare bore into him. He wasn't just talking to colleagues... this was Mia's supervisor. Whatever he said now could affect her job, and the last thing he wanted was to bring more trouble to her door.

"I know her," he admitted, his voice gravelly with restraint. "And before you ask—no, she wasn't some casual hookup from my past. I met her when she was fifteen. I was sixteen. We dated for ten years."

"Holy shit," Todd muttered, his surprise breaking the charged silence.

"The one from your past," Cole added, his tone laced with realization.

Devlin hesitated, debating how much to reveal. A team thrived on trust, but revisiting the pain of his history with Mia felt like walking barefoot on shattered glass. Still, honesty was nonnegotiable.

"She didn't just get away," he said, his voice quieter now, the weight of his admission dragging it down. "I pushed her away. Ten years ago, I broke her trust, and I know I broke her heart. What she never knew was that mine was broken, too."

He glanced up, his gaze locking on Margarethe's. Vulnerability clawed at him, leaving him feeling strangely exposed under her unwavering stare.

"Fuck," Cole mumbled under his breath.

"You can say that again," Devlin replied with a grim nod.

Margarethe leaned back in her chair, her expression

carefully neutral, though her piercing eyes missed nothing. "I only have one question for you."

Devlin stood straighter, bracing himself. "What's that?"

"Is this going to be a problem?"

"No." His response came quickly, too sharp, and even he knew it sounded defensive.

Her brow arched again in a silent challenge. "Are you sure about that?"

He opened his mouth, but the truth caught in his throat. With a frustrated exhale, he looked down at his boots, hands resting on his hips as he collected his thoughts. When he raised his head again, his eyes were steady.

"I hope not," he admitted, his tone softer but resolute. "Mia is dedicated to her cause, and I'm just as committed to keeping her safe. Whatever happened between us before—it won't interfere with the mission."

Margarethe studied him for a moment longer before nodding and standing. Her commanding presence made the gesture feel like a dismissal. "All right. I'll take your word for it. For now. I suggest you all get some rest. I'll review the files tonight, and we'll regroup in the morning."

Devlin released a breath he hadn't realized he was holding as she walked out. His thoughts, however, refused to settle. His team might have accepted his assurance, but the storm between him and Mia wasn't over. Not by a long shot.

Cole hefted the chairs and carried them down the stairs with Todd close behind, their easy camaraderie filling the space. Devlin trailed them, his mind elsewhere. As they descended, his eyes scanned the warehouse, searching instinctively for Mia. The place buzzed with activity. Voices overlapped as workers moved supplies, but she wasn't among them.

He headed out into the cooler evening air, the scent of dust and faint traces of cooking fires mingling in the breeze. Just as his hopes began to wane, he caught sight of her.

Mia sat in a Jeep parked at the edge of the warehouse, her profile illuminated by the sun low in the sky. She looked so achingly familiar yet like a stranger all at once. Alone in the vehicle, she seemed small but undeniably resilient.

For a moment, Devlin felt the ground tilt beneath him as he waged a silent war within himself. The pull to run to her, to finally say what had been locked in his heart for a decade, battled against the walls of restraint he'd built over the years.

As if sensing his gaze, Mia turned. Their eyes locked.

Everything else—the clamor of the camp and the distant conversations—faded into oblivion. The air between them crackled with their shared past and unspoken words in that suspended moment. Her expression shifted, something raw flickering in her eyes. Then, as if she'd made a decision, Mia took a sharp breath, turned away, and faced forward. The Jeep's engine sputtered, and the vehicle jerked forward, rolling onto the uneven lane and away from him.

Devlin stood frozen, the space where she had been now filled with emptiness. He barely registered Margarethe's voice until she turned toward him.

"Good night," she said simply, dipping her chin. Her steady gaze lingered on him and he felt assessed and warned. Then she paused, her expression softening ever so slightly. "Mia means the world to me, Devlin. I'm trusting you to do right by her."

Her words landed with the weight of an unspoken threat. "Understood, ma'am," he said firmly.

She studied him a moment longer before nodding and walking away, her figure fading into the shadows of the camp.

When he finally turned, he found Cole and Todd watching him, their postures relaxed but their gazes sharp.

"I'm not even going to suggest we get someone else to take your place," Cole said, crossing his arms. "I'm a firm believer that things happen for a reason. You being here, her being here—it's not a coincidence."

Devlin nodded slowly, Cole's words echoing the deep pull he felt in his chest. "There hasn't been a day in the past ten years when I haven't thought about her," he admitted quietly, his voice rough with emotion. "But I figured that ship had sailed." He paused, his gaze turning toward the direction the Jeep had gone. Determination hardened his tone. "Now that I have this chance, I'll right the wrongs of the past. That's a promise. After that...we'll see if she's willing to forgive."

The sound of soft, measured footsteps broke the moment. Devlin turned to see Farid approaching. The wiry man stopped a few feet away and met Devlin's gaze with calm intensity. "Al-qalb alladhi yuhibb la yatab," Farid said, his accented voice warm.

Devlin frowned slightly. "I'm sorry—I don't understand."

Farid's lips curved into a knowing smile. "It means, 'The heart that loves never grows weary.'"

"I—" Devlin faltered, caught off guard by the weight of those words.

Farid tilted his head, his expression kind but penetrating. "Don't worry, Mr. Devlin. I can see it in your eyes. Regret. Hope. Love. Life gives you all of those, but mostly love." Farid inclined his head toward Cole and Todd in a goodbye gesture before stepping away, his figure disappearing into the soft glow of the evening lights.

Devlin exhaled deeply, his chest expanding with the pungent mix of cooking spices and wood smoke that filled the air. He wasn't just here to investigate stolen food supplies or protect the camp. This mission had become something far more personal—an opportunity to bridge the chasm between him and Mia, to lay his heart bare, and hope she might do the same.

"Did you guys find out where the dining hall is?" he asked, breaking the silence.

Todd smirked, clapping him on the shoulder. "Yeah. Let's go."

The three men made their way toward the guesthouse and staff quarters, their steps falling into an easy rhythm. When they reached the dining tent, the setup was all too familiar—long tables under canvas, the clatter of utensils, and the faint aroma of rice and beans wafting in the air. It mirrored countless meals Devlin had shared on military missions before.

Soon seated at the end of the table, he looked down at their trays, noting that each had not taken much food. While the three large men could burn through calories, they were aware of being in an area where a simple beans and rice meal was a feast. Devlin absently poked at the rice on his tray while Todd and Cole fell into easy conversation.

His eyes kept scanning the tent, restless and searching. He noted Robert seated at a table with a small group of staffers, his posture relaxed as he spoke with them. But Mia was nowhere to be seen.

Devlin's stomach clenched as his gaze lingered on Robert. Something about Robert's earlier concern for Mia set Devlin's nerves on edge. And then came the thought he didn't want to entertain but couldn't shake—had Robert and Mia been close? Were they close now?

It's been ten years, he reminded himself, his grip tightening on his fork. *Who knows how many people she's let into her life since then?* The idea of Mia sharing herself, her heart, with someone else stirred a jealousy he had no right to feel.

"What the fuck is wrong with you?" Todd's voice broke through his spiraling thoughts.

Devlin jerked his head toward him, his brow furrowed. "What?"

"You're glaring, man." Todd leaned back in his chair, shaking his head. "We're supposed to be sliding in here quietly, not scaring people off. We don't need to cozy up to anyone, but we definitely don't want to piss them off right out of the gate."

Devlin grimaced, leaning back and running a hand over his face. "Jesus. I told you all this wouldn't be a problem. Maybe I was wrong."

Cole leaned forward then, his forearms resting on the edge of the table, his tone calm but direct. "Listen, you're one of the sharpest guys I know, and you've come back from worse—hell, you've survived things most of us can't even imagine. You can handle this. But you've gotta stay focused. I'm not saying you can't think about Mia. Damn, I'm rooting for you, brother. But if you lose your focus now, you'll regret it later."

Devlin met Cole's steady gaze and nodded slowly. "Yeah, you're right."

As he glanced back toward Robert's table, his chest tightened. The man had stood and was walking out of the tent, leaving behind a woman still finishing her meal.

Devlin's jaw tightened as he stood, pushing his chair

back. "You two head back if you want. I'm going to check in about Mia. I don't like not knowing where she is."

Todd straightened immediately. "You want us to help look for her?"

"Not yet." Devlin shook his head. "Let me see what I can find out first. I'll let you know if it's anything to worry about."

With a nod, Todd and Cole exited the tent, their figures disappearing into the dim light outside. Devlin turned his attention to the lone woman still sitting at the table.

"Excuse me," he said, stepping closer. His tone was polite but edged with urgency. "I'm sorry to interrupt your meal, ma'am. I was wondering if you know Mia Duff."

The woman looked up, startled by his sudden presence. She blinked, then dabbed her mouth with a napkin before offering a small smile. "Yes, I know Mia. She's a good friend of mine. Who are you?"

He hesitated briefly before answering. "I'm one of the security team members with the WFP. I saw her leave earlier in a Jeep, and I haven't seen her since. I just wanted to make sure she's okay."

"Oh, nice to meet you," the woman said warmly, her accent lilting and musical. "I'm Ritah, the head protection officer." She extended her hand, delicate but firm in its gesture. "Don't confuse that with a security officer like Moses. My work focuses on the protection of vulnerable groups—women, children, and the elderly. Most of my time is spent with women who've endured gender-based violence or children in need of safeguarding."

Devlin nodded, a flicker of respect crossing his features. He could only imagine the weight of her role and the emotional toll that came with witnessing such pain day after day. "That sounds like incredibly important work, but I'm sure it's not easy."

Ritah gave a small, tired smile. "It's not, but it's worth it."

"I appreciate your time," he said, stepping back slightly. "I'm sorry to have bothered you, ma'am."

"Not at all," she replied with a wave of her hand. "But I haven't seen Mia since breakfast." She tilted her head thoughtfully. "Though I haven't been back to my quarters today. Mia and I share a container apartment. She has her own place on one side, and I have the other side."

"Container apartment?" he asked, curiosity edging his tone.

Ritah chuckled, a light, airy sound that softened the weariness in her eyes. "Yes, the staff quarters. They're old shipping containers converted into small apartments. Just efficiencies, really, but each has its own bathroom. We still use the communal showers, but it's nice to have a bit of privacy. Most of the other staff are in dorms."

Devlin nodded, the description sparking memories of makeshift accommodations during deployments. "We had something similar in the military," he said, his voice tinged with familiarity. "Again, I'm sorry for interrupting your meal, and thank you for the information."

"You're welcome," Ritah said with a kind smile.

8

As he stepped back into the night, the cool air did little to temper the unease gnawing at his chest. Darkness had fallen, and the thought of Mia out in the camp unsettled him. The idea that she might have driven off because of him sent a fresh wave of guilt rolling through him.

But as he approached the food distribution warehouse, a flicker of relief coursed through him. The Jeep she'd driven earlier was parked in the same spot, now a welcome sight.

He exhaled slowly, some of the tension easing from his shoulders. She'd come back.

The warehouse's front door was locked, but as he walked around the side, he spotted the large cargo sliding door open, the glow of interior lights spilling onto the gravel outside. A few workers still milled around the loading dock.

Inside, the space was brightly lit, but the noise of earlier activity had vanished. The silence was almost eerie, broken only by the faint rustle of fabric and a soft voice muttering in the distance.

Devlin's ears perked, and he followed the sound toward the back of the warehouse. As he moved through rows of stacked crates, he finally caught sight of her.

Mia was perched on a ladder, her small frame leaning precariously as she tugged at the edge of a tarp covering several crates. Her dark braid swung over her shoulder, catching the light with each movement.

He stopped in his tracks, unwilling to startle her while she balanced so high up. Instead, he allowed himself a stolen moment to simply watch her.

She was thinner than he remembered, her frame more delicate, and he wondered uneasily if she was eating enough or pushing herself too hard. Knowing Mia, she probably worked herself to the brink without a second thought.

Her hair, pulled neatly back now, brought back a rush of memories he wasn't prepared for. He could still feel the silky strands sliding through his fingers, the way they'd spill over her shoulders in waves when she let it down. He remembered waking up to find her hair strewn across his pillow like dark silk.

And then his mind betrayed him, conjuring images of her in his lap, her body moving against his, her hair cascading around them like a curtain, shutting out the world. Those moments had felt sacred like nothing and no one else existed but them.

His body stirred at the memory, heat pooling low in his stomach. *Not now,* he scolded himself silently, willing the rush of arousal to subside. The last thing he needed was to approach her while battling the evidence of his desire.

Her long-sleeved khaki shirt, now tied around her waist, revealed a fitted white T-shirt that clung to her breasts. Devlin's gaze swept over her, catching on the curve of her hips and the way her khaki pants stretched over her figure. The sight tugged at a memory he couldn't suppress—the first time he saw her nearly twenty years ago, chained to a goalpost, defiant and wild-eyed. Even then, her presence had been impossible to ignore. The thought brought a wry smile to his lips.

She straightened on the ladder, her movements deliberate and careful. He called out once he was sure she was steady, his voice cutting through the silence. "Working late?"

Mia whirled around, her braid whipping from one side of her chest to the other. Her sharp gaze searched the dimly lit warehouse before landing on him below. Her eyes narrowed, and her mouth twisted into something between a grimace and a frown.

"Did you get lost on the way to the guest quarters?" she asked, her tone clipped.

Devlin tilted his head, the hint of a grin tugging at his lips. "If I say yes, will you give me a tour?"

A sound escaped her lips—a low, frustrated growl even at this distance. Without another word, she began climbing down the ladder. Devlin stepped forward, his hand steadying the frame instinctively.

She stopped when she reached the last rung, their faces suddenly level. The moment stretched, charged with tension and the unspoken weight of the years between them. Then she descended the final step, and Devlin's gaze dropped to meet hers.

She barely came up to his shoulder, just as he remembered. The memory of her tucked into his side flickered in his mind—her arm wrapped around his waist, her thumb looped through his belt loop, holding tight as though letting go might make her lose her balance. She'd always said being with him made her feel safe. Back then, he'd considered it his mission in life to protect her, even when she didn't know it.

Now, standing before her, the ache of how he'd failed her spread through his chest like a slow, gnawing fire. Mia dusted her hands off on her pants, drawing his eyes briefly before she glanced up at him, her expression unreadable.

"Still checking the inventory?" he asked, keeping his tone neutral and professional. It felt safer—less likely to end with her kneeing him where it would hurt most.

She crossed her arms, one brow lifting slightly. "Someone has to."

He allowed himself another moment to drink her in now that the initial shock of seeing her again had passed. The years had only sharpened her beauty. Though there were faint lines at the corners of her eyes, her features held the same striking balance of strength and softness that had captivated him all those years ago.

A flood of questions rushed to his mind—about her family, her work, how her life had unfolded since he'd last seen her. But he kept them locked behind clenched teeth. He hadn't earned the right to ask those things, not yet. The weight of that truth settled heavily in his chest.

Mia shifted, glancing down at her boots, her hesitation palpable. When she finally looked back up, her shoulders sagged with a deep sigh. "You want a tour?"

Devlin almost staggered with relief. It wasn't an invitation for conversation, but it wasn't a dismissal, either. For now, that was enough.

"Absolutely," he said, keeping his tone even but warm. "I'd be honored."

She opened her mouth as if to say something, but no words came, only another soft exhale. Without further comment, she turned, and he fell into step beside her. As they walked the length of the warehouse, she pointed out the careful organization of crates and supplies. Her tone was even and professional, though her voice had a faint edge of weariness.

He followed her lead, listening as she explained the intricate logistics of running the warehouse. And though her words were measured, every step they took together felt like progress toward reclaiming something he thought he'd lost forever.

"In some ways, it's like a grocery store," he observed, gesturing toward the aisles of goods.

"Same principle," Mia agreed. "It makes it easy for us to get an order from a village—whether they need rice, potatoes, dairy, or vegetables. We can quickly figure out how much we have, how much they need, how many trucks to load, and how much personnel I'll need to send to make the transfer."

Devlin nodded, his mind half on her words and half on the guarded tone she maintained. She was answering his questions, but her answers were precise. Personal details were noticeably absent.

At the end of the warehouse road, Mia abruptly stopped, her expression tightening as though a sudden thought had struck her like a physical blow.

"Mia?" Devlin's voice was laced with concern.

Her gaze met his, heavy with emotion, and then, as if she couldn't hold it back any longer, she blurted, "Did you know?"

He frowned, unsure of her meaning, and stayed silent, waiting for her to elaborate.

Did you know I was here?" she pressed, her voice sharper now, the demand slicing through the humid air like a blade.

The question hit him square in the chest, knocking the breath from his lungs. He knew this was a moment he couldn't afford to fumble. One wrong word, one hesitation, and she'd be gone—not just physically, but in every way that mattered. But he'd promised himself that with Mia, he would only offer the truth.

"No, I didn't," he admitted, his voice measured and careful. "My boss… he knew Margarethe, and when Margarethe got your email, she wanted to handle things privately. She was the one who coordinated the WFP contract with us."

He braced himself, waiting for the storm to hit, but Mia's expression remained unreadable. That was worse. That eerie stillness, the silence stretched so thin it felt ready to snap. But her eyes searched his, digging, peeling him apart to see if he was lying.

Finally, she nodded… slow and deliberate.

The silence stretched between them, taut and fraught with unspoken words. Devlin wanted to say more, to explain the circumstances fully, but he sensed this wasn't the time. Not here and not now.

"Of course," she murmured, voice flat. "Convenient how life works, isn't it? That after ten years, after—" She exhaled hard, like she refused to give breath to the words choking her.

Devlin swallowed. "I'd like to talk more," he said gently, his voice softening as he held her gaze. Her eyes—so familiar yet distant—searched his, and he felt as though he were drowning in their depths. "Mia—"

She held up a hand, stopping him cold. "You want to talk?" she asked, her tone deceptively mild. "Now you want to talk? Because the last time you had the chance, you said nothing. Not a word." She scoffed. "Not that anything you could have said would have made a difference."

The accusation landed like a punch, and he flinched despite himself. "I didn't want to lose you."

Her laughter was bitter, humorless. "Wow. That makes it so much better. You didn't want to, but you did it anyway. Well, that makes one of us because I sure as hell didn't want to be gutted and abandoned without so much as an explanation."

Devlin's chest tightened. "I—"

"No." The single syllable cracked through the air like a whip. "You don't get to stand here and act like this accidental reunion is a chance for two old friends to catch up." Her eyes burned with something deeper than anger. "You were my whole world, Jim." She spat the name like it tasted bad. "And then you obliterated it."

Devlin exhaled slowly, trying to keep his voice steady. "I know I hurt you—"

"Hurt me?" She scoffed. "You destroyed me. And you think one awkward conversation outside a warehouse will fix that?"

He had no answer for that.

Mia's shoulders slumped, her expression weary as she closed her eyes and dropped her chin to her chest. The weight she carried seemed almost tangible, and he would have given anything to lift it from her. She shook her head, crossing her arms tightly as if physically holding herself together.

When she finally raised her head, her voice was firm but low. "We can't talk here. Even if we seem alone, someone could always be nearby. I'm not about to air my business in front of people I work with."

Her words cut deep, but he knew he deserved the dagger she'd just driven into his chest. Pressing his luck, he asked softly, "Then where? What about your room?"

Her eyes flashed with disbelief before narrowing into dangerous slits. "For all you know, I share a room with twenty other women."

He didn't flinch. "You don't."

Her sharp inhale told him he'd made a mistake.

"You already knew that, didn't you?" Her voice dropped to something cold and lethal. "Who did you ask?"

He hesitated a second too long. "I asked someone in the dining hall."

Her brows shot up. "You what?"

He raised his hands, palms out, in surrender. "No, no. It's not what you think. I told her I was with security and hadn't seen you in a while. She said you might be here or in your room. She also explained the shipping container apartments. She said she shared one with you, and I recognized the setup from my military days."

Mia's glare lingered before she finally tilted her head as though weighing his words. "We can talk… sometime. But not now. And definitely not in my room."

He should have let it go. Should have known when to quit. But dammit, he'd already lost her once. He wasn't about to let her slip away again. "It would be private," he pushed, his tone edged with something dangerously close to desperation.

Her hands landed on her hips as her lips curled in a humorless smirk. "Yeah, well, I don't invite strange men to my room."

Devlin took a step closer, his voice softening with emotion. "Oh, Mia… you know me."

"Do I?" she shot back, her voice cold. "Jim? Devlin? Whoever you are now?" She scoffed, her tone turning biting. "Farid thought Margarethe called you Devil."

Devlin chuckled ruefully. "You remember… that was my call sign."

Pain flashed in her eyes, swift and cutting. "At one time, many years ago, I thought I did know you." Her voice dropped to something almost fragile. Then just as quickly, it hardened again. "But I didn't. And nothing in the last decade has changed that."

She turned on her heel and walked away, leaving him standing in the deepening shadows of the warehouse.

He followed at a distance, watching as she lowered the door and locked it securely. Then she slipped back into the world with no place for him anymore. A world she had carved out when he let her walk away. Her steady voice was professional as she called out to another worker. "No more deliveries tonight. See you in the morning."

As they rounded the corner, her demeanor shifted, and she tossed a wave and a smile to a group of staff and refugees passing by. It looked like a mask, one she wore with practiced ease.

Devlin hesitated when they reached the guest quarters, then said, "I promise I won't push you to talk anymore tonight. But let me walk you to your room. Please."

Mia looked as though she might argue, but then she sighed and inclined her head.

They walked side by side, the silence hanging like a heavy weight between them. When they reached her container apartment, she turned to face him. "This is me."

He nodded toward the structure. "Ritah mentioned there are staff showers. Will you be safe?"

Mia scoffed, the sound soft but tinged with exasperation. "I'm not inviting you to see for yourself." Her lips pressed together as though she wanted to say more but had to stop herself from speaking. Inhaling deeply, she finally said, "I'm fine. Plenty of people are around. I'm in no danger."

He waited as she unlocked her door and stepped inside. Just before it clicked shut, he thought he heard her whisper, "Good night, Jim."

His chest tightened, his heart swelling. For a long time,

he just stood there, staring at the closed door. And for the first time in ten years, he realized he hadn't even begun to atone.

Turning, he walked back down the lane, his voice low as he whispered to the breeze, "Good night, my Mia."

When he returned to the guest quarters, he found Cole and Todd studying the maps of the whole camp as well as the villages. He immediately sat down with them, looking over the information.

"We need to drive the perimeter tomorrow," Cole said. "Look for the other roads and entrances here where a truck could leave. Check out what security is at those checkpoints."

Devlin was grateful for the distraction. His focus needed to remain sharp on the mission, but now the mission had expanded. It wasn't just about protecting the camp—it was about proving to Mia, step by step, that he was still the man who would do anything for her.

9

Mia pressed her back against the cool metal of the door, her breath catching as she tried to make sense of the storm swirling inside her. The day had been a relentless assault on her emotions, each one clawing for dominance—anger, confusion, and a flicker of something she didn't want to name. She felt like a dam ready to break.

Jim Devlin. Seeing him again had been like ripping open an old wound, one she thought long since scarred over. When he asked to talk, the words she'd buried for years nearly spilled out. *Go to hell.* She wanted to say it. She wanted to scream it. But the haunted and pleading look in his eyes had stolen her voice, leaving her standing there, clutching at the tattered remains of her resolve.

He'd blown them apart once, wielding their love like a stick of dynamite. Yet there was still a painful, aching pull she couldn't ignore. It infuriated her.

A bitter snort escaped her lips as she leaned her head back, staring at the ceiling as if the answers might be written there. What could he possibly say to make any of this better? The scars he'd left behind weren't the kind that words could heal.

And as he had walked away, she'd heard the faint crunch of gravel through the open window next to her. Then his voice drifted through the night air, soft as a prayer. "Good night, my Mia."

The breath in her lungs stilled. *My Mia.* The endearment hit her like a whisper from the past, an echo of a memory she thought she'd locked away forever.

The first time he'd called her that was at the high school junior dance. She could still feel the way his arms held her close, the warmth of his gaze as their bodies swayed in perfect rhythm. He'd kissed her then—tentative, tender, as though he was afraid to break the moment. When he pulled back, his lips hovered over hers, and he'd whispered, "My Mia." Those two words had been a vow, a promise, and for years, she'd believed it with everything she had.

Hearing it now, after all this time, after all the pain... it unraveled her. She lost all sense of time until a sharp knock on the door yanked her from the spiral of memory. She straightened, her heart thudding as she wondered if it was Devlin again. Her fingers hesitated on the doorknob, torn between the desire to send him away and the reckless urge to confront him.

But when she opened the door, it wasn't Devlin standing there. It was Elizabeth, holding a bottle of wine, flanked by Ritah, Prossy, Karen, and Doreen, their faces alight with curiosity and concern.

"What's going on?" Mia asked, blinking at them in surprise.

Elizabeth raised the bottle with a sly grin. "Ritah spilled the beans about the handsome man who was asking about you. Now, you need to tell us who he is. And if you say no, we're bribing you with this." She shook the bottle, adding with a sheepish smile, "Okay, it's not the best wine, and it's already been opened. But I figured it was worth a shot."

For a moment, Mia wanted to shut them out, to bury everything deep where it couldn't hurt her anymore. The story of her and Devlin wasn't something she shared lightly—it was too raw, too personal. But as she looked at their eager faces, something inside her softened. These women had seen her at her strongest, but maybe it was time to show them her scars, too.

"Come in," she said, stepping back to let them pass. "But if you want the full story, it's a good thing I have another bottle."

As they settled into her small space, the women lounged beside each other on the bed, legs stretched out with their backs against the wall. Mia perched on the chair after she grabbed a few plastic cups from the shelf. The wine was poured, and five pairs of eyes fixed on her, patient but expectant. For the first time in years, Mia felt the tiniest crack in the wall she'd built around herself.

She took a deep breath, swirling the wine in her cup. "Okay," she said softly. "Here's how it started... and how it ended."

Mia let her gaze sweep over her friends, marveling at how different yet perfectly they fit together. Ritah and Doreen, both Ugandan, exuded quiet strength. Ritah, poised and confident, was a natural leader in her department, while Doreen's shyness masked a deeply compassionate heart. Karen, the head nurse with a fiery Irish temperament, was the steady anchor of Doc Elaine's team. Her humor kept everyone grounded. Then there was Elizabeth, the sharp-witted American, heading the Economic and Livelihood Program with her husband. And Prossy, a brilliant and tireless South Sudanese teacher who worked in the children's education centers. These women represented the best of humanity, a rare and beautiful gathering of resilience, humor, and heart.

Mia hesitated for a moment, the weight of her story pressing against her ribs. But then she smiled softly. For the first time in years, she felt ready to let someone else carry a piece of it with her.

"I was fifteen years old when I first met Jim Devlin," she began, her voice steady but tinged with nostalgia.

Ritah's eyes immediately widened, and Karen's sharp gasp filled the room.

Mia laughed, shaking her head. "If that shocks you, I'm not sure you're ready for the rest of this story."

"You're right," Elizabeth said, her grin wry. "Good thing you've got more wine. Keep going—I have a feeling this is just the beginning."

She paused, a rueful smile tugging at her lips. "I was with the environmental club outside the school, protesting about the cafeteria's wasteful practices. When the principal brushed me off, I decided to stage a protest. So I marched down to the football field during practice, pulled out a chain, and locked myself to the goalpost."

Elizabeth burst into laughter, nearly spilling her wine. "Oh my God! I can *so* see you doing that!"

"What a little rebel you were!" Doreen added, her shy grin emerging.

Mia couldn't help but chuckle at their reactions. "The football team was livid, the coach was apoplectic, and the principal came storming down the hill with two police officers in tow. I stayed polite but firm, even when one of the officers didn't appreciate being made a fool of. He started to grab at me, and before I could even react, one of the football players stepped between us."

She leaned forward, her voice softening as she replayed

the moment. "He was fully suited up in his uniform and pads, towering over everyone. He told the officer that they could talk to me, but no one was laying a hand on me."

The room went still as her friends absorbed the moment. Karen's eyes shimmered with awe. "That is so sweet," she whispered.

Mia's smile faltered, the memory tugging at her chest. "I didn't want him to get in trouble, so I unchained myself. The police left, and the principal begrudgingly agreed to hear the environmental club's requests. When I turned around, I finally looked at my protector—really looked at him. And there he was. Jim Devlin. Those piercing blue eyes... I couldn't believe it."

Elizabeth let out a dramatic sigh. "Please tell me this is like a Hallmark movie, and you two started dating right away."

"What's a Hallmark movie?" Ritah asked, her brow furrowed in confusion.

Elizabeth gasped. "Oh, girl, it's like reading a romance novel—only you're watching it instead. Handsome guy, beautiful girl, and no matter how crazy things get in the middle, you know they'll end up together."

"That sounds amazing," Prossy said, her shy smile brightening.

The laughter that followed filled the room, a lightness Mia hadn't realized she needed. But even as her friends' mirth bubbled around her, she felt the familiar weight pressing against her chest. The more she spoke, the harder it became to contain the ache swelling inside her.

She took another sip of wine, her smile bittersweet. "The truth is, it was a lot messier than a Hallmark movie. But at the time, I thought maybe we were that kind of love story."

Her voice trailed off, and her friends exchanged

glances, their expressions softening. They didn't press her, seeming to sense there was more to the story and knowing she would share it when she was ready.

For now, Mia held on to the comfort of their company, grateful for the distraction as her heart wrestled with the ghosts of the past.

"We started dating, and we didn't stop for almost ten years," Mia said, her voice soft but steady.

The women gasped again, but none of them spoke, their silence urging her to continue.

"We never broke up during that time," she said, her gaze dropping to the empty cup of wine in her hands. "Sure, we had our arguments, like any couple, but we grew up together. He graduated a year ahead of me, but we kept dating. When it came time to choose a college, I picked the same one. Not just because of him but because they had the program I wanted.

"I worked hard, taking extra classes while he studied and played football, so we graduated at the same time. Then I went straight into a master's program, and he joined the military. He wanted to become a SEAL, and I wanted to save the world. For me, that meant getting my master's in public health. We were both chasing dreams, but we were also making plans. Marriage, kids, growing old together... we had it all mapped out."

Her voice cracked slightly, and she stopped, staring into her cup.

"What happened?" Prossy's whispered question was almost drowned out by the stillness of the room.

Mia drew in a long breath, letting the memories wash over her. They came like flashes—fragments of a life she'd once believed was unshakable. Shared smiles. Sweet kisses. Fierce hugs. Nights tangled together in the dark. Lying in bed, his arm heavy and protective around her waist.

Dancing under the stars and laughing until their sides ached.

She shook her head slowly. "We were in love... until we weren't."

The weight of her words settled over the room, and no one dared to speak. The silence felt both comforting and suffocating, but she pushed forward, the words tumbling out even as they tore at her.

"Something changed after one of his missions," she said quietly. "When he came back, he seemed... lost. He couldn't—or wouldn't—talk about it. He was distant. I didn't know how to reach him. By then, I was almost finished with my master's and looking at job opportunities. We knew we'd face challenges with our chosen careers, but other families managed, so why couldn't we?"

She gave a small, bitter laugh, the sound devoid of humor. "But he started saying things like, 'You should take whatever job you want. Don't stay back for me.' When I asked about his missions, he'd just grimace and say he couldn't talk about it. I thought it was a phase. I thought our love could conquer anything, everything. But looking back, I can see now that he was pulling away.

"It became a dance. He'd step back, and I'd step forward, trying to fill the space between us. But then one day, he stepped back, and instead of me following, I was shoved so far away I couldn't close the gap."

Her throat tightened, and she swallowed hard, trying to keep her voice even. "It was the morning I returned from a monthlong work trip to Haiti. When I walked into our apartment... there was a woman in our bed."

Another collective gasp rippled through the room, but Mia didn't lift her eyes to meet theirs. She didn't want to see the shock or, worse, the pity.

"He wasn't in the bed with her, but she wasn't wearing

anything," she continued, her voice flat, as though that would make it easier to say. "Barely covered by the sheet. And all I could do was stand there, stunned. The shower was running, but it might as well have been thunder with how loud my pulse roared in my ears. And then it turned off."

She paused, her lips pressing into a thin line as the memory hit her again, sharp as a blade. "He walked out of the bathroom, a towel slung around his hips. He looked at me, then at her, then back at me. She was sitting up by then, pulling the sheet tighter around herself, her eyes darting between us."

"What did he say?" Ritah asked, her voice thick with emotion.

Mia let out a shaky breath. "Nothing. Not one word. He just… stared. For a split second, I thought I saw something in his eyes— maybe regret or pain. But then it was gone. His eyes went blank, like I was just someone he used to know. My heart was breaking, and all I could do was whisper that I'd come by later to get my things, and I didn't want him there when I did."

The room fell deathly silent, her words pressing down on everyone.

"And he still didn't say anything?" Karen asked softly.

"No." Mia shook her head, her voice tight with the effort of holding it together. "A few hours later, I went back. The apartment was empty. He wasn't there to try to explain or deny it or even apologize. He didn't leave a note. Nothing.

"I called a couple of friends, and we packed up everything that was mine. When I walked out, I left the key on the kitchen counter. And that was it."

She looked up at her friends then, her expression one of

quiet resignation. "Other than a plain apology letter, I never saw him or heard from him again. Until today."

The air in the room felt thick, heavy with the weight of her confession. For a long moment, no one said anything, and Mia let herself breathe, letting the ache in her chest settle.

10

After the girls left, Mia sat in her room for a long time, her thoughts tangled and her emotions churning. Her phone rang, and she hesitated to see her mom's name on the caller ID.

She answered, forcing a cheerful tone. "Hey, Mom."

"Good evening, sweetheart." Her mother's voice was warm and familiar, wrapped in the soft Midwest accent of home. "I figured I'd catch you before you went to sleep."

Mia sipped from the water bottle she'd pulled from her small refrigerator. "It's lunchtime in Kansas, isn't it?"

Her mother scoffed. "You know us. We rose early and spent the morning in the garden. We were hungry by noon, and I just had to heat leftovers. Now, tell me what's going on over there."

Mia hesitated, fingers tapping against the plastic of her water container. She hadn't planned on saying anything. She could keep this light, casual, just another day in camp. But as soon as she took a breath to respond, the truth slipped out before she could stop it. "Jim Devlin is here."

A sharp intake of breath was heard, then silence lasted for several seconds. "What did you say?"

Mia winced. "Jim Devlin is here at the camp."

Her mother's gasp was loud, followed by a biting tone. "Jim Devlin?"

Mia rolled her eyes. "Yes, Mom. The one and only Jim Devlin."

"Lord have mercy," her mother muttered. "You mean to tell me that man just—what? Showed up? Walked right back into your life after all these years? In Uganda?" The last words were practically shouted.

Mia exhaled, her cheeks puffing out with the effort. "Not exactly. He's here investigating some thefts from the camp. Strictly business."

"And that's all?"

Mia hesitated again, her face scrunching into a wince, which was answer enough.

Her mother sighed, long and knowing. "You've talked."

"A bit," Mia admitted. "But not about us. Or what had been us. He's just here to do a job, and then he'll disappear."

Her mother was silent for a moment. "I... I... oh, Mia, I don't know what to say."

"I know, Mom. I don't either. He said he wants to talk to me, but I don't know if I'll ever be ready."

After another moment of silence, her mother said, "When he broke your heart, it broke my heart as well. And your dad's and your brother's. And his parents. There was a ripple effect, and he must have known that. His mother certainly let him know."

Mia pressed her lips together, then agreed. "Maybe we could have talked back then. Maybe things would have been different—"

"Nope," her mom said. "You were too raw. It was too

fresh. The hurt would have overtaken anything he could have said."

She picked at a loose thread on the hem of her blanket, pondering what her mother was saying. "So… you think we should talk now?"

"I'm not saying that, Mia. Only you can answer that question. But after all these years, I know your hurt is still there, even if it is less raw. Maybe you can have that conversation now. Maybe you can get things off your chest that you've always wanted to say. Maybe he can offer an explanation as to what was going on that made him act so abominably."

"It was so weird to see him today. He did say that he didn't know I was here. That just seems so random, doesn't it?"

"Hmm…" her mom hummed. "People don't walk back into your life for no reason. Maybe this is your opportunity to let him know what he did to you. Perhaps it's his opportunity to ease the pain or let you know he really was a poop."

Mia snorted. Her mom wouldn't use the word *shit*, but had no problem calling someone *poop*. "I love you, Mom," she said.

"You know we love you, too, sweetheart. Anyway, I don't guess you can avoid him, but if he hurts you again, he'll answer to me!"

She laughed, and they soon said goodbyes. Mia thought about what her mom said. Maybe her mother was right. Maybe Devlin being here wasn't just a coincidence. But Mia had no idea whether it was fate, unfinished business, or just a mess waiting to happen. For now, she just had to figure out what came next.

Looking at the time, she hurried to the staff showers, desperate to wash away not just the day's grime but the tangle of emotions dredged up by their conversation. The warm water cascaded over her skin, soothing her body but doing little to calm her restless mind. No matter how hard she tried, thoughts of Devlin pushed through, stubborn and unrelenting, until they claimed center stage.

Back in her room, she slipped into her pajamas, the soft fabric a fleeting comfort. She went through her nightly routine mechanically, brushing her teeth and tying her hair back before climbing into bed. A book lay on her nightstand, one she'd meant to lose herself in, but after reading the same page three times without registering a word, she gave up and tossed it aside. The room was quiet now, save for the faint hum of the fan, and the stillness only amplified her thoughts.

Memories of Devlin rushed forward, vivid and insistent. She'd told the girls only the basics earlier about how they'd met, the outline of their years together, and the inevitable unraveling. But now, in the solitude of her room, every detail came flooding back, so clear it was as if she were reliving it.

She smiled, bittersweet, as she thought of their teenage years. She'd often wondered if Devlin was embarrassed to be dating her. She was the bookish girl who preferred the protest rallies to pep rallies. The cheerleaders had certainly given her enough side-eyes and whispered plenty of nasty things behind her back. "It won't last," they'd said. "He's only with her because she puts out." Even her friends had been stunned that she'd captured the attention of someone like him.

But Devlin had made it clear from the start that there was no one else for him. The way he'd taken her hand the first time, his touch warm and steady, told her everything she needed to know. At sixteen, he hadn't been shy about claiming her, holding her hand in crowded hallways, or pressing a kiss to her temple as they parted for classes.

When he left for college her senior year, the whispers started again. "He'll find someone else. He'll cheat." And though the thought had scared her, she'd known in her heart it wouldn't happen. He wasn't that kind of person. Their connection was too strong, their love too deep. They talked through every fear and doubt until they'd made a pact to hold on no matter what.

By the time her college acceptances came, she hadn't even considered going anywhere else. His college became her first choice—not just because it had her major but because it was close to home. *Close to him.*

Her parents had adored Devlin from the start. Even her father, who was famously hard to win over, had warmed to him quickly. Devlin's parents had welcomed her just as readily, treating her like another daughter. Holidays were spent together, the two families mingling easily, cementing what everyone already believed—that she and Devlin were forever.

She thought about those college years, a rush of memories filling her mind. They'd navigated crowded dorm rooms and tiny apartments, stolen moments, and shared dreams. She grinned at the memory of his dorm bed, so narrow they'd had to tangle themselves together to make it work. When desperation struck, they'd sneak off to park on some deserted road, making love in the back seat of his car.

Later, she'd gotten her own tiny apartment. It was little more than an efficiency, but it was hers. She'd worked two jobs to afford it, and Devlin had practically moved in, his clothes hanging in her closet and his scent lingering on her pillow. By her final year, they lived together full-time, falling into a rhythm that felt like a preview of marriage.

Mornings started with sleepy kisses and hurried breakfasts. Evenings ended with him pulling her close, her head resting on his chest, lulled to sleep by the steady beat of his heart.

Her chest ached as she thought about those nights, their intimacy growing in that first apartment. Devlin's body had always mesmerized her—strong, solid, and so achingly familiar. His arms had been her favorite, both for the power they held and the gentleness they offered. She thought of how they'd wrapped around her, pulling her close, making her feel cherished and adored.

But holy hell, even missionary sex was amazing. His weight was held above her chest by his strong arms. As he drove into her, with soft and gentle thrusts when they made love or pounding where she gave as much as she took, it didn't matter. His body was made for her.

With all the memories flooding her mind, suddenly Mia was flushed. Heat moved through every cell of her body and pooled in her core. Her breasts felt heavy, her nipples needy.

She whipped off her T-shirt as she lay back on her bed. With her eyes closed, imagining him over her, she slid her fingers into her panties. Her other hand drifted over her breasts, kneading them as she tugged on her nipples. She hadn't brought her vibrator with her to Uganda, and while she usually found her hands to be a poor substitute for the real thing, she was so primed with remembrances of how sex was with Devlin it didn't take long for her climax to hit. She rode the feeling until the last pulses had eased, and she could catch her breath again.

She pulled her shirt on and settled onto her back, staring at the ceiling as her cheeks heated with the memories. She hated how overwhelming thoughts of him could be and how easily he could slip past her defenses.

Rolling to her side, she pulled the mosquito netting over her bed, tugged the covers up to her chin, and closed her eyes. Her mind drifted to the way he'd spoon her at night, his body warm and protective against hers. She'd always felt safe with him, not just physically but in every way. Making love with him had been incredible, but it was the quiet moments afterward that she'd cherished most—when his arms were around her and his breath evened out as he drifted to sleep.

Her lips curved into a sad smile as the truth settled over her like a heavy blanket. It wasn't just biology. It wasn't just memories. It was him. It had always been him. And as she lay in the quiet dark, she couldn't help but wonder what that meant for her future. How has he changed? *We're not the same people we were ten years ago. If I give him power over me again, he'll have the power to break my heart... again.*

Devlin lay on his back, staring at the dim ceiling of the guest room, knowing sleep was out of reach. The hum of the fan was a distant vibration, but it did little to calm the turmoil in his mind. Memories surfaced, sharp and vivid, cutting through the years as if they'd happened only yesterday.

No matter how often his football buddies or college friends had told him not to commit, to keep his options open, or to avoid getting tied down, he'd known Mia was different. From the moment he'd turned around that afternoon and saw her, he'd been hooked. Her voice was calm but determined as she unchained herself from the goalpost to save him from trouble. She wasn't like anyone he'd ever met. Her eyes, wide and intelligent, held a passion and fire that drew him in. She'd captivated him with just a soft touch and a shy, radiant smile.

It had been almost twenty years ago, and the memory still had the power to twist his heart.

A soft snort escaped him, and he quickly turned his head, glancing at his bunkmates. Cole, sprawled out, was snoring loud enough to rattle the walls, while Todd lay flat on his back, mouth agape, dead to the world. Devlin sighed in relief. They hadn't noticed him.

But the snort had been earned. He couldn't help but smile at himself as another memory surfaced. The way he and Mia had contorted their bodies to fit on her tiny dorm bed, limbs tangled as they searched for closeness. It didn't matter how cramped or uncomfortable it got, they'd always made it work, driven by the simple need to be together.

Sex with Mia had been nothing short of extraordinary, even from the beginning. They'd been each other's firsts, fumbling at times but always fueled by an intensity that made the awkwardness irrelevant. He'd heard enough from his teammates and friends to know that what they had was rare. Mia had looked at him like he hung the moon, her gaze full of trust, admiration, and love. It had filled him with a pride he couldn't quite explain. Not because he thought he deserved it but because it was her. She'd always been the better half of their story.

In the years without her, Devlin had learned that nothing compared to what they'd shared. No matter how many women had crossed his path, no relationship had lasted longer than a weekend. The hollow flings only reminded him of what he'd lost and what he'd foolishly let slip away.

His thoughts shifted to the years after their breakup. His career as a SEAL had given him purpose, even after the injury that ended it. During his recovery, he'd befriended an attorney who worked with tribal councils, and the work had drawn him in. Helping others, fixing what was broken—it had felt like something Mia would do. Maybe, deep down, some part of him had been trying to mirror her unwavering dedication.

When Logan approached him about joining Lighthouse Security Investigations, he hadn't hesitated. And when he'd learned Sisco was part of the team, it had sealed the deal. Once again, he'd found a purpose, a place where he belonged. But no matter how much satisfaction his work gave him, there was still a void he couldn't fill. He'd had the great love of his life, and he'd let her go.

He exhaled slowly, his chest tightening as he thought about Mia. He'd resisted looking her up over the years, afraid of what he might find. The idea of seeing her married, smiling in family photos, or holding the hands of children who weren't his had always been too much to bear. While he wanted her to have everything she deserved, he couldn't risk shattering what little peace he'd managed to carve out for himself.

This morning, though, everything had shifted. Seeing her again had shaken him to his core. He'd stared at her ring finger, holding his breath as he noticed it was bare. No pale indentation, no shadow of a ring long worn and recently removed. It didn't necessarily mean she was unattached, but it had ignited a flicker of hope he hadn't allowed himself to feel in years.

If even the slightest chance to reconnect existed, he wanted it. Needed it. But the weight of his mistakes hung heavy on him. His jaw tightened as the words he'd have to say ran through his mind. *I was such a fucking idiot.* It wasn't enough to capture the depth of his regret, but it was a start.

With a last glance at the sleeping forms of his fellow

Keepers, Devlin rolled onto his side. His body ached with exhaustion, but his mind wouldn't let go of her. When sleep finally came, it wasn't restful. Dreams of Mia filled his restless slumber.

In his dream, she walked toward him with a seductive smile. He was lying in bed with the TV on, watching a game he had little interest in, just to kill time until she came out of the bathroom. Her thick, glossy hair floated around her shoulders, and her beautiful smile aimed his way with a twinkle in her eyes.

His mouth dropped open as his heart pounded, all the blood running to his cock as she sauntered toward him in a silky nightie that left little to the imagination. It didn't matter that he'd seen her body and worshipped every inch. Each time, it was like unwrapping a new present at Christmas.

She stripped off the nightie and, with no panties, continued toward him completely naked. He clicked off the TV and tossed the remote to the nightstand, not caring when it skidded across the surface and landed on the floor.

Just as she reached the bed, he shucked his boxers down and kicked them to the side, freeing his cock. It bobbed up, and her gaze dropped to his erection. Her smile widened, and she leaned forward, placed her hands on the mattress, then crawled up the bed until she straddled his legs.

With her hands on his hips, her breasts dangled, teasing the hair on his thighs as she licked her lips. Fisting his cock, she opened her mouth and took him in. With the first swipe, his eyes rolled back in his head.

With the ease and practice that came from being together for years, she knew exactly how to drive him wild. He reached down and fondled her breasts, tugging on her nipples until she moaned, the sound reverberating through his cock, making him swell even more.

Just when he was ready to come, he slipped his hands under her armpits and dragged her upward. She shimmied up his thighs and then lifted, placing the tip of his cock directly at her entrance. She slowly lowered her body down until he was fully sheathed, and once again, he felt his eyes roll back in his head.

With his hands on her hips, he guided her as she lifted and plunged, taking them both to the edge of the cliff. He pressed his thumb on the bundle of nerves, and she shattered, her fingertips digging into his shoulders. With her head thrown back, she cried out his name as he groaned, "My Mia."

Devlin gasped, his eyes flying open, and he realized he'd just had the most erotic dream he'd ever had in his life. His cock was rock hard, and if he just fisted himself, he would come. Jerking his head to the side, he ascertained Cole and Todd were still sound asleep. Thank God! No way would he give in to his dream and rub one out with them in the room.

Crawling out of bed as quietly as possible, he pulled on a T-shirt, slid on a pair of sweatpants, and shoved his feet into his shoes. He slipped out of the room and jogged to the guest bathroom, where he went straight into one of the private shower stalls.

With the warm water coursing over him, he grabbed his cock, and with one hand on the side of the shower and the other pumping his erection, he clamped his jaws tightly shut so he wouldn't cry out her name. It only took a moment of still thinking of her, and he jerked off, finally coming as he sprayed his release down the drain.

For the past decade, when he'd jerked off to thoughts of Mia, it had always been to a past memory. This time, he had her firmly in his mind as she was now. Everything about her still called to him.

Rinsing off, he dried, redressed, and returned to the guest quarters. When he stepped into the room, Cole and Todd were just waking.

"You took a shower already?" Cole asked, looking at Devlin's wet hair.

"Yeah, I figure it would be good to go ahead and get in before it gets busy."

"That makes sense. I should do the same."

While Cole and Todd headed to the showers, he dressed for the day, then sat on the side of his bed, his forearms on his knees. He let out a deep sigh, wondering if he was destined to just rub one out to thoughts of Mia for the rest of his life.

11

Devlin sat on the edge of his bunk with maps and spreadsheets spread haphazardly across the bed. His fingertips traced invisible lines over the paper, mapping out possible routes, trying to visualize where the thefts were happening and how the stolen supplies were transported. But no matter how much he focused on the logistics, his mind drifted to Mia—back to the past and forward to the conversation he needed to have with her. She was here, in this camp, working tirelessly to help people who had lost everything. And despite all his training and all the years he'd spent shutting down distractions, she was the one thing he couldn't push from his mind.

The door opened, and Todd and Cole stepped inside. Devlin looked up as Todd dropped onto his own bunk. "What kind of satellite view can Sadie get for us?"

"She's good," Cole answered. "But if we want a deep dive, we might need to loop in Mace's team in Maine. He's got a power couple on staff who can pull just about anything."

"I forget you've got a tie-in with the other LSI locations," Todd said.

"I worked with your brother Blake... well, William."

Todd nodded, as he looked at Devlin. "My younger brother, William Blake, works for Mace in Maine. My younger sister now works for Carson in California and is married to another Keeper."

Devlin pulled out his phone and dialed LSIMT. It was the middle of the night there, but LSI was a twenty-four-hour operation. Someone would pick up.

"Devlin? You've got Casper."

"Now that we're boots on the ground, it's clear we won't be able to pinpoint what's happening without satellite support. Cole thinks we might need to bring in Mace's people. Logan can make that call, but we need visuals on nighttime truck activity in the meantime—particularly heading west toward the Congo border. Start with the refugee village of Sweswe, but expand to all the villages if possible. We need to know who's coming and going at night. Especially if they're heading to the west and the Congo border."

Casper let out a low whistle. "That's a tall order, but I'll get Sadie on it. Logan will be briefed first thing, and I'll update you as soon as I have something."

"That's all I can ask," Devlin said. "And I'll check with the FSO here. I'll pin down dates and times. That'll give Sadie more specifics."

Casper added, "Everything going okay there?"

Devlin hesitated, his eyes flicking to Todd and Cole, who watched him closely. They might not know everything, but they could sense when something personal weighed on a man.

"For now," Devlin answered. "Nothing we can't handle."

Disconnecting the call, he leaned back against the wall,

exhaling heavily as he gathered the maps and notes. The room remained silent, but he could feel the weight of his teammates' stares. They were patient.

He clenched his jaw, hating talking about his history. Hated the vulnerability of it. But this wasn't just his past. This involved Mia, and whether he liked it or not, that meant his teammates deserved to know at least the basics. Todd and Cole mirrored his posture—seated, forearms resting on their thighs, waiting until he was ready to speak.

Finally, Devlin sighed. "Alright. I'll give you the short version so you know what I'm facing."

"You don't owe us anything," Cole said, shaking his head.

Todd nodded. "Your past, your business."

"I appreciate that," Devlin admitted. "But when it comes to Mia, you need to understand. Especially since my mission here isn't just about this case any longer. I need to protect her. And I also need to reconnect with her if she'll let me."

They nodded, giving him the space to continue.

"You already know the beginning... high school sweethearts. Dated all through college, stayed together after. I went into the Marines, then SEAL training. Mia went to grad school near the base. We made it work, even with the separations. By the time I finished BUD/S, we were living together and talking about marriage, kids, the whole thing."

Todd let out a low whistle. "Sounds like the great American love story."

Devlin held his gaze, surprised by how true the words felt. "It was. Until I blew it to hell."

He exhaled slowly, rubbing a hand down his face. The words were hard to say, even now. "We had a mission that went sideways. Two of my team members died. A few others were injured. One of the guys was married and had kids. When I got back, I had to watch his wife crumble. The team was given a few weeks off to deal with everything, and I spent most of them at the bottom of a bottle."

He shook his head. "Every time I closed my eyes, I saw Mia getting that same knock on the door. I kept thinking about how she was at the point in her program when she was looking at jobs—figuring out where in the world she might want to work. And it got in my head. Messed me up. I convinced myself that maybe I should let her go, give her the freedom to make choices without me tying her down."

A heavy blanket of silence settled between them. Todd was the first to speak, his expression dark. "I swear, man, the only thing I can think of that would've blown that apart was cheating. But I know you. And even though I didn't know you back then, I know you wouldn't do that."

Devlin nodded, his throat tight. He had worried they might look at him differently, but neither man's expression held judgment—only understanding.

"There are things I need to say to Mia first," he admitted. "She deserves the full truth before anyone else. But let's just say that something happened, and I knew it would make her walk away." His voice dropped lower, thick with regret. "Because I didn't have the fucking strength to just let her go."

Cole and Todd exchanged a glance.

"You broke her heart," Todd said quietly. "But you never betrayed her."

Devlin nodded once. "Not even at my worst."

Todd muttered a curse under his breath, and Cole simply shook his head.

Devlin didn't want their sympathy. He just wanted a chance—one goddamn chance—to fix what he'd broken. A knock on the door shattered the heavy moment.

"Come in," Cole called, sitting up straight.

Jonan poked his head in, grinning. "I was about to grab breakfast. Thought you might want to join me."

Without hesitation, all three men stood. Enough dwelling on the past. It was time to move forward. It was time to protect Mia. And it was damn well time to figure out who was behind the black market operation.

As they walked, Jonan fell into step beside Devlin, his voice low. "I have someone I want you to meet."

Devlin glanced at him, noting the way Cole and Todd kept their attention forward but were clearly listening. "Who?"

"A nurse. Works under Doc Elaine." Jonan paused. "He's Congolese."

That was enough to stiffen Devlin's spine.

Before he could ask more, they reached the dining hall. His gaze swept the room automatically, searching for Mia. She sat at a table across the room, engaged in conversation with others, and he was glad to see Robert wasn't present. Hustling through the breakfast line, he took a small tray and cup of coffee and started toward her.

Devlin's gaze landed on Mia as she turned and looked up at him. She simply stared with a thoughtful expression on her face. His breath caught in his lungs. For a moment, everything else faded. There was something in her eyes, something he couldn't quite name. But whatever it was, it wasn't hate. And right now, he'd take any damn positive step he could get. He gave her a small nod, a half smile playing at his lips before starting toward her.

Jonan interrupted as he nudged Devlin. "Come, sit over here."

Reluctantly, Devlin tore his gaze from Mia and followed Jonan. A man and woman seated at the table straightened as they approached.

"May we join you?" Jonan asked, a broad smile on his face.

"Of course," the man said, his white teeth gleaming against his dark face.

Jonan made the introductions as the three Keepers slid into seats. "These are friends of mine. Alain Taty and his wife, Dena. Alain is one of the lead nurses here at the clinic, and Dena is a nurse's aide."

"Nice to meet you," Devlin said as Cole and Todd echoed the same greeting. Dena was dark and pretty, her smile shy as she nodded at them.

"I told Alain that you would like to hear his story."

Devlin wasn't sure what information Alain had to impart but was willing to see what Jonan had for them.

Alain immediately nodded. "We are Congolese. I worked at a hospital in Goma, Congo. In the Kinshasa Providence—"

"We know it," Devlin said softly, thinking of a SEAL mission he'd been on in the Congo years before.

Alain held his gaze, then nodded slowly. "We had... problems."

Devlin's stomach tightened. *Goma. The heart of the conflict.*

Dena reached out, placing a hand on her husband's arm. He covered it with his own before continuing.

"If you'd rather not talk here, we can go somewhere else. Somewhere more private," Cole offered.

"No, this is fine," Alain said, shaking his head. "My story is not new, but I thank you all the same."

Dena's fingers twitched, and Alain rubbed her hand before continuing. "There is so much death and war in our country. At first, M23 insisted that we treat the wounded rebels first before anyone else who might have a need.

Several of our medical team who disagreed with the edict disappeared."

Devlin's chest ached for the man's plight. Alain was a healer, but being forced not to heal those who might've needed him the most.

"We had family in Beni, but there was little we could do to help them, being caught between the violence. My father had already died, then we received word that my brother was killed in the uprising." He and Dena exchanged another glance before he added, "We knew we needed to leave. So we asked to visit Beni to bring my mother back with us. The story was she would look after our children so that Dena could work as a nurse's aide, providing more help for the insurgency. Given permission, we drove to Beni but took our three children with us and had the car loaded with everything we could. We picked up my mother, and then in the middle of the night, we drove back down through the pass that leads through the National Forests. We got as close as we dared, then contacted another nurse who had made it into Uganda. He gave us directions, and we were sent to a boat where we loaded our possessions and family. We successfully crossed Lake Edward into Uganda. We went first to a refugee camp near there, then we accepted the offer to come to this camp where we would all receive assistance and, in turn, be able to practice medicine the way we always wanted to."

Devlin listened, the weight of Alain's words settling in his chest. The story was all too familiar—ordinary people forced to make impossible choices just to survive.

Alain's eyes were now filled with tears, but he smiled. Dena reached out her other hand, clutching his as they lay on the table.

"It takes a helluva lot of courage to do what you did," Devlin said, admiration in his tone. "I'm glad for you and your family." Devlin glanced over at Jonan then, knowing there was more to Alain's situation than hearing about his daring escape to freedom.

Now, with lowered voices as they finished their meal, Jonan whispered, "You are curious about the black market and the Congo. You will find that Alain knows a great deal about medical supplies that find their way there. With his knowledge, they were able to stem the flow of a lot of the products moving from a refugee camp across the border to be sold. I thought you would find his story interesting."

Devlin nodded, now understanding. He looked at Alain and Dena as they stood. "It'll be nice talking to you more at another time."

Alain dipped his head. "I look forward to it. Jonan will arrange a time."

Jonan stood with his tray in his hand. "I'm going to drive Margarethe around this afternoon as she works on inventory. I know Mia will be at her office before visiting some of the villages. Alain will walk his wife to the medical clinic and meet us at Mia's office."

Devlin nodded, then watched as Jonan walked away. He glanced toward Cole and Todd. "He seems eager."

"Can't get a read on him," Cole said. "Can't tell if he's here to lead us in one direction or is working with us."

"We'll talk to Alain and find out what he has to say."

"Maybe Mia will have more information on him for us," Todd added.

Devlin agreed, but the more he thought of Mia in the middle of a black market investigation, the more his breakfast sat like a rock in his gut.

12

Mia sat at the long, worn wooden table, surrounded by the quiet hum of morning conversation. The scent of strong Ugandan coffee mixed with the earthy aroma of fresh bread, but her appetite was nonexistent. She lifted her cup, fingers wrapped around the warmth, but her mind was elsewhere as her gaze constantly flicked toward the entrance of the dining hall. She wondered if Devlin had already had breakfast or would be coming in soon.

She exhaled sharply, inwardly chastising herself for the attention she was giving to a man she had walked away from. Why should it matter? But she was nothing if not self-aware, and deep down, she recognized the truth. A decade with Devlin wasn't something she could continue to pretend had never existed. No matter how much pain came at the end, she had loved him for too long to simply erase him.

She shook her head and scoffed quietly to herself. Years together, then years apart. *Maybe we're destined to have something different happen to us each decade.*

"Are you okay?"

She jerked slightly, pulled from her thoughts. The three people at the table were watching her now, their expressions expectant. Damn. She had completely tuned them out and had no idea what they'd been discussing.

"Yes, I'm so sorry," she said, forcing a small smile. "I slept poorly last night, so my brain is a little foggy."

"Well, that explains the blank stare," one of the women across from her teased before her expression shifted. Her eyes widened as she sat up straighter. "Holy shit. Who the hell is that trio?"

Mia didn't have to turn around to know exactly who had just walked in.

A strange, familiar energy settled in her chest, prickling along her skin, and even though she told herself she wouldn't, she gave in and turned. Devlin. Her gaze locked onto his immediately, as if pulled by an invisible tether, and just like yesterday, she found his eyes already pinned on her.

Unlike their first unexpected encounter, she felt no shock today. No jarring realization that he was suddenly here, in this world she had built without him. But the emotions coursing through her were impossible to name.

A rush of heat flooded her as last night's dream came roaring back, so vivid it made her stomach tighten. Then there was the conversation. He had said he wanted to talk. About what?

Did he want to rehash the past? She wasn't sure she could do that, not without reopening wounds she'd carefully stitched closed. Was he here to apologize? That thought stirred something bitter inside her. She didn't need an apology—she needed to move forward.

But a darker, more vulnerable fear slithered through her mind. What if he wanted to tell her about *her*? The woman he'd been with that night. Or worse—about all the women who had come after. Or maybe he was still with her.

She swallowed hard and forced herself to study him with a clinical eye. He wasn't the same man who had left her. The sharp edge of testosterone-fueled arrogance that had defined him in his early SEAL years had softened. He looked... deeper. More introspective. As if the years had forced him to stop running headfirst into every situation and actually think first.

She hadn't realized how long she'd been holding his gaze until she suddenly jerked, breaking the moment. Devlin dipped his chin in acknowledgment, his lips curving into the hint of a smile.

For a second, she thought he would come over. But then Jonan leaned in, murmuring something to him, and just like that, Devlin turned.

Mia watched as he and the other Keepers moved toward a table where Alain and Dena were seated. Instead of relief that she wouldn't have to talk to him just yet, disappointment crept in. Her eyes lingered on them as they quickly fell into deep conversation.

She had met Alain and Dena before. Karen had spoken highly of them. While Karen was the lead nurse at the camp's main clinic, Alain oversaw the satellite clinics in the villages. He was Congolese, but beyond that, Mia knew very little about his past.

But Devlin was listening to him now, leaning forward with sharp focus, his expression unreadable. *What does this have to do with the stolen food?* She didn't have time to ponder further.

"Are you coming?"

She startled again, her friend snapping her out of her reverie. *Dammit.* Pushing her chair from the table, she quickly gathered her tray and returned it, her steps brisk.

She didn't look back to sneak another glance toward Devlin. Instead, she shoved her way out of the dining hall and into the sun-drenched lane, forcing her feet to move with purpose.

As she walked, she muttered, her frustration bubbling over. "I have a job to do, and it's not spending my day staring at him."

"Hey, wait up, Mia!"

She turned to see Robert jogging toward her. She smiled at the sight of Ravi watching from the side and then breaking into a run to see who could reach her first. Holding her arms out wide, she waited for them to tag her hands. Somehow, this had become a game between the two men. The loser would buy the winner and Mia a dessert from one of the refugee families that baked and sold mandazi. The sweet dessert was known as African donuts, a particular favorite of hers.

At the last second, Robert tagged her hand first, then turned and grabbed Mia around the waist, twirling her in a circle as he called out, "I won, I won!"

She laughed as he set her feet on the ground, then glanced over to see Devlin standing just outside the dining hall, his eagle-eyed glare pinned on her. Returning his glare with one of her own, she turned and walked with the two men toward the camp's food distribution center.

Mia twisted her head to glance up at Ravi, shielding her eyes from the glare of the sun. "When will you be ready to start borehole drilling at Sweswe?"

"The equipment arrived yesterday, so we're starting today," Ravi replied, his gaze shifting to Robert. "I'll need you to coordinate the water trucking until we get the new source operational."

"Not a problem." Robert nodded. "I was already planning to review the trucking schedules today."

Mia crossed her arms. "Do we need to remind the camp that they should only use the trucked-in water for washing food? I'll be making my rounds to Sweswe this afternoon and can make sure my food security team gets the word out."

"Good thinking," Ravi said. "Once they see us drilling and hit water, some people might assume it's safe to use before it's tested."

"Farid can coordinate with his team at each camp as a reminder. I'll tell him to pay extra attention to Sweswe."

"Sounds good," Ravi said before pivoting toward the admin offices. As he walked away, he glanced over his shoulder with a grin. "I'll bring the mandazi when I come back! And I'll grab a few extra for tomorrow because I have a feeling I'll lose again!" His laughter echoed as he vanished into the distance.

Mia chuckled as Ravi disappeared into his office. Robert draped an arm over her shoulders, steering her toward the food storage center. He leaned in, his breath warm against her ear. "I have a feeling the big guy trailing us isn't too happy about this."

Mia rolled her eyes. "Are you seriously trying to make someone jealous?"

"Is he jealous?"

She peered up at him. "What are you really getting at, Robert?"

Robert chuckled, shaking his head. "Fine, I'll be blunt. Do you know him?"

Mia tapped her finger against her chin in mock thoughtfulness. "Why, yes! I was introduced to all three of them when they arrived at camp."

"Smart-ass," he muttered, grinning.

Then his expression softened, his gaze searching hers.

"You know, no matter how close we were, a part of you always held back."

Mia's heart gave a familiar twinge. "Oh, Robert, why bring this up now?"

He leaned in, his forehead almost touching hers. "Because I still care about you. We may not be together anymore, but that doesn't mean I stopped looking out for you."

Her heart ached at his sincerity. "That's one of the things I've always admired about you. We stopped dating, but we never stopped being friends."

"And what about the guy who looks like he wants to tear my liver out?"

A giggle slipped out, and she shook her head. "I knew him years ago—many years ago. We didn't end well, but before that... we had a lot of history."

"History has a way of repeating itself."

Mia scoffed. "I never want that kind of heartache again. That's probably why I've never been able to completely let it go."

Robert tilted his head. "I'm not talking about pain. I'm talking about the kind of emotion you must have shared for it to have hurt so much."

She pursed her lips. "You're very wise. Also, a pain in my ass."

"Good," he said with a smirk. "Then I'd say my job for the day is done."

They were still laughing when they stepped into the storage center's loading dock, where Farid and his assistant were already unloading another truck.

"If he's got everything under control, let's review the trucking schedules. I want to make my rounds this afternoon," Mia said.

"No time like the present," Robert agreed.

As he turned, Mia caught sight of Devlin approaching, his expression unreadable. His attention flicked over Robert dismissively before settling on her with a gentle smile. "Good morning, Mia."

"Good morning, Jim... um... Devlin." She inclined her head to acknowledge his companions. "Cole. Todd."

Devlin's gaze never left hers. "What's on your agenda for the day?"

"Robert and I are reviewing trucking schedules—"

"Good. We need details on where the trucks come from, who owns them, where the drivers are from—"

"Whoa, whoa, whoa." Robert interrupted, hands raised. "That's a hell of a lot of questions for someone who's just here for security."

Devlin's gaze turned sharp. Mia felt the tension thicken and quickly intervened. "They came in with Margarethe. They're investigating shortages."

Robert's expression darkened. "What shortages?"

"Some food doesn't make it to the refugees," Devlin said evenly.

"I was asking *her*," Robert bit out.

"And I'm telling *you*," Devlin shot back.

"Oh, for the love of—" Mia threw up her hands. "Enough with the testosterone showdown! Robert, they're trying to determine why food supplies aren't reaching the people who need them." She sighed, thinking she had given up all hope of keeping her fears to herself. By now, everyone would know she had called in someone to discover what was happening to the food.

Robert's jaw tightened. "Are you saying there's theft happening here?"

"We're trying to find out," Mia said softly. "Something systematic is happening with the food. We're stretched thin as it is, but I refuse to let people go hungry because someone's profiting off what they steal."

Robert exhaled heavily. "Alright. I have nothing to hide. Logistics in a camp this size is chaotic—we contract out trucks and drivers to whoever we can. But we can't oversee every single truck, every single person, every single day."

Devlin crossed his arms. "Someone's stealing."

Robert muttered a curse. "Point taken. But theft happens everywhere. Medical supplies, toiletries, even toilet paper. You can't track it all."

"We're not blaming you, Robert," Mia said gently. "But we need to figure out where the leaks are."

He sighed. "When were you going to tell me?"

"Dr. München has just found out from Margarethe. We wanted to keep things close. We don't know who's involved."

Robert nodded slowly. "Fine. One of you can come with me to my office. I'll show you how we coordinate a few hundred trucks in and out every day."

"I'll go," Todd volunteered.

"I'm heading over to Farid to check on the process," Cole added before walking off.

As the others dispersed, Mia realized only she and Devlin remained. She turned to him, crossing her arms. "We have to work together. It'd be easier if you didn't glare at me all the time."

"I don't glare at you all the time."

"Only when I'm near another man, right?"

Devlin exhaled, rubbing a hand over his face. "Yeah, I guess so."

Mia arched a brow. "You know that's fucked, right? You, of everyone in the world, have no right to wonder who I might be knocking boots with."

"I know," he admitted, his voice low as his face

contorted in a wince. "Believe me, I've reminded myself of that every day for ten years."

A bitter laugh escaped her. "And whose fault is that?"

"Mine. All mine." His jaw clenched. "And I've felt it every single day."

A heavy silence stretched between them.

"Are you dating Robert?" he asked at last.

Mia's mouth opened in disbelief. "I can't believe you're asking me that."

"I just want to know."

She inhaled deeply, steadying herself. "No. I am not currently dating Robert. Or anyone else, for that matter."

Devlin nodded, but his gaze remained intense. "Have you dated him before?"

Exasperated, she nodded. "Yes. Several years ago. It lasted six months. I ended it. We stayed friends. There, are you satisfied?"

"Not even close." His voice was raw.

She bristled, but before she could snap back, he continued, "I have no one to blame but myself for pushing you away. I'd like to say I'm glad you found companionship, but the truth is, it hurts."

Mia's anger faded slightly as she snorted. "I appreciate your honesty."

His gaze softened. "We need to talk."

She sighed, wanting to continue to deny him the chance. But part of her was curious... *what could he possibly say after all this time?* "Okay, this evening," she said, her body weary. "I have a full day ahead of me and need to concentrate. I know you have work to do, too. But I'll set time aside for you to finally unburden whatever the hell you think you need to tell me."

Once again, he surprised her when he stepped close, reached down, and wrapped his fingers around hers just long enough to give a little squeeze. Then he stepped back and inclined his head. "Okay, let's check the food coming in and out."

As always, just like in the past, her heart clenched at just the touch of his fingers. As she walked toward the loading dock, she was acutely aware of the man following and of the past still lingering between them.

13

Devlin didn't push Mia any further. Instead, he stayed by her side, his eagle-eyed gaze scanning the operation as the day unfolded. His admiration for her only deepened as he watched her move seamlessly between roles. One moment, she was the no-nonsense professional, tracking lists of food and trucks, and issuing orders to drivers with unwavering authority. The next, she was in the villages, overseeing food distributions, her face lighting up as she greeted the refugees with a warmth that never felt forced.

She was everywhere at once, ensuring the camp's food supplies for over a hundred thousand refugees ran as efficiently as possible without losing sight of the people it was meant to serve. She spoke to the men with respect, gave the women reassuring smiles, and knelt to embrace the children who ran into her arms, their laughter ringing out like a balm against the hardship that surrounded them.

"She's wonderful, isn't she?" Enock's voice cut through Devlin's thoughts.

Devlin turned to the man at his side, Moses's second-in-command. He gave a slow nod, his gaze drifting back to

Mia. He noted the way Enock watched her, and the admiration in his expression was clear. Possessiveness twisted in Devlin's gut, but he didn't sense any deeper interest from Enock—just respect. That eased something inside him, if only slightly.

Still, Devlin remained suspicious. Whoever was behind the thefts had connections and resources. But Enock exuded the same trust and ease around the refugees that Mia did. The people weren't afraid of his uniform or the gun holstered at his hip.

"Have you worked here long?" Devlin asked.

"Five years." Enock nodded. "When I was a child, I watched the police officers in town." He chuckled. "I liked their uniforms. I liked the way the ones in charge carried themselves. They'd smile at us, and I knew then that I wanted to do the same one day."

A group of men called Enock over, and as he walked away, Devlin moved toward the back of the Sweswe village food center's loading dock. He found Mia standing slightly apart, watching as a truck was unloaded.

He followed her gaze. The efficiency of the process impressed him—the truck drivers unloaded crates as the refugees lined up with ID cards and baskets, each person receiving their allotted share. There was no chaos, no pushing or shoving, and no anger. Just patience, gratitude, and quiet relief as they walked away with their meager rations, ready to bring food back to their families.

"What can I do to help?" Devlin asked.

Mia turned to him, her eyes widening slightly. "You're supposed to be watching while I work."

"I am."

Her eyes now narrowed. "I think that entails keeping an eye on more than just me."

He held her gaze. "Keeping an eye on you is my most

important job," he admitted. "At the same time, the more I learn about this process, the more I can see where things might be going wrong."

"Got any ideas yet?"

He exhaled, rubbing a hand over his face. "Honest to God, there are so many places where things could go missing, it's almost laughable. The easiest way? If the drivers aren't getting the full shipments to begin with. Not all of these trucks come from an organization."

"And we have deliveries day and night."

He nodded, then motioned toward a group of men clustered around Enock. "What's your read on Enock?"

She studied him, her expression shifting. "Do you mean, do I trust him?"

"That, too. But mostly how his team operates."

She glanced away, her gaze fixed on the distance before meeting his again. "Honestly, I've never really thought about it. Everything here works because we don't have time to do anything but our jobs. We have to trust that everyone else is doing the same."

"So you don't have time to wonder if someone is committing a crime."

She grimaced. "When you put it like that, it doesn't sound great, does it?"

He stepped closer, fighting the urge to tuck a stray strand of hair behind her ear. "It's not bad, my Mia. It's just reality."

Her eyes widened slightly, and he realized too late that he'd let the words slip. My Mia. But she didn't snap at him. She didn't stiffen or glare. Instead, she dropped her gaze and simply nodded. He swallowed hard, resisting the urge to exhale in relief.

Dragging his focus back to the operation, he scanned the dozens of workers unloading food. They weren't going to catch this by watching the ground-level movement. If the thefts came from the top, they needed to follow the money trail.

While Mia moved away to continue supervising, Devlin stepped outside, finding a quiet corner to call LSIMT.

"Frazier. Devlin here. How's it going?"

"Busy. How's it on your end?"

"Too many moving pieces. Hundreds of trucks are in and out, day and night. Dozens of hands are involved every time a shipment arrives. If this is an organized operation, we need to follow the money, not the food."

"Logan had the same thought. Casper and Sadie are already on it. We're looking into international and Ugandan banks. If you have any names, that would help."

"Robert Ellyson." Devlin hesitated, glancing around to make sure Mia wasn't nearby. She wouldn't be happy, but Robert oversaw the trucks. If someone was moving stolen goods, he was in a perfect position to facilitate it. "Check Moses Kamanga and Enock Kasule, too. They're with camp security."

"Got it. Who else?"

"Jonan Muwange. Farid Hussein." He cursed under his breath. "Hell, Frazier, I could give you every single person's name here."

Frazier chuckled. "You're narrowing it down, though. That's a start."

Devlin rattled off a few more names, including Ravi, Charlie, and Dr. München. "See if they've received any unusual payments. Let me know what you find."

"Will do. And Devlin?"

"Yeah?"

"You doing okay?"

Devlin exhaled, rubbing a hand over his head. He had given Logan the heads-up about what he was facing here.

"I'm managing. At least she can talk to me without wanting to kill me. I think."

Frazier's laugh was warm. "You got this. No matter what happens with Mia, you'll be all right."

"Thanks," Devlin muttered before ending the call.

He stared at his phone, rolling his shoulders. Frazier was right—he had the mission. But he also had something more. The possibility of Mia. And that, more than anything, was the fight worth winning.

He looked over and spied Alain making his way toward him. Devlin nodded, saying, "I'm sorry you had to track us down here."

Alain grinned broadly. "I am used to walking. Since I oversee the medical nurses for each village, this is a good place for me to start today."

"Mia is inside. I'd like for her to be with us if that's okay?"

"Of course," Alain said.

While Todd and Cole remained with Alain, Devlin jogged back into the building, his sharp gaze scanning the throng of workers. His eyes locked onto Mia's, and she moved toward him without hesitation, curiosity flickering across her face.

"Hey, what's up?"

"I know you're busy, but I have Alain. He has some information for us, and I'd like you to hear it."

Her initial confusion shifted into interest, and she nodded. Without thinking, Devlin placed a hand on the small of her back, guiding her through the organized chaos of the warehouse. They maneuvered around wooden crates stacked high and reed baskets filled with supplies. Even through the thick air filled with the scent of grains and earth, the barest touch of his fingers against her back sent a familiar, electric tingle through him. After all these years, something as simple as touch still carried the weight of memory.

When they reached Alain, standing beneath the shade of a towering tree, Devlin forced himself to pull his hand away, but he immediately missed the contact.

"Alain," Mia greeted warmly, offering him a smile. "It's nice to see you. I talk to your wife and children when they head to school."

Alain returned her smile, and Devlin once again noted Mia's unique ability to make people feel seen. She never simply greeted someone—she made them feel important as if their presence truly mattered.

"And I see you are busy as always," Alain replied.

Mia laughed, a soft, cheerful sound that made Devlin's chest tighten. "I imagine you could say the same about the clinics."

"You are right. People will always need food and medical care, which is why we are here."

Mia glanced up at Devlin, and without a word, he knew she was silently signaling him to take the lead. He turned to Alain. "Jonan told me you have information about the black market."

Alain's easy smile faded, his expression darkening. "Yes, I'm sorry to say. When I worked in the hospital in Congo treating insurgents, it was not hard to notice that while the Congolese people starved, the insurgents had food. It was even brought into the hospital for their use." His voice dropped lower, burdened by the weight of his memories. "It was even offered to us—the medical staff treating them."

His face contorted as if remembering left a bitter taste. "As a healer, I took a vow to help anyone in need. But as a Congolese, it broke my heart to know that the food I was eating had been stolen, given to men who would leave the hospital only to continue their killing spree."

Mia reached out and gently laid her hand on Alain's arm, a gesture of quiet understanding. "We can only be responsible for the choices we make, Alain. There are times we can influence others and guide them to do the right thing, but sometimes all we can do is mitigate the damage. Your job was to heal, and you did. You followed your calling, and you protected your family. That is what matters."

Tears glistened in Alain's eyes as he stared at Mia, as though absorbing her words into the very marrow of his bones. Devlin held his breath, recognizing the moment for what it was—one of Mia's gifts. He had seen it before, so many times, watching her offer comfort with a single touch, a single word. And now, standing beside her, he was struck all over again by just how remarkable she was.

His gaze lingered on her, the pull of old emotions swirling within him, mingling with something new. She had once loved him with all her heart, and the thought of earning back that love consumed him.

Realizing Mia and Alain waited for him, he cleared his throat and refocused. "Alain, what information do you have for us now?"

Alain exhaled heavily. "The black market for food that feeds the insurgents in the Congo mostly comes from Uganda. The reason is simple—Uganda takes in refugees freely, and the smugglers take advantage of the aid coming into the country. The theft happens at every level."

"Can you give specifics?" Cole asked.

"Some steal directly from the farmers, raiding fields, selling crops at high prices, and smuggling them across the border. Others divert food meant for the refugee camps before it even reaches its destination. And then there are the warehouses—raided or bribed officials letting trucks through without questions."

Devlin felt the weight of Alain's words pressing on his shoulders.

"So the trucks from our warehouses can drive straight into the Congo?" Mia's voice rose slightly, edged with frustration. Devlin instinctively placed a hand on her shoulder, a calming touch. She turned to him briefly, and instead of bristling, he felt the tension in her muscles ease under his fingertips. She nodded and turned back to Alain.

"What I learned," Alain continued, "is what I saw when we crossed Lake Edward. The lake is vast and impossible to guard completely. It divides Uganda from the Congo, and once food makes it onto a boat, there's virtually no stopping it before it reaches its destination."

Todd crossed his arms. "We know Congo has the Allied Democratic Forces and the M23 rebels, but do you have any idea who might be stealing from this camp?"

Alain shook his head. "If I knew, I would have gone straight to Dr. München. But my best guess? The M23 rebels. They control most of the smuggling routes in eastern Congo. If food is being stolen from this camp, they're likely involved, or at least the ones at the end of the line."

Devlin watched as Alain sagged slightly, exhaustion evident in every line of his face. Before he could speak, Mia stepped forward again, both hands clasping Alain's.

"Alain, you must know that for all you do—for the refugees, for your wife and children—you are a good man."

A tremulous smile broke across Alain's face, and Devlin saw the way he straightened his shoulders as if those simple words had lifted an invisible weight from him. "Bless you, Miss Mia."

Alain turned to Devlin. "If you have more questions, I

will try to answer them. But I believe I have given you all I know."

Before Devlin could ask anything else, Alain added, "Before I go back to the clinic, I will say this. Small-scale theft happens everywhere—desperation drives some, greed drives others. But if this is bigger, if the theft is more than a few stolen sacks, it's organized. And it goes much higher up."

He winced as if the admission pained him, then bowed his head. "Good luck," he murmured before turning and walking away, leaving the three Keepers and Mia standing in silence, watching him go.

14

Mia looked up, exhaustion pressing down on her like a heavy weight. Alain's explanation of the black market and smuggling drained her with every bleak word. She had offered him comfort, but she realized her energy was waning as she stood there.

Her gaze flickered toward Devlin, only to find him already watching her, his expression conveying his understanding of her mood. Their connection had been forged in something deeper than time, and even after years apart, it remained.

She shook her head slowly, pulling herself back to the present and turning to Todd and Cole. "This camp is too big to monitor. It's over two hundred square kilometers. I don't even know why I thought we could uncover this ourselves."

"We've got our people working on it from their end," Devlin said.

She squinted up at him, her nose wrinkling. "I don't even know what that means."

Cole chuckled. "It just means that sometimes a person

sitting behind a computer, poring through information and intel, can see patterns we can't see on the ground."

She worried her bottom lip between her teeth, hating how lost she felt in the intricacies of their world. Devlin, of course, seemed to sense it.

"We have access to all kinds of information," he explained. "And if we don't, we have contacts who can get it for us. Since the WFP has asked for our help, our people back home can tap into bank records and follow the money trail."

Understanding dawned in her eyes, widening them slightly. It struck her then how different their work was, almost like something out of a movie—the kind that left ordinary people in awe of what was possible while secretly wondering if such things happened in real life. Except now, she was living in it.

"What do you know about the security here?" Devlin asked.

Mia folded her arms. "Moses has a massive security team. Some are UN hires, but many are just refugees given jobs to help keep the peace."

"In most places, flashing a little money can make someone look the other way," Todd said.

Mia nodded slowly. "I know you think I'm naive, but I've worked in enough camps to know we deal with the same problems every society does. So yes, I can easily see a guard taking a payoff to let an entire truck filled with food drive away."

"But someone would have to organize it," Devlin reminded her. "Sure, a truck driver could slip a guard some cash to get through a checkpoint, but that's opportunistic. What's happening here is systematic."

She hesitated. "Do you think Moses is involved?"

Devlin exhaled. "I don't know. You know him best."

Mia recalled her conversations with Moses, then slowly shook her head. "I don't know. I've always liked talking with him. That makes it hard to imagine he'd do something like this." Her mind slipped into darker places, ones she had fought to leave behind. "But then... how well do we really know anyone?"

The moment the words left her lips, she saw the pain flash across Devlin's face. Her heart twisted, hating that she'd hurt him. There was a time when she would have done so without hesitation, but that time was fading away. Faced with food stolen that was intended for those who needed it the most, the pain from Devlin seemed like it had existed in another lifetime.

She drew in a deep breath, blinking away the tears burning the edges of her eyes. Clearing her throat, she continued, "This camp contains too many people for me to vouch for who is or isn't trustworthy. Even good people can be susceptible to bribery. Margarethe believes someone in leadership might be involved. She is going to express these concerns to Dr. München. I've worked with, laughed with, and shared meals with these people. I just... I just don't know."

Exhaustion threatened to drag her under, and it wasn't even noon. And then, there was still tonight when she'd agreed to meet with Devlin, who wanted to talk.

Cole checked his watch. "I'll call headquarters and see if there's any update for us."

"Hey, Mia!"

She turned as Charlie pulled up in a Jeep, waving wildly with his signature grin. She shook her head, unable to suppress a chuckle.

He parked and gestured toward the van pulling up behind him. "Some mission volunteers wanted to see how food distribution is handled. They're assigned to me. Some are journalism majors, so they're here to see how we make miracles happen. You know, the whole 'fishes and loaves' routine."

Mia laughed, glad for the levity. "Some days, that's exactly what it feels like." She nodded toward the warehouse. "They can observe. If they want to help, that's fine too."

Charlie turned to his assistant, who guided the visitors inside, then sauntered over. "You're smart to have your powwow under a tree. Shade and a breeze? Genius."

"Charlie, have you met these gentlemen? This is Devlin, Cole, and Todd. And this is Charlie Anderson, our information reporting officer."

After a round of handshakes, Devlin asked, "What exactly does your office do?"

Charlie threw his arm around Mia's shoulders and grinned. "Well, my passion is finding beautiful women to hang out with."

At times, Mia loved Charlie's easygoing attitude, but right now, she hated how he appeared unprofessional and didn't seem to mind involving her at the same time.

Mia heard the growl rumbling deep inside Devlin's chest and quickly stepped away from Charlie's arm to maintain a professional distance. "Cut the crap, Charlie."

Charlie clutched his chest dramatically. "Aw, you wound me. Always breaking my heart."

The joke fell flat. Devlin, Todd, and Cole simply stared, unimpressed. Charlie cleared his throat. "Okay, okay. I know my humor gets away from me. It's just… it's tough here, and I try to make people laugh."

Mia, hoping to salvage the awkward situation, smiled at him. "And most of the time, it's appreciated."

Charlie smirked. "See? That's why you're the best. You always make people feel better."

Devlin cut in. "So what does your job entail?"

Charlie sighed. "All the leadership heads send information to me, and I collate it for reports. Information like camp numbers, the demographics of the refugees, resource needs, and just about everything you can think of. Then I prepare the reports on our camp that are sent off to our funding organizations, such as UNHCR, Red Cross, WHO, WSB, and all the NGO... nongovernment organizations."

"Charlie likes to act like his job isn't important," Mia said, "but of course it is. His reports help us get funding. Lets the officials know if we get too crowded. Lets Dr. München know the state of our resources so he can ask for more." She turned to Charlie and shook her head. "So don't sell yourself short."

Charlie shrugged. "What can I say? I crunch numbers and drive a Jeep."

Someone called his name, and he turned. "Looks like I'm needed. Nice to meet you."

As he jogged away, Mia's phone vibrated. She checked the message, then looked up. "We need to go to the admin building. Margarethe is getting ready to leave."

The four of them climbed into the Jeep and headed back to camp. Inside Dr. München's office, they found Margarethe waiting.

Not skipping a beat, Margarethe said, "I'm heading back to Germany first thing tomorrow. Two nights were all the time allotted for this trip. After reviewing the records, I have assured Dr. München that I can attest that you are correct. Systematic thefts are occurring of the food sources."

"Do you have any insight as to who might be instigating it?" Mia asked.

"I didn't do any investigating, my dear. I leave that to

the professionals," she said as she inclined her head toward the men.

Dr. München interjected, "As much as it pains me to think that it's one of my heads, I have listened to Margarethe's suggestions and want you to continue to turn over every stone until you find who is perpetuating the organized stealing and smuggling."

Margarethe nodded. "But I also know that as soon as you plug one hole, others will pop up."

Mia's heart ached at hearing the experienced woman's words. "So we do nothing?"

"Mia, my dear, you will do what you do every day. Help those you can with what you have. Sometimes that's all we can hope for."

After standing, she leaned over to shake Dr. München's hand, then turned and did the same with Devlin, Cole, and Todd. Finally, she pulled Mia into a heartfelt hug, rubbing her back gently.

Just as Mia thought the woman would pull away, Margarethe whispered, "The heart has an amazing capacity to heal from past hurts. It keeps on beating, evidence of life all around us. But we have to be willing to take that chance of finding happiness again."

Before Mia had a chance to respond, the woman tightened her arms, then let go. And with a wave to all, she walked out of the room, leaving Mia staring in her wake.

Hours later, she'd made it to the end of the day without seeing Devlin again. He and his coworkers had gone off to places unknown, which was fine by her. She needed to concentrate on taking care of her job without worrying about anything else. Of course, her peace was short-lived as thoughts of him crept through her mind continually.

She was almost grateful when a truck broke down just outside the warehouse, and they all had to pitch in to unload the food, carrying it the last fifty feet into the food center. Several of the men tried to stop her and the volunteers who were around. She laughed them off. "I'm not afraid to get my hands dirty, and I can certainly carry a few boxes," she argued.

Ugandan women worked hard, so she could only imagine the driver was uncomfortable with the idea of a white woman assisting or that it was her position in the camp that made him uneasy. But with everyone pitching in, the truck was soon emptied. She walked over to the truck one last time to find the drivers as they stood in the back of the cargo trailer. "Thank you!" she called out.

The two men rushed forward, nodding and bowing. "Thank you, ma'am. We are getting someone to come get the truck started or towed."

"It's okay," she said. "You're not in the way of the other trucks coming." With that, she headed inside to find Farid. "I'm leaving, but I also don't want you to stay late tonight."

"Don't worry about me. You look like you've had a hard day, Mia. Go home and take care of yourself."

She managed a smile, but her stomach clenched at the thought of her evening. Offering a wave, she walked down the dusty lane to the housing area. Deciding to at least take care of her shower first, she grabbed what she needed and went to the women's showers closest to her room. Five minutes. Not long for hot water but another quick scrub and shampoo, and she was dressed and walked back to her room.

Looking up, she spied Devlin standing at her door, two trays of food in his hands, and she froze.

Of course, he'd show up now. The timing sucked when she was exhausted, raw, and barely holding herself together after the day's chaos. Her defenses were already worn thin, and now he stood there like some kind of penitent offering, holding food as if that could erase ten years of silence.

Her chest tightened, but she forced a small, detached smile, nodding toward the trays. "You must be hungry enough for two dinners."

Devlin's expression was cautious, like he wasn't sure if she was joking or ready to slam the door in his face. But he managed a small smile, his voice quiet yet sure. "I figured after the day you had, you'd probably appreciate somebody bringing food to you."

A surprised chuckle slipped out before she could stop it, but it carried more disbelief than amusement. "I haven't had someone bring me food in... hell, I can't even remember."

He took another step closer, his presence filling the small space between them. "Then I'm glad I'm the first."

The words hit like a slow, burning ache, seeping into places she thought were long healed. Her breath caught. She was trapped in his gaze, the air around them thick, charged. Memories surfaced—ones she'd long tried to suppress, ones that made her chest ache with longing, and something far more dangerous. Before she could stop herself, the words tumbled out, unbidden. "You were all of my firsts, Jim Devlin."

The second she said it, she wanted to snatch it back. She felt exposed. Too much of herself laid bare. But there was no point in pretending. He already knew. He knew exactly what he'd meant to her—how much of herself she'd given to him, blindly, completely.

Her chin lifted, forcing herself to meet his gaze. "I'm not sure why I should even let you in."

There was something solemn in his eyes. "If you don't, I'll sleep on your stoop."

She narrowed her gaze. "You'd do it, too, wouldn't you?"

"Damn straight."

She shouldn't have doubted him. The Jim she remembered had always been quietly tenacious. The weight of his gaze never left hers. The stubborn set of his jaw and the quiet conviction in his voice should've irritated her. Instead, it twisted something deep inside, something too dangerously close to hope. And she couldn't afford that.

Finally, she huffed, turning toward the door and unlocking it. Throwing it open with more force than necessary, she growled. "Come on in. I'm hungry and tired, but we might as well get this over with."

The door clicked shut behind them as they stepped inside, the sound oddly final. Mia motioned to the small desk in the corner. "You can set the food there. I have a couple of water bottles in my fridge."

She pulled out two bottles and handed one to him before picking up the tray with the least amount of food. Without a word, she walked over to her bed and settled in. Devlin took the chair across from her, his movements slow and deliberate. But his eyes never stopped watching her. As if he were studying her, searching for something she wasn't ready to give.

For a few moments, neither spoke as they ate. The meal was simple—beans, rice, and makati with bread and fresh mangoes. The silence between them was tense, pressing in all around them. She hated that he could still make her feel so many things she didn't want to feel.

When she finished, she handed him her empty tray, and he stacked them together on the edge of her desk before turning his chair to face her completely. Mia reached for the thin blanket folded at the foot of her bed and wrapped it around her shoulders. It was a flimsy and useless barrier, but it was something. His gaze was too intense, and she was terrified of whatever words he thought he needed to say. She folded her arms tightly, bracing herself, her pulse hammering against her ribs.

He broke me once before. There's nothing else he can say that will break me again. With that thought, she lifted her chin, bracing herself. "Okay. You're here to talk. Go for it." Now, she just hoped her heart would still be intact by the time he finished.

15

Devlin sat in the stiff, uncomfortable chair that barely fit in the cramped container room Mia called home at the refugee camp. The space was small, military-issue, utilitarian—bed, chair, a desk shoved into the corner. But bringing a non-military brightness to the room, the space reflected the woman he remembered. A framed photograph of her family on the desk—a family that he remembered well but hadn't seen or talked to for as long as they had been separated. A bright green and blue cover over the bed. A local beaded decoration hung on the wall behind the bed.

But now, the woman who sat across from him was wrapped tightly in a blanket like she could shield herself from the storm of words he was about to unleash.

His heart pounded in an uneven rhythm, a beat he couldn't steady no matter how much he tried to regulate his breathing. He had imagined this moment for a decade —over and over, rehearsing what he would say, how he would explain, how he would make her see. But with Mia sitting on that narrow bed, her body curled in on itself like she was bracing for an impact, he felt all those well-rehearsed words slipping through his fingers like dry sand.

She was silent, watching him. Waiting. And as he stared back, the weight of what had been left unsaid for ten years pressed down on him like a physical force. He cleared his throat, forced his spine straighter, and spoke, his voice rough. "I fucked up."

Mia didn't flinch. Her only reaction was a tight press of her lips and a slight dip of her chin. It was a familiar sight—her restraint when she wanted to let him speak or knew he needed to get the words out first. It was one of the things he'd always loved about her. If they were in a heated argument, she fought passionately, unafraid to speak her mind. But in moments like this, when he needed to lay himself bare, she listened.

"I've looked back on everything that led up to my colossal fuckup. I've analyzed it from every angle, torn it apart, and studied every reason, every doubt, and every mistake. I've forced myself to relive it. Every fucking day. I tried to understand why I let it all spiral, why I let you walk away without stopping you." His throat tightened. He swallowed hard and kept going. "Everything I ever said to you—every promise, every word, every dream we shared—was real. I loved you. I saw a future with you."

Her face remained impassive, but he saw the slight tension in her fingers where they clutched the blanket.

"When I graduated from college and told you I wanted to join the Marines, you supported me. When you told me you wanted to save the world but knew you'd have to narrow that focus, I was all in for that. When I told you that I wanted to go to BUD/S and become a SEAL, we talked about what that would look like for our future. We knew there'd be times when we'd be separated. We knew there'd be times when I couldn't talk about what I was doing. We even said that the time apart would make us stronger."

He forced his eyes to stay on her face, wanting to see her expression. What he saw, he recognized... her full attention just on him. Mia's breath was so shallow, he wasn't sure she was even breathing. The weight of her attention pinned him in place, urging him to keep going before she cut him off.

"I knew you made choices to be closer to me," he admitted, his voice quieter now. "At the time, I was worried you were limiting yourself for me. You swore you weren't. You said the graduate program at a university near where I was stationed was exactly what you wanted. You excelled, like always. But when you started looking for jobs, all I could think was that you were making sacrifices for me."

She opened her mouth slightly, then shut it again, and his stomach twisted. He wasn't sure he wanted to hear what she was about to say.

"You were always supportive of me, Mia. Those were my own doubts. Looking back, you'll remember that my SEAL team had two members going through divorces. Another was breaking up with the woman he'd been with for about three years. I saw the stress and difficulties. But I still felt like you and I could make it work, even if we didn't sleep in the same bed every night."

The instant he said the word bed, he grimaced. By the look on Mia's face, he knew exactly where her thoughts had gone, but he wanted to explain more before going there.

Still hurrying to get out what he came to say, he rushed forward. "The month you were in Haiti, I went on a mission. It was only supposed to be a three-day mission. That's why you and I were out of communication. But the three-day mission extended into a week. A god-awful fucking week. Our intel wasn't accurate. We came against insurgents more heavily armed than we had anticipated." He scrubbed a hand over his face, pressing his fingers into his eyes. The ghosts of his fallen brothers were still with him.

A small gasp left her lips, and his eyes popped open to see her gaze remain pinned on him. He could see it in her eyes… the sympathy. *Christ, how did I manage to be so lucky to have that beauty, that passion for life, and a caring person in my hands for so long?*

He cleared his throat. "We lost Markowski and Whitten. Searles and Rubio were injured." He once more scrubbed his hand over his face and sighed heavily.

"I'm so sorry, Jim," she said softly, using his first name the way she had the years they'd been together. "I should've been there for you instead of in Haiti."

He shook his head, sharp and violent. "No."

She flinched at his vehemence but stayed silent, waiting.

"I wasn't in a good place. None of us were. You were in Haiti, where you needed to be. And I… I was burying my teammates. I watched as Markowitz's wife and children fell apart. I spent the next two weeks drunk off my ass. We all had to see a base counselor, but we each handled our grief differently. Logan just got quiet, and Sisco headed off to see his family. Me? I raged, I cried, I wanted to hold you tight, and I wanted to push you away."

He watched as she swallowed deeply, then dragged her tongue over her dry lips. "All that was a normal reaction to that kind of trauma, but if I had been there, I could've supported you. Made sure you got to counseling. Given you someone to lean on. Helped mitigate the grief."

He looked at her face and couldn't believe she was still offering comfort under the circumstances, with everything he was telling her and knowing what he'd done. "I would never have wanted you to see me like that. Rock-bottom. Staring at the world through the bottom of a whiskey glass."

"So you decided to push me away."

He shook his head. "It wasn't a plan. I knew we needed to talk. Your internship was the last thing you had to do before you graduated, and you were looking for jobs. You had so much passion inside you, and I wanted you to fly. And all I could see was that I was a huge stone around your neck. During some of those whiskey-induced stupors that I was in during those couple of weeks, I thought maybe our time had come. Maybe we were meant only to be what we had, but not what future we thought would be ours."

She shifted again, drawing the blanket tighter, giving evidence that she was shielding herself from the pain still to come.

"Before I say anything else, I need to let you know that I never cheated on you—"

This time, it wasn't just a gasp that left Mia's lips. A full-blown scoff burst forth as her eyes bugged out. "Devlin, I always trusted that you'd never lie to me, but then I'd never thought you'd cheat. I know what I saw. I know what you didn't say at the time. I don't think anything you can say will make that day right."

It didn't escape his notice that she was calling him Devlin. "Please, hear me out. I'll be honest to say that I spent more time being drunk than sober. I couldn't have even told you what day it was when I should've been planning a welcome home celebration for you. I didn't even realize it was the day you would come home."

Another bitter laugh escaped Mia, sharp and cutting. "And that made it all right? That you were so drunk you didn't even know I was coming home, so it was fine to have another woman in our bed?" Her voice rose with every word, each syllable a blade slicing into him.

Devlin swallowed against the tightness in his throat. "No, no, that's not what I'm saying." He rolled his shoulders and cracked his neck, needing to relieve the mounting tension threatening to strangle him. "I was home alone... drinking like I had been every day and night, when she showed up. I knew her. She was one of our support people. She and her boyfriend had a fight after drinking at a party, and he locked her out of their apartment. She was drunk, crying, pissed off, and because he lived in the same complex, she came over and banged on the door. She asked if she could sleep on our couch until she sobered up enough to drive."

Mia's face was a storm of emotions—disbelief, fury, and something far deeper that made his stomach twist. She had never been able to hide what she felt, and seeing it now was like a punch to the gut.

Her voice was quiet and measured, but the ice in her tone was worse than her shouting. "So you let her in. But she was clearly in our bed, not on the couch."

He nodded. "Yes, but *I* slept on the couch."

He hadn't expected Mia to jump for joy, but her tight jaw and thinly pressed lips made him even more nervous. "And before you ask, she had her clothes on underneath the covers. She wore a strapless dress when she'd been out with her boyfriend, but she was dressed the whole time in our apartment."

Her brow lifted, skepticism clear.

"The following morning, I woke up and reeked. I stank of unwashed clothes and an unwashed body due to too much fucking alcohol." He exhaled. "I was a fucking mess, Mia."

Her expression didn't soften. If anything, she looked even more disgusted.

He pushed forward, needing her to hear it all. "I slipped through the bedroom to see she was still sleeping and went into the bathroom. I looked in the mirror and knew it was time to straighten up. So I got in the shower and washed off. I couldn't remember what day it was, but I knew you were coming home soon."

"Soon, as in you expected me to walk through the door and see that woman, appearing naked, in our bed?"

"No, absolutely not. Honest to God, I didn't know that was the day you were coming home. I mean, I knew you would be home sooner rather than later. But as I was in the shower, the alcohol finally leaving my system, I knew that you and I needed to have a heartfelt and probably painful conversation. I could not let you sacrifice any goals you had just to try to stay with me, as fucked up as I was."

"So you were just going to decide we needed to be apart?"

Her legs uncrossed, feet dangling off the bed, and his gaze caught on them for a second—small and delicate. He used to love how they looked against his and fit so perfectly between his larger ones when they sat together. A memory of one of their teenage summers at the pool flashed through his mind as she lay with her back against his chest, her laughter ringing in his ears as they compared foot sizes.

But that was another lifetime ago.

His chest ached, but he forced himself to look back at

her face, finding her staring at him with an expression so guarded, so wounded, that it made his stomach turn.

He blew out a breath and shook his head. Looking at her face, he realized he'd allowed his mind to wander down the path from years ago while she awaited an answer. "Mia, at that time, I wasn't thinking clearly. I barely knew what day it was, let alone what I was going to say to you."

"Okay," she murmured, voice deceptively calm. "So let's get back to the morning you finally had this epiphany. The morning you showered, stood in front of the mirror, and decided I deserved better. You found yourself wondering all sorts of things about us... the *us* that I will remind you had been together for almost ten years. The same morning I walked in to find another woman in our bed."

The words landed like a slap, and Devlin flinched despite himself.

He swallowed hard. "I took a shower and realized I hadn't brought clean clothes in with me. I peeked out and saw that Cheryl was still asleep, so I shut the door, dried off, wrapped myself in a towel, and was just going to grab some clothes from the closet."

Mia's jaw was so tight, he swore he heard her teeth grind. "And I walked in."

It wasn't a question. It was a statement.

He nodded slowly. "Yes. You walked in just as I opened the door."

Her lips rolled inward, blinking rapidly, and he prayed she wouldn't cry. He deserved every bit of her anger, but seeing her in pain and knowing he was the reason was unbearable.

Mia's voice turned razor-sharp, slicing right through him. "You knew what it looked like. You knew what I thought and did nothing to fix it." Now, her tone was harsh. Mia's face didn't crumple, but the pain was there, raw and exposed. It was still a wound that hadn't fully healed. And it was his fault.

His throat felt tight, his lungs constricted. "Yes." Silence stretched between them, thick and heavy, threatening to cut off his breath.

Mia blinked, but her gaze didn't waver, her hands clenched into fists in her lap. "Ten years, Devlin. Ten fucking years. Do you have any idea what that did to me?"

His stomach churned. "Mia, I—"

"No." She cut him off, shaking her head. "You don't get to explain away what I went through. I spent years—*years*—questioning everything. Hating myself for trusting you. Hating myself for loving you." Her voice cracked, but she pushed through it. "You broke me. And the worst part? You let me believe I wasn't enough. That I wasn't worth fighting for."

His hands clenched into fists. "That was never—"

"But that's exactly what you did," she interrupted, her eyes burning into his. "You didn't chase me. You didn't try to explain. You didn't attempt the long conversation about how we might be better apart. You just let me go after I'd seen the worst."

Her voice trembled at the end, but she sucked in a sharp breath, steadying herself. "And now you think you can just… what? Show up with dinner and talk your way back in? Ten years, Devlin." She let out a shaky laugh, but there was no humor in it. "I had to rebuild myself from the ground up because of you. And you think you get to waltz back in and just… throw out an explanation, and it's all fixed?"

Devlin's chest ached, but he held her gaze, refusing to look away. "No." His voice was rough and raw. "I don't think that. I don't think I deserve anything from you, Mia."

Her lips parted slightly as if the admission surprised her.

He swallowed hard. "But I do know one thing. I regret it. Every single day, I regret it. And I will spend the rest of my life proving that to you if you let me."

Mia studied him for a long moment, her eyes unreadable. Finally, she exhaled and shook her head.

16

Mia's heart had been pounding ever since she'd sat on her bed, facing Devlin. The air in the small, container-like room felt stifling, pressing down on her. She instinctively knew that whatever they talked about tonight would alter both their lives. Yet in truth, her heart had been hammering from the moment she'd first laid eyes on him again.

But in her wildest dreams, she'd never imagined the words that had just come out of his mouth. *He hadn't cheated.* The shock of it stole her breath and left her momentarily frozen as her mind struggled to process. Others might whisper that he was lying, but Devlin never lied. That had always been one of his defining traits. It was why, if he had opened his mouth and told her the truth ten years ago, she would have believed him. But he hadn't.

He'd let her suffer. He'd let her grieve their relationship, their love, and their future. He let her believe he had destroyed it with another woman in their bed. And now, this?

She stared at him, unblinking. Not because she was

overwhelmed with relief—there was none. No weight lifted off her chest. No breath of fresh air filled her lungs after a decade of suffocating pain. If anything, the air grew heavier, thick with another layer of betrayal. She grappled with the bitter truth that he had let her believe the worst, knowing the agony it would cause. There was no relief in this confession, only another layer of betrayal.

He had known what she thought, what she'd gone through, and he'd let her. Let her hate him. Let her mourn him. Let her leave. And now, his unwavering gaze remained locked onto her, the tight clench of his jaw revealing his own turmoil. His hands flexed open and shut, a nervous tell she had learned years ago.

Her thoughts tangled, unable to settle or land anywhere except on the unshakable truth. He had broken her then, and now he was twisting the knife all over again.

The blanket around her shoulders suddenly felt suffocating. She let it drop and straightened her spine. "I think you should leave."

He blinked, then shook his head as he stood. "No, Mia. I'm not leaving."

Her chest tightened at his defiance, at his absolute gall to stand there and act like he had any say in this. Her jaw locked, and she could barely spit out, "You're not leaving?" She stared in disbelief, her gaze sharpening into something lethal.

His arms spread wide, palms up in a pleading and insistent gesture. "No, I'm not. That's the whole problem, Mia. I let you walk away ten years ago thinking the worst, and I've hated that ever since. But I told myself that by doing so, you could live your life, and I had to deal with it, even though it hurt both of us."

She let out a sharp, humorless laugh. "Hurt both of us?"

she echoed. "You have no fucking clue what I went through, Devlin. None."

He swallowed hard but pushed forward. "I wrote you a letter—"

She jumped to her feet. Her scoff cut through the air, sharp as a knife. "A letter? A goddamn apology letter that didn't explain anything other than you were sorry it ended the way it did! Do you hear yourself? You let me believe I wasn't enough, that I wasn't worth the truth, and you think a 'gee, I'm sorry you're hurt' letter was supposed to fix that?"

She stepped closer, her anger vibrating under her skin, nearly unbearable. "Tell me something—when you wrote it, did you intend to send it? Or was it just something you did to make yourself feel better? Another way to justify letting me go?"

He winced. "I realize it wasn't enough to repair the damage. And I get that... it was stupid of me."

Her heart twisted painfully, fury warring with something dangerously close to devastation.

He held her gaze as he pointed down at the floor. "But, Mia, we're here. Right now. Together," he rasped. "Don't you think that means something?"

Mia inhaled sharply through her nose. "Maybe it means I should have my head examined for even listening to you," she growled.

"You know me—"

"I *used* to know you—"

"No, you know me," he ground out. "There are things about us that aren't the same, but deep inside, you know me." His voice dropped to a low intensity, his words forceful like a storm about to break. "If I thought for one moment that the best thing for us was for me to walk out that door right now, letting you hate me, I would do it. But what we had was worth fighting for, and I didn't fight for it years ago. If you don't think it's providence that we randomly ended up in the same place, at the same time, on the other side of the fucking world, then I know you're lying. And one thing about you, my Mia, is that you don't lie."

Her heart clenched so tightly in her chest that she winced, and she plopped down onto the side of the bed again, afraid her legs would no longer offer support. Her nails dug into her palms, rage bubbling along every nerve because part of her did know him. That was the problem. Because if there was one thing she could still do after all these years, it was fight.

And if Jim Dev thought he could just walk back into her life, say a few words, and expect everything to fall into place—oh, no.

Mia felt the air shift as Devlin crossed the small space. His long strides ate up the distance between them before she could react. He sank down beside her on the bed, one leg bent, the other foot planted on the floor as if he belonged there.

His nearness was suffocating. The warmth of his body and the quiet confidence in his posture was too much. It stirred something deep in her, something she had buried beneath layers of bitterness and self-preservation.

"Let me have it," he said softly.

Her gaze snapped to his. "What?"

His expression didn't waver. "Let me have it. Yell at me. Cuss me out, up one side and down the other. Tell me how you feel and how you felt back then. I didn't give you the chance to do that. I let you walk away, and I've asked myself why I didn't explain for years. Why I didn't fight for us. The problem was, I was too fucked up to do any of those things. So I let you go." His voice roughened. "But I'm not fucking letting either of us walk away right now."

Mia trembled, the shiver starting deep and spreading like wildfire throughout her body. She opened her mouth, ready to scream at him, to unleash every ounce of pain she had swallowed for a decade. But nothing came out.

Her entire life had been about fighting—for justice, for others, for what was right. But now, with the man who had once been her whole world sitting barely a foot away, the words stuck in her throat. Overwhelmed, she closed her eyes.

The bed shifted, and she thought that he was getting up to leave. Instead, warmth brushed over her shoulders. She startled, eyes flying open as he gently pulled the blanket around her again, his fingers lingering for half a second before retreating. He leaned back, resuming his position as if nothing had happened.

The tenderness of the gesture made her stomach twist painfully. It was such a small gesture. After all these years of nothing, why did he suddenly decide she deserved comfort? Where was this care and thoughtfulness when she had been breaking apart from the inside out?

Some might say it was too little, too late. Perhaps, years ago, it would have been. But they weren't those same people anymore. She inhaled deeply, filling her lungs before exhaling slowly. His scent filled her. When she opened her eyes, he was still there. Still waiting.

"Why did you leave the SEALs?" she asked. The question surprised even her. Of all the things she could have said, those were the words that came out.

Devlin didn't hesitate. "Four years after you and I... after I let you go, I was on another mission that went fubar. I was shot in the chest—"

She gasped, one hand flying to his knee as though anchoring herself to him. "Oh my God."

He didn't react to her touch. He didn't acknowledge the way her fingers curled against him like she could somehow turn back time and undo what had happened.

"I went down before reaching the helicopter. We were under enemy fire." His lips pressed together briefly before he sighed. "Logan turned back for me. He managed to get me up and carry me toward the bird, where Sisco and the others waited. Then there was an explosion. Logan took the brunt of it, and I crashed down on top of him. He tore his knee to hell, but the others dragged us in." His expression tightened, eyes distant. "Sisco went to work, shooting Logan up with enough morphine to keep him comfortable. Then he worked on me. He saved my life. They both did."

A breath shuddered from Mia's lungs, but she couldn't stop the tears that slipped down her cheeks. *I could've lost him. I could have lost him without ever having this chance—to argue, to talk, to figure things out.* For ten years, she had hated him, resented him, tried to forget him. But if he had died? If she had never gotten the chance to see him again... *Oh God.*

She pressed her free hand against the ache in her chest, her other still gripping his knee as if she could tether herself to this moment, to him.

"I'm so sorry, Jim," she whispered, her voice thick with emotion.

He shook his head but hesitantly reached down. His hand covered hers, warm and solid. He squeezed, just barely, before letting go.

Mia exhaled slowly, trying to steady the riot inside her.

"Logan had to get out, too. His knee was never going to let him jump from planes again," he continued. "He moved to Montana and started flying rescues over the mountains.

He… also started running a few under-the-radar ops. After I healed, I spent time with my family, but every day in Kansas, I kept vigilant, terrified I'd see your parents, and I didn't want to see the disappointment in their eyes. It was bad enough from my parents."

Then I started using my skills to help people. I ended up working with a man in tribal security. Eventually, I followed him from Kansas to Montana, not far from Logan. He came looking for me and practically discovered me in his own backyard. We found Sisco in El Paso, and he and I were the first two hires. I've been with Logan for about two years now."

For several minutes, neither of them spoke. The thick silence pressed against Mia's chest as though a tangible weight. Thoughts stormed inside her mind, a chaotic tangle of emotions and memories, each vying for dominance. She lifted a trembling hand from where it rested against her heart and rubbed her temples, squeezing her eyes shut as if that would still the chaos within her.

The bed shifted again, the small space amplifying even the slightest movements. Then she heard footsteps. Opening her eyes slightly, she turned just in time to see Devlin disappear into her tiny bathroom. She frowned, listening as he rummaged around, followed by the unmistakable rattle of pills. A moment later, he emerged, crossing the room with steady steps.

He held out a few ibuprofen tablets and a bottle of water.

"If I thought a shot of whiskey would help, I'd try to find some for you," he said, his voice low and edged with something she couldn't quite name. "But I spent too much time at the bottom of a bottle to recommend that. Water and pain relievers will do the trick."

A soft, unexpected snort escaped her. Shaking her head,

she took the offering, swallowing the pills and finishing the water. When she lowered the bottle, she saw that he was still waiting, his hand extended. Silently, she passed it back to him, and he returned it to the nightstand before resuming his spot on the bed, facing her once more.

The air between them felt dense, filled with the past decade's unspoken words. There was still so much to say, so much she needed to process. Everything he had told her tonight had already altered the foundation of what she had believed for years.

She could hold on to her anger, demand that he leave, and vow never to see him again. But out of everything he had said, one fact lodged itself deep into her mind—the sheer impossibility of them meeting in a refugee camp in Uganda. What were the odds? Perhaps it meant nothing. Or perhaps, it meant everything. She owed it to herself and to him to think before making any life-altering decisions.

Had she been too hasty all those years ago? Should she have fought harder for the truth? She had made an assumption, and he had let her believe it. But the man she had loved with all her heart—the man she thought she knew—would never have cheated.

She sighed heavily, rubbing her temples again, unsure if her headache would ever go away.

"I was so broken," she finally said, her voice barely above a whisper. "When I saw the look in your eye as you leaned against that bathroom door… dressed only in a towel, hanging low on your hips… and that woman in bed behind you, with what looked like sex hair and no clothes…"

She winced at the memory, the sharp pain of it slicing through her all over again. "I looked at you, waiting for you to tell me it wasn't what it looked like. That I had it all wrong. But you said nothing. You just cocked a damn brow at me and stood there so casually, like you were daring me to say something. And when I ran... I thought you'd come after me. I sat in the parking lot for a few minutes, waiting, sure that as soon as you got dressed and realized I'd left, you'd follow. But you didn't." Her voice cracked slightly. "And my heart broke. I've never felt pain like that before. Not in the past ten years. Not even once."

She exhaled shakily. "After that, I wondered if everything you ever told me was a lie."

"Mia," he rasped, his voice thick with emotion, "I swear, I have never lied to you. Not once. I let you believe the worst because... at first, I was shocked that you were standing there. And then, I realized that letting you believe it would set you free. And maybe, just maybe, you'd be better off."

Mia swallowed hard, but the lump in her throat refused to budge. She could barely look at him, could barely hold the weight of his words, because the sheer audacity of it—of him deciding she needed to be set free, of him choosing for her—was almost too much to bear.

Her voice came out cold, flat. "You thought you were doing me a favor?"

Devlin flinched, the guilt on his face stark in the dim lighting. "I—"

"No." She cut him off, her eyes burning. "You don't get to do that. You don't get to sit here and act like some noble martyr. You shattered me. And you had a choice. To fight for me. To tell me the truth. And you let me walk away."

She exhaled sharply, pushing off the bed to put some space between them. Because if she stayed too close, she wasn't sure if she'd lash out or completely fall apart.

Pacing the small room, she ran a shaking hand through her hair. "Do you even know what it did to me?" She turned back to him, her eyes flashing. "Ten years, Devlin.

Ten years of believing I wasn't enough. That I was a fool. That everything we had meant nothing. And you let me believe it, knowing it would rip me apart."

His jaw clenched, but he didn't try to argue.

She inhaled deeply, trying to steady the trembling in her hands and voice. "I was broken. And instead of pulling me back, you let me drown."

His head dipped forward, his hands scrubbing over his face. He looked exhausted, worn, wrecked. But that didn't change anything.

When he lifted his gaze, his eyes were red-rimmed, filled with something she wasn't sure she wanted to name. "I thought I was doing the right thing," he rasped. "I thought… maybe, if I was gone, you'd be free of me. That you'd go after your dreams instead of trying to save me from myself."

Mia exhaled sharply. "You don't get to decide what's best for me."

He nodded slowly, his throat bobbing as he swallowed. "I know that now."

Her breath was uneven, her body trembling. She should still be furious. She was furious. But beneath it, something else clawed at her ribs—grief. The loss of all those years. The life they could have had.

She clenched her jaw and forced herself to push past it. "And what about that letter?" she demanded. "The one where you didn't deny a damn thing and only said you were sorry?"

His jaw tensed. "Because after you left that day, I lost it. I went into a rage. Cheryl felt awful—she was crying, saying she'd talk to you and try to explain. But all I could think about was that you deserved better than me dragging you down. So I told her not to worry about it. Later, I found out she tried to call you, but you had already changed your number." He let out a slow, bitter breath. "A couple of weeks later, I was drowning in regret. I wrote you that letter because I never meant to break your heart."

His eyes squeezed shut for a moment, and she could see the pain radiating from him. When he looked at her again, his voice was a hoarse whisper. "I swear on my life, my Mia, I never meant to break your heart. But I did. And my own broke right along with it."

She let out a shuddering exhale, pressing her fingers against her temples, hating the way her body reacted to those words. The way a traitorous part of her wanted to believe him. Because this was the Devlin she had loved. The one who never lied. If she had thought he cheated, it was only because he let her believe it. The silence between them stretched tight, fragile, neither of them moving.

Finally, she exhaled sharply and wiped at her cheeks, hating how vulnerable she felt. "You still don't get it, do you?" Her voice was soft but razor-sharp. "It wasn't just about what I thought happened that day. It was about everything after. You let me leave. You let me go."

His face crumpled, pain slicing through his expression. The words hung between them, heavy and raw.

17

Mia let out a slow breath, her heart thudding unevenly in her chest. The weight of the past ten years sat between them, thick and unmoving, but something was shifting, something she couldn't quite put words to yet.

Devlin had always been solid and unwavering. Even now, with the raw confession of his regrets laid bare, he had a steadiness, a quiet certainty that made her pulse race in a way she wasn't prepared for.

"What did you do to get help?" she finally asked.

He exhaled sharply, rubbing his hands over his jeans. "I did what my captain ordered. I worked with Markowitz's wife and kids, and made sure they had what they needed. I contacted your parents and best friend, but they shut me down. I leaned on my parents, and they wanted me to find you. But when I tracked down one of your classmates, they told me you'd taken a full-time job in Haiti. So I let you go."

"And other women? Other relationships? It's been ten years. How often have you been in love?" She wasn't sure why she asked those questions because she didn't really want the answers. But the words were already out, and she could hardly pull them back in.

His lips pressed together, and for a moment, she wasn't sure he would answer. Then he spoke, his voice raw. "Other women? Yeah. Not as many as you might think. Other relationships? No. Been in love?" He shook his head. "Not once. The longest anything lasted was a weekend."

"Why?" she whispered.

He didn't hesitate. "Because I never looked. I had the gift of the perfect woman for me. And I lost her. I knew there was no one else for me, my Mia. And I was willing to stay single for the rest of my life."

She blinked, stunned. She had assumed he had moved on. Had found someone else. That he had been able to do what she hadn't—find love again. But he hadn't. And the revelation rocked her.

His gaze softened as he studied her reaction. "I guess that sounds strange to you, doesn't it?"

Slowly, she shook her head. "No. Or rather, it sounds strangely familiar. I assumed I was destined only to have one love in my life, too."

A spark ignited in his eyes, the first sign of hope she had seen all night. And suddenly, she realized she had given him something—an opening.

Her thoughts were a tangled mess, refusing to fall into any order. She squeezed her eyes shut for a second before meeting his gaze again. "Devlin... what do you want? What do you want from this? From me? Closure? If so, I guess we have that."

He shook his head. "No. Seeing you again was like waking up from a ten-year-old, suck-ass dream that keeps playing on repeat and never gets better. I don't expect you to jump into my arms. Hell, I'm lucky you haven't decked me yet. But I'll take whatever you're willing to give me. If it's just friendship, I'll take it. We have so much history, but I want a future, Mia. Whatever that looks like—I'll take it."

Mia dropped her chin, offering a pointed glare. "You'll only be here a few more days. You'll finish your job and leave, and I'll still be here," she argued. "That's hardly time to figure anything out between us."

"Mia, honey, I've gone years without you in my life. And I've hated every fucking minute of not being with you. I want to be in your life somehow."

She snorted. "Pen pals?"

His lips quirked ever so slightly, but his eyes remained earnest and pleading. "If that's the best we can have, I'll take it. But it needs to start with me earning your forgiveness."

Silence stretched between them as she searched her heart. The animosity she had clung to for so long was ebbing. Truthfully, it had faded long ago, though she had never admitted it. A heavy sigh left her lips. "I don't hate you, Jim. I did... or maybe that was just the heartbreak talking. But I don't hate you. If forgiveness is what you seek, you have it. You meant the world to me. Moving past that emotionally took time, but my life went on."

She had spent years learning to be whole on her own. She had picked up the broken pieces and forged something new, something strong. She shrugged, lifting her shoulders in a gesture of surrender. "Maybe we were always meant to be apart for these past years. Maybe that time apart let us grow into the people we were always meant to be."

The words hung between them, and as she heard them aloud, she realized they rang true. They had both grown, becoming the people they had once dreamed of being.

"Maybe so," Devlin agreed. "But I'm grateful for your forgiveness. The way I ended us was wrong. It was fucked up, painful, and inexcusable. But I'm not that same person."

She nodded, believing him in a way she hadn't expected. "So what happens now?" she asked, studying the man in front of her. He was no longer the man she remembered, but looking into his eyes, she could still see the teenager who had once shielded her from the police when she'd been strapped to the goalpost. A little smile curved her lips at the memory.

"We start new," he said, his voice edged with hope.

"New?" she echoed, her brows lifting.

"We had ten years of good, Mia. And now we've had ten years of pain, mistakes, hard work, career changes, and figuring out what matters. Then, against all fucking odds, we run into each other on the far side of the world."

"That's scary," she whispered, feeling more vulnerable than she had in a long time.

"I'm suggesting we start something new, knowing that all our decades from now on will be whatever we decide together they'll be. And you're right. It's scary as hell. But that doesn't make it wrong."

Silence stretched between them again, thick with possibility. She felt like she was standing on the edge of something massive, a decision that would determine whether she truly lived or simply continued existing. And, God, she wanted to live.

"Okay," she murmured.

Devlin inhaled sharply, his eyes widening slightly. Before he could misinterpret her meaning, she quickly added, "We're not the same people we were. Friends might be all we ever are. But like you said, I'd rather have you in my life than not."

He reached for her hand, his fingers wrapping around hers, completely engulfing them. Warmth traveled up her arm, settling in her chest. Still holding her hand, he stood and gently pulled her to her feet.

"I'd like nothing more than to stay and keep talking all night," he admitted. "But I can see the exhaustion on your face, and I never want to be the source of your pain again. So I'm going to say good night, but I ask for a promise from you."

She tilted her head, peering up at him. "What promise?"

"Don't backpedal. Don't talk yourself into thinking you were hasty by agreeing that we can work on becoming close again. Don't overthink it. Just let it be, Mia. Sleep. Rest. And tomorrow, we can talk some more."

It had been a long time since someone had cared for her like that. The words she might have spoken fell away, and she simply nodded.

He leaned in slightly, his massive body towering over her, and for a moment, she wondered if he would kiss her. Instead, his lips landed on her forehead. The warm, steady pressure made her eyes close, and the tension in her body ebbed away. When he pulled back, she missed his closeness.

He walked to the door, pausing just before stepping out. "Good night, my Mia."

For the first time in years, the thought of those words didn't make her chest ache. It wasn't long before she climbed into bed, fatigue pulling at every muscle. But she reached over to grab her phone. She only hesitated for a moment, the urge to talk to someone who knew it all overpowering all other emotions.

"Hey, sweetie," her mom greeted. Her voice was warm as always but now held a tinge of caution. "What's going on?"

"He told me a little about what happened back then. Why he left," she blurted, then paused before adding, "It wasn't what I thought had happened. And... well... we've agreed to be friends."

Her mother made a noncommittal noise, one Mia knew well. It was the skeptical hum of a mother who wasn't buying what her daughter was selling.

"He broke your heart, Mia." The words were gentle but firm. "You were devastated when he left. Now he's just back, after what? Ten years? And you think friendship is going to be that easy?"

"No," Mia said honestly. "But it's…different now. We're different."

Her mother was quiet for a moment, then sighed again. "I always loved Jim. I always thought he was a good man. Until he hurt you."

Mia's throat tightened, but she pushed past the emotion. "I know."

"Be careful, baby," her mother warned. "I don't want to see you hurting like that again."

"I will," Mia promised, and then, because she couldn't help herself, she added, "But I can't shake the feeling that maybe this is a good thing."

"How so?"

"At the time, all I felt was hurt. But I moved on… lived my life my way on my terms. He did, too. And now, it's like we're two different people from who we were back then. Two people who still have a long history."

Her mother huffed. "We'll see. I just want you to be sure. To be careful. I don't want your heart broken again."

"I know, Mom. Me, too." She picked at a thread on her blanket. "But I have discovered that I really want him in my life, however that looks."

"I know you'll take care of you, sweetie," her mom said, resignation in her tone. Then a small chuckle sounded. "You know who'll be thrilled about this?"

Mia already knew the answer. "His mom."

"Of course. You know how much that woman loved

you. If she finds out you two are even breathing the same air again, she's liable to start planning a wedding."

Mia laughed despite herself, shaking her head. "Let's not get ahead of ourselves. Right now, we have to see if the past ten years overshadow everything from our first decade together."

"I wish you only the best, but trust you to make the right decision for you."

"I know. And that's why you're the best mom in the world, and I love you," Mia declared, her heart lifting again.

With loving goodbyes, she tossed her phone to the side and slid under the covers. As she lay in bed, replaying the past hours in her head, her heart was strangely at peace.

18

Todd and Cole were still awake when Devlin returned, their sharp gazes locked onto his face when he stepped inside. It only took them a second to read him—his talk with Mia had gone well. Or at least, it hadn't gone horrible. Both men offered chin lifts and knowing grins.

"Hate to bring you back down to earth," Cole said, amusement lacing his tone, "but we've got plans for tomorrow."

Devlin sat on the edge of his bed, running a hand over the back of his neck. "What's up?"

"Casper called," Cole continued. "Jonan is exactly who he said he was. Ugandan. Served in the military for several years before transitioning into health, welfare, and safety. The WFP currently contracts him for security. No suspicious activity. His finances are clean."

Devlin nodded, pleased.

Todd added, "He's offered to take us to Lake Edward tomorrow, and with him cleared, we're good to go."

"It'll give us a chance to see where the food might be crossing over," Cole confirmed.

"One of us should stay back and keep an eye on Mia," Todd interjected. "Figured you'd want it to be you."

Devlin's grin widened as he remembered something she had mentioned in passing to Farid. "Just so happens, she's got the day off." His heart kicked up at the thought, though a flicker of doubt tried to settle in. What if she had plans? Then again, if she did, he'd find a way to change them.

They turned in soon after, but Devlin found sleep elusive. Not that it mattered. Years of operating on minimal rest had conditioned his body to push through exhaustion, but this was different.

The vise grip that had clenched around his heart for years had loosened. The familiar ache of being without her had shifted and transformed into something else—something sharper, more urgent. Instead of drowning in the past, he was now restless with anticipation and eager for the hours ahead, for the time he'd have with her.

By the time the first streaks of dawn brushed across the horizon, he was up, showered, and dressed. The camp was already stirring, dust rising in lazy swirls as people moved between the tents. Devlin made his way to Mia's door and knocked. Silence greeted him. A frown creased his brow.

"Mia?" he called, his stomach tensing. He prayed she hadn't spent the night overthinking everything.

A door creaked open, and Ritah's head popped out from next door, a bright smile on her face. "Good morning, Devlin. Mia's already gone. I think she headed to breakfast."

He exhaled, relief unfurling in his chest. "Thanks." With a wave, he strode toward the dining hall. The scent of warm chapati and eggs filled the air, mingling with the ever-present smoke from nearby cooking fires. The moment he stepped inside, his gaze sought her out as precise as a marksman locking onto a target.

She was seated at a table, laughter lighting up her face. Her skin glowed, her hair shone, and her eyes twinkled. For a moment, he tried to steady his breathing, remembering how much he'd lost in the past years since she'd been in his life.

She wasn't alone. Robert, Charlie, Ravi, Percy, and Karen surrounded her, their laughter blending with the morning chatter. But Devlin noticed immediately—Robert and Charlie were vying for her attention.

His steps slowed as a ripple of possessiveness flared in his chest. He observed the way Robert leaned in and how Charlie grinned a little too widely in her direction. Of course, they were vying for her attention. Why wouldn't they? She was beautiful. Intelligent. Sweet. And as far as they knew, she was single.

Technically, she was still single. But Devlin hoped to change that soon. With an easy confidence, he slid into the empty chair beside her. The moment she turned toward him, her eyes brightened, her lips curving ever so slightly, sending warmth flooding through his chest.

"Good morning," he murmured, leaning just enough that his shoulder brushed against hers.

"Good morning to you," she responded, her voice soft, intimate, as if the rest of the world had fallen away.

"Sleep well?" he asked.

"Yes," she said, holding his gaze. "Surprisingly well."

The others greeted him with nods and casual acknowledgments, but Devlin didn't miss the way Robert's jaw tensed and Charlie's brows lifted in curiosity. Karen, however, smirked knowingly, her gaze bouncing between him and Mia. *She knows,* he thought. Mia must have told her. Good. Let the gossip spread. Let it be known that Mia wasn't available. At least, not to anyone else.

"I thought I should warn you," Mia said, her voice softer now, meant only for him. "Our parents know we're both here at the same time."

His brow lifted. "Oh?"

"I talked to my mom last night. I mentioned you were here for work. I asked her not to say anything to your parents, but..." she hesitated, her lips twitching, "I got a message from her this morning. Apparently, your mom hopes we'll have a chance to talk."

Devlin chuckled, shaking his head as he shoveled a bite of beans onto his fork. "What did you tell her?"

"I just told her that we talked and, after a long conversation, decided that we could try friendship." She glanced around the table, ensuring the others were distracted, before leaning in. "In case you're wondering, I haven't seen your parents since... well, in a long time."

"I know," he said, voice thick with regret. "And I'm sorry. That's on me. They missed you. I haven't been home much, so I haven't seen yours either. Though, I doubt yours wanted to see me."

Before Mia could respond, Charlie leaned in with an exaggerated expression of intrigue. "What are you two whispering about over there?"

"Charlie, mind your own business," Percy drawled in his haughtiest British accent, playing up the theatrics.

Robert, however, didn't play along. His tone was darker, more assessing. "Yes, I was curious about that myself."

Devlin didn't hesitate. "We knew each other years ago."

Mia nodded. "We were just catching up on each other's families."

"How delightfully cozy!" Percy declared, pressing a hand to his chest in dramatic flair.

Devlin chuckled as Mia rolled her eyes, the warm glow of nostalgia settling over him. Let them tease. Their history was his leverage—one that would keep Mia close while he showed her what they could still be.

The table erupted in laughter, but Devlin caught the way Robert's smile didn't quite reach his eyes. Let them laugh. Let them wonder. He wasn't worried about anyone else at this table. The only thing that mattered was Mia—keeping her safe and having a chance to prove that they weren't just a part of each other's past but also meant for each other's future.

As he finished his breakfast, he kept an ear on the conversation, watching as Robert and Charlie continued to angle for Mia's attention. Ravi, meanwhile, had barely looked at her, too preoccupied with stealing glances at Ritah when she walked in and sat beside Karen.

Then Robert made his move. "I thought you might want to go check the water stations with me today," he said, flashing Mia a confident smile. "I know it's your day off."

Devlin's jaw ticked. He hadn't told her about their plans yet, but he wasn't about to let Robert wedge himself in. "She'll be with me today," Devlin said smoothly, his voice leaving no room for argument. "We're taking a little trip."

Mia turned to him, curiosity flickering in her gaze.

Before she could ask where they were going, Charlie wiggled his eyebrows. "Oh, a date?" he teased, feigning shock. "Mia, you're stepping out with one of the investigators? That's very daring of you. I haven't seen you go out with anyone since you've been here." He sighed dramatically. "Not that I haven't tried."

Percy cackled. "That's because Mia has standards, and you, Charlie, are simply too easy."

Laughter rang out again, but Devlin didn't miss the way Robert remained silent, his gaze assessing. When Devlin turned to Mia, he found her watching him, a silent question in her eyes. But she didn't ask where they were going. She didn't challenge him.

Her trust meant everything. Now, he just had to make sure she knew she could trust him with so much more.

A few hours later, Devlin sat in the back of the van beside Mia, his head swiveling from side to side as he took in the breathtaking scenery of the Ugandan countryside. They were at the edge of the Queen Elizabeth National Forest. Vast stretches of emerald-green forest spread out in the background. Their dense foliage provided the perfect backdrop to the blue sky as they drove along the hard-packed dirt road.

"It's beautiful, isn't it?" Jonan asked from the driver's seat, his voice carrying a note of quiet pride.

Cole rode shotgun beside Jonan, his arm resting lazily on the open window, while Todd occupied the middle bench seat, scanning the landscape with quiet curiosity.

Mia turned toward Devlin, catching his gaze. "I don't know why I expected barren land when I first came here." She scoffed, shaking her head as she looked out the window again. "I was so surprised at how lush the forests are."

"Yes, yes," Jonan agreed, his dark eyes flicking toward her in the rearview mirror. "With Lake Victoria to the south, Lake Edward on our western border, and Lake Albert to the north, our forests grow plentiful."

He came to a stop as a small herd of elephants meandered across the road on a well-worn path. "Oh my God!" Mia's arm reached out to grab Devlin's arm as she whispered in awe of the sight before them. She held up her phone to snap pictures of the mother elephants with a few babies lumbering to keep up.

"Give me your phone and turn around, Mia," he said.

When she did as he asked, he snapped a picture of her with the elephants in the background. Then impulsively, he flipped the camera and shifted next to her to snap a selfie with both of them in front of the savanna vista.

He wondered if she would complain at his high-handedness, but as they sat, she perused through the pictures. "This is good. Mom will love the one with me in it."

She didn't mention him, but he was glad she didn't immediately delete the one with him beside her.

As they settled for the next leg of the trip, Devlin rested his arm on the back of their seat. His fingers brushed against her shoulder in a tentative touch as he pointed out another baby elephant hustling by. Mia glanced at him, her lips still holding the faintest smile she had when she'd spied the elephant. That small, simple reaction sent a quiet sense of relief unfurling in his chest. She didn't object, and he kept his arm resting across her back as they turned to view the passing landscape.

The overland journey stretched across several hours, the road winding through thick jungle and small, scattered villages. Jonan served as their guide, pointing out landmarks and sharing stories.

"It takes longer to get to the lake than a hornbill can fly," he explained, his voice warm with pride. "We have to travel north to enter Queen Elizabeth National Park because Kigezi Game Reserve is south of it. But we are heading to Kisenyi, a small fishing village on the lake's edge."

"How do Uganda and Congo handle the fishing rights on the river?" Todd asked.

"With diplomacy and great difficulty," Jonan answered

with a wry chuckle. "While there is an arbitrary line down the middle of the lake, we are always arresting Congolese fishermen who cross over."

"So there's a Ugandan police presence on the water?" Devlin asked.

"A small one. But as you know from Alain, the lake is also a crossing point for refugees and, of course, for smugglers bringing goods into the Congo. The same happens on Lake Albert, to the north."

As they crested a hill, the forest suddenly gave way, revealing the village ahead. Mia let out a quiet gasp. "Who would've thought that right at the edge of the forest, they would carve out this place?" she murmured in wonder.

"It is a prosperous little village," Jonan said, his tone light but firm. "Because of the fishing. There is a church, a mosque, and even a hotel."

"Hotel?" Mia repeated, her brows lifting in surprise as they passed a squat building with a thatched roof. A hand-painted wooden sign out front declared it the Lake Edward Retreat.

Devlin studied her face, wondering if she'd be disappointed at the modest town, but there was no trace of dismay. Only awe. He liked that she wasn't the kind of woman who needed luxury to be impressed.

They reached the end of the road and parked. "Let's get out and walk," Jonan suggested. "Then we'll eat at one of the little cafés before heading back to camp."

The midday sun blazed overhead, casting shimmering reflections off the water as they stepped onto the sandy path leading toward the shore. Dugout canoes—ebiso, as Jonan called them—were lined up along the water's edge, their hulls carved from ancient trees. Fishermen crouched beside their boats, mending nets with long needles, their hands moving with the practiced precision of men who had done this every day of their lives. Others waded knee-deep into the shallows, dragging in baskets overflowing with freshly caught tilapia and Nile perch.

Mia wrinkled her nose, tilting her face up to Devlin. "The long, thin boats are certainly practical, but aren't big enough to smuggle anything significant."

"They could be used for small loads of drugs or medical supplies," Cole mused.

She nodded, but the crease between her brows deepened, her thoughts clearly still turning over the information.

"Look over there," Jonan said, pointing at a wooden dock farther down the beach. Several boats, larger than the ebiso, were tied there, their hulls boasting small outboard motors. "Those could easily make it across the lake in half the time. Some are small, but I've seen others that could carry larger crates."

Mia exhaled, her voice quieter now. "And they just pay off whoever they need to, right?"

Devlin watched as frustration flickered across her features, her lips pressing into a thin line. Without thinking, he lifted a hand and brushed his thumb over the furrow between her brows, smoothing it away. Her lips twitched at the tender gesture, and he allowed himself the smallest of smiles in return.

"It doesn't take much," he said, his voice low. "Here, even a small cut of the profits is enough to make it worth looking the other way."

Mia's fingers curled into her palm. "It's hard," she admitted, her voice carrying the weight of too many battles fought in places just like this. "We work so hard to get food to people who need it, but then so many more are suffering just across the border. And when smugglers steal, they don't take it for their own families. They funnel it straight to insurgents while their own people starve."

She exhaled sharply as if pushing the weight of the world from her shoulders. "I was always told not to take it personally when I got into this work. That I should do my job and not let the world's problems affect how I do it. But I don't know how to turn it off."

The four men exchanged glances, but Devlin reached out again, tucking a stray strand of hair behind her ear. His fingertips lingered on her jaw for half a second longer than necessary.

"You've always cared. That's what makes you... you," he murmured.

She turned her face upward to peer intently at him before he nodded slightly.

Jonan introduced them to several of the fishermen. Though some were wary, a few admitted that at night, boats often left from hidden ports, laden with crates. When they returned from the other side, they were empty.

By the time they climbed back into the van, Mia was quieter, staring out the window in thought.

"Hey." Devlin drew her gaze to him. "What's on your mind?"

She let out a humorless laugh. "The stealing. The smuggling. It'll never stop. It's like Margarethe said... plug one hole, and ten more open."

He nodded, understanding her frustration. He hated that she felt the loss so personally, but at the same time, he knew her heart too well to think she'd ever stop caring. "You're right," he admitted.

She snorted. "Wow. Great pep talk, Devlin."

He chuckled. "We can't stop the smuggling, Mia. But we can stop whoever is running it from inside the camp. That will keep you safe."

Todd turned in his seat. "If we can identify the leader, we can at least shut down their operation for a while. Sure, another will take its place eventually. But that takes time."

She nodded but remained quiet as they reached the small café nestled at the edge of the Queen Elizabeth National Forest.

By the time they'd finished their meal, laughing over Jonan's childhood stories and listening to Cole and Todd talk about adjusting to life in Montana, Devlin was relieved to see Mia smiling again.

And if he was lucky, he'd spend the rest of his life making sure that smile never faded.

19

The next day, Devlin strode down the narrow lane, his boots kicking up soft puffs of dust as he took in the familiar sights and sounds of the refugee camp. The mingling scents of wood smoke, earth, and cooking food filled the air, and the lively chaos of conversation and activity wove through the breeze. He glanced sideways, unable to suppress the small smile tugging at his lips.

Mia walked beside him, her presence a quiet warmth at his side. He watched as she greeted the refugees and workers they passed. Her dark eyes held a kindness that never wavered. He'd known she was special the first time he'd truly seen her all those long years ago. The way people responded to her—offering smiles, nods, murmured words of gratitude—only deepened his admiration.

When they had returned from the previous day's excursion, Mia had immediately hurried to the food storage center to check with Farid, ensuring the day's deliveries had gone without problems. Last evening, they had talked for a short while, catching up on each other's families and sharing anecdotes about where they'd worked over the past years of separation.

The conversations were punctuated with the reality of how much time had passed, yet it flowed as though they were old friends. He could see the fatigue pressing in on her and had reluctantly left her room early to give her a chance to rest. He wanted to take care of her, but knew if he pushed too hard, she might retreat. He wasn't about to yield an inch of what he hoped they were building.

Now, as they walked, he instinctively wanted to reach for her hand, to feel her touch, and let her know he was steady at her side. But he held back, uncertain how she felt about public displays of affection in the camp. He reminded himself that he could be patient.

Yet, deep down, patience warred with something else. Now that they had stepped beyond mere polite words and declared the rekindling of their friendship, he wanted more. Hell, he wanted everything.

As they moved down an empty stretch of the lane, she suddenly slowed, then stopped altogether. The camp noises seemed to fade, leaving only the whisper of the wind and the faint noise of the others behind them. When she turned to him, her gaze steady, her question caught him off guard.

"Tell me about your job. Is it a lot like when you were a SEAL?"

He chuckled, shaking his head as he considered how best to answer. "No, not like that." A slight shrug accompanied his words before he added, "There are a few similarities, but nothing was as intense as my time on the teams."

Mia didn't respond right away, but her gaze remained fixed on his, patient, expectant. Encouraging.

So he went on. "The SEALs, like all special forces, work under strict military protocols. But we also had a lot of autonomy in the field, making split-second decisions that could mean life or death. Being in the private sector is different. There's more freedom. We get to choose which cases we take and decide how to run the business."

She pressed her lips together, a thoughtful crease forming between her brows. "Why is it called Lighthouse Security Investigations?"

A grin pulled at his mouth. "It sounds weird, I know. But I promise it'll make sense once you hear the story."

He saw the curiosity in her eyes sharpen, and he loved that she was interested. "There was a former Army Special Forces leader who retired back to his home state and started a security and investigations firm. It just so happened that he owned a decommissioned lighthouse on the Maine coast. He built his business, Lighthouse Security Investigations, there and started hiring other former Special Forces operators. After a few successful years, he partnered with a friend on the California coast to expand the business. That's how LSI West Coast was born."

Mia's eyes widened, glinting with amusement. "Oh, please tell me there was a lighthouse there, too?"

Laughing, he nodded. "Yep, there was."

She stepped into the center of the lane, placing her hands on her hips, the golden light of the late afternoon catching in her hair. "While I may have forgotten some geography, the last time I checked, Montana was a landlocked state."

He smirked. "No, you haven't forgotten your geography." He held her gaze, appreciating the spark of humor in her expression. "Remember how I told you my boss, Logan, flew helicopters for rescues over the mountains?"

She gave a small nod.

"Most mountain ranges used to have light towers to guide planes over dangerous terrain. Some countries still use them. But when satellite navigation became the norm, the US decommissioned and tore most of them down. Montana, though? It still has six standing."

Her lips curved knowingly. "And one of them is close to where you are."

"Yep."

She tilted her head, studying him. Something softened in her expression, and for a moment, neither of them spoke. In a voice touched with nostalgia, she murmured, "You know, I remember when we were together, you always took the time to talk to me. Explain things. Tell me about your day, or your job, or your class. Even the missions when you could. You'd listen, keeping your focus on me as though you had nothing else better to do."

His chest tightened at her words, at the truth in them. "It was easy," he admitted, his voice rougher than he intended. "Being with you was the best feeling in the world."

So many emotions passed through Mia's eyes as she sucked in a deep breath before tilting her head slightly as if considering her next words carefully. "So back to your work. Is the motto to keep people safe?"

Devlin recognized the subtle shift, her return to a topic that felt secure, one that wouldn't stray into deeper waters. He smiled, playing along. "The business doesn't have a specific motto, but yeah… that would be the idea."

A light gust of wind swept between them, stirring the dust along the lane and tugging at a loose strand of her hair. Without thinking, he reached out, tucking it gently behind her ear. His fingers skimmed her skin, and he felt the faintest hitch in her breath. He let his hand drop but held her gaze. "In fact, we're known as Keepers."

Her eyes widened in surprise. "Really?"

"Yeah... after the lighthouse keepers who guided others to safety."

She nodded, and her face softened. They fell into step again, moving down the narrow path. The murmurs of the camp surrounded them once more—children's laughter, the clang of a cooking pot, the distant calls of relief workers moving supplies.

"What kinds of things does security entail?" she asked, her curiosity still evident.

"We design security systems and contract out to vetted businesses for installations. We also provide personal security for specific reasons, but we don't have ongoing contracts with any one person or organization."

"That sounds kind of exciting," she said, the interest still in her voice. "And the investigating?"

"We have access and contacts to be able to find out a lot without going through some of the same channels we had to with the military."

She stopped and turned her gaze up to him again, but this time, a furrow creased her brow. "Did you ever check on me?"

His breath halted, and his mind raced to think of what to say that might not sound as bad as he was afraid his words would. But he came up empty. "Um... no."

The instant her expression fell as she started to turn from him, he rushed to explain. "Not because I didn't think about you, but it would hurt too much. I was... afraid."

She scoffed. "You? Afraid?"

"Yes, Mia. Afraid." He heaved a sigh. "Afraid of seeing pictures of you happily married to someone else. Having kids with someone else."

She lifted a brow. "And whose fault would that have been?"

"Mine," he said without reservation. "All fuckin' mine."

He dropped his head back for a moment, then lowered his chin and speared her with his gaze. "I tortured myself into thinking that not knowing was better than knowing."

She nodded slowly. "Am I asking too many questions?"

Devlin shook his head. "No way, Mia. You can ask anything you want. In fact, I'm glad you're asking."

"Why?"

"Because that tells me you're interested in what I do."

"Because I am." She swallowed audibly before adding, "I never looked you up either. I guess for the same reasons as you."

Another group of women passed by, greeting them with friendly smiles before whispering to one another, giggling as they moved on. The heavy moment was broken.

Mia inhaled quickly, then reached out to touch his arm. The simple touch sent a jolt through him, grounding him to the moment. She leaned closer, lowering her voice to a conspiratorial whisper. "I think we're giving them some village gossip."

She started to pull away, but he caught her hand, tucking it into the crook of his arm as they continued walking. The simple, instinctive act felt as natural as breathing.

Bringing the conversation back to where they'd started, he said, "We're asked to investigate activities or possible crimes. Sometimes we're hired by individuals and sometimes through government contracts. A lot of times, the lines get blurred between who's in charge of what."

"Wow. So you can do your own thing without having to follow too many rules." She shot him a teasing look before bumping her shoulder lightly against his. "That kinda sounds like the Jim Devlin I remember long ago."

"Me?" He feigned exaggerated surprise, placing a hand

over his chest. "What about you? Tying yourself to the goalpost?"

She threw her head back and laughed, the sound rich and unguarded. "I was just so angry that Principal Martin wouldn't pay attention to the environmental club's requests. He had the temerity to shoo me out of his office. I was not going to let anyone shoo me out of their office!"

"You go, girl." He smirked. "And remember, if anyone gives you a problem, they have to deal with me first."

She slowed again, and this time, there was no teasing in her expression. Her laughter faded, replaced by something quieter, more introspective. He felt the shift in the air and sensed something important coming before she spoke.

Mia reached out, taking his hand between both of hers, cradling it against her chest. The heat of her palms seeped into his skin, but it was the emotion in her eyes that truly made his breath catch.

"You will never know how much that single act meant to me."

His chest tightened. "Oh, my Mia. You've thanked me many times while we were together for that."

She shook her head slowly, her grip tightening around his hand. "Yes, but I was younger. Still in school, then in college. But now that I've been out in the world, seen the best and worst in people, that single act stands out in my mind."

Devlin barely breathed as he stared down at her, struck by the quiet honesty in her words. He had always known Mia was strong, but in moments like this, he realized just how deeply that strength ran.

"To this day, I can still remember looking at the back of you in your larger-than-life football uniform and pads, standing between me and the two policemen and Principal Martin. And you told them they couldn't lay a hand on me without going through you." Her voice wavered, but she kept going. "And I can still see your name on the back of your jersey. Devlin. I had no idea at that moment what we would become."

She gave a small shrug, still holding his hand. "And maybe to some, they would hear our story, shake their heads, and ask how on earth could I move past what was a betrayal of the heart."

His stomach clenched at the reminder of the pain he had caused her. He had no defense for it, no way to erase what had happened. He could only accept it, own it, and hopefully have them move forward together.

He exhaled slowly. "Even though I'm more grateful than you can imagine, for the past twenty-four hours, I've wondered the same thing. How you can move past the hurt."

"Because when I lay in bed last night, I did think about things, Devlin." She blinked back tears as she slowly shook her head. "And what I kept remembering was seeing you standing between me and danger."

A lump formed in his throat.

She inhaled deeply before finishing, her voice barely above a whisper. "And even though you didn't know it was me when you came here, you're still standing between me and danger."

Devlin's breath hitched.

He had no words for that, no way to express how much her trust meant to him, how fiercely he wanted to keep it. But as she stood there, looking at him with that unwavering honesty, he knew one thing for certain.

No matter what happened next, he would not fail her again.

Devlin no longer cared who was watching or what whispers might follow. Wrapping his free arm around

Mia's shoulders, he pulled her close, and without hesitation, she melted into his embrace. Her hands loosened their grip on his, allowing them to hold each other tightly, as if letting go would shatter the fragile shift between them.

Her cheek rested against his chest, right over his heartbeat, her head tucked beneath his chin. She fit there. She had always fit there. And here, in the middle of a world filled with poverty, want, and need, something between them changed. It wasn't a rekindling of the past. It was something new. A beginning.

He could have stood like that forever, content to simply hold her and pretend for a little while that nothing else existed beyond this moment. But he had something important for her and didn't want to give it to her in public.

He loosened his hold reluctantly but didn't let her go completely. Keeping one arm securely around her waist, he guided her back toward the staff quarters.

When they reached her door, she turned, searching his face. "You want to come in?"

His answer came without hesitation. "I don't want to be anywhere else but where you are."

Her lips curved slightly as her gaze held his. That tiny smile was a light in a place inside him that had been dark for ten years. He had spent a decade convincing himself he didn't need it, but she made him realize just how wrong he'd been with one simple expression.

Inside her room, he reached into his pocket, fingers closing around the small object he'd kept there for the last few hours. When he pulled it out, the silver charm caught the dim light, the sturdy chain pooling in his palm. The tiny lighthouse gleamed.

"I want you to wear this at all times," he said, his tone unyielding. "Day and night. Don't take it off."

A teasing glint appeared in her eyes. "It's a little early in our burgeoning friendship for jewelry, don't you think?"

"This isn't just any necklace," he countered. He let the weight of his words settle before continuing. "There's a tracer inside. That means I can find you anywhere you might go."

As he held her gaze, he saw the moment she understood. The amusement faded from her features, replaced by something more serious.

"You think I'm in danger, even if you're here."

"We're narrowing down who might be heading up the smuggling ring," he admitted. "I'm not going to take a chance. So as long as you have this, I'll know where you are and can get to you."

Mia gave a slow nod, then lifted her hair as he fastened the clasp at the nape of her neck. The chain settled against her skin, and she immediately curled her fingers around the tiny charm before slipping it beneath her shirt.

Then without a word, she stepped forward, resting her forehead against his chest. A heavy sigh shuddered from her, and he slid his hands down her back, holding her there.

He was caught between two warring emotions—thrilled that fate had led them back to each other and tortured by the knowledge that she was now in danger. He would always stand between Mia and whatever threatened her, but the problem was, right now, he didn't know who the threat was.

When she looked up at him, he slid his hands to cup her cheeks, thumbs tracing the soft skin beneath her eyes. He bent slowly, giving her every chance to stop him, to pull away.

She didn't. Instead, she rose onto her toes and met him halfway.

The moment their lips touched, it was as though time collapsed, the years apart dissolving in an instant. It wasn't tentative or uncertain—it was rediscovery, a surge of everything they had been and everything they could be.

He started slow, savoring her, but the instant her fingers curled into his shirt, pulling him closer, restraint shattered. A low groan rumbled in his chest as he wrapped his arms fully around her, molding her against him. He deepened the kiss, angling his head to claim more of her, to taste what he had been missing for far too long.

They shifted at the same time, bodies tangling until they tumbled onto the small bed. A lesser frame would have given under the sudden weight, but the military-grade metal held firm.

Fully clothed, they pressed together, lips moving in a desperate, aching rhythm. Mia's breath was warm against his skin, her body soft where his was hard. He was aware of everything—the way her hands gripped his shoulders, the way her leg slid against his, the way his arousal pressed insistently against her belly.

Then she moaned, and it nearly broke him.

He wanted her more than he had ever wanted anything in his life. But he knew they weren't going to have sex tonight. Not because he didn't crave it—because he did, with a need so fierce it burned through him—but because this moment deserved more than urgency. It deserved patience.

He wasn't going to rush this. He wasn't going to let the weight of the past dictate the choices of the present.

Most of the women he had been with in the past decade had been fleeting. Kisses were just a means to an end, foreplay for something without meaning. But this? This kiss was different. This was an offering, an unspoken promise, a piece of himself that he was handing back to her.

He had no idea how long they stayed like that, lost in each other, before reason finally clawed its way back to the surface. With a groan, he pulled away, pressing his forehead against hers as he tried to catch his breath.

She winced and shook her head. "Maybe I'm crazy."

He waited as she lifted her gaze to him. "Why? What makes you say that?"

Shaking her head, a little snort escaped. "I'm well aware that you have no idea what a groveling romance book is, but I feel like I'm in one and skipped ahead a few chapters."

He blinked, keeping his arms around her but wondering what the hell she was talking about. "I'm going to need you to spell it out, Mia."

Her lips rolled between her teeth as she inhaled deeply. Letting the air out, she said, "In some stories, the guy does something really bad like cheats or maybe just really stupid—"

"Like me," he said with a sigh.

Nodding slowly, she agreed. "Yeah, like you." She shrugged after another sigh. "A long period of groveling is usually what the woman has the guy do… Readers get pissed if she forgives the guy too soon."

"So if the guy has spent years being miserable without her but finally connected again and will do anything to have the woman forgive and give him another chance to be in her life… it's not real unless a long groveling occurs?"

She pressed her lips together again. "When you put it like that, a long groveling seems unnecessary, doesn't it?"

"All I know is that this is *our* story. We do what is right for *us*. And I don't give a shit what anyone else thinks. They don't know that you're one of the most giving people in the world. They don't know that I have groveled inside every day we've been separated. And they don't know that we are now who we need to be for us to come together again."

"I know it's crazy, but I really want to ask you to stay," she murmured, her gaze dropping to their still-clasped hands.

He exhaled sharply, running a hand through her hair before shaking his head. "It's killing me, but I'm not going to."

She didn't argue. She simply studied him, her expression unreadable.

He bent again, pressing his forehead to hers. They stayed like that, breathing each other in, before he leaned back and met her eyes.

"I want us to be sure," he told her, his voice rough with emotion. "I know I am, but I want to make sure you have time to make the right decision for you. Because, my Mia, when I have you again, I will never give you up and never let you go."

They stood, hands still linked, and walked to her door together. At the threshold, she turned, and he pulled her close one last time.

Her lips parted slightly, and then, with infinite tenderness, she reached up, cupping his cheek, her fingers threading lightly through his beard. Their lips met again, and this kiss was different. It wasn't goodbye. It wasn't even good night. It was a beginning.

20

The air inside the food distribution center in Sweswe was thick with heat and tension. The shuffle of workers moving crates, the conversations of the refugees gathering for their rations, and the clatter of metal as supplies were stacked created a chaotic symphony. But none of it distracted Mia from the slow-burning anger curling in her gut.

She stood rigid, her arms crossed tightly over her chest, frustration tightening her features as she scanned the dwindling supplies. The lines of refugees had already begun forming, their patient but weary faces a stark reminder of what was at stake. Beside her, Farid stood just as tense, his expression mirroring her own frustration.

"How the hell could we be short again?" she growled, the edge in her voice sharper than she intended.

Farid exhaled heavily. "You know the answer to that as well as I do." His voice was low, resigned, and filled with the weight of experience. He turned and signaled one of the workers.

"Did you get all the food off the trucks last night?" Farid asked.

The worker shook his head, looking nervous. "I didn't get here until early this morning when my shift started."

Farid let out a curt breath, waving the man away with a flick of his hand before turning back to Mia. "I have the night shift on a rotating schedule. Sometimes even a surprise schedule."

Mia's brow furrowed. "What do you mean a surprise schedule?"

"One that they don't predict. It makes it harder for them to plan." He rubbed the back of his neck, his dark eyes shadowed with worry. "That's why we usually have unmarried men on the night shift. I mix up their nights so they can't plan with one of the truck drivers."

"That's a good idea." She nodded.

He gave a half-hearted shrug. "Sometimes my ideas are not born of genius but more of desperation."

Mia studied him, sensing something deeper behind his words. "What do you mean?"

Farid hesitated before sighing. "A married man working the night shift could be more susceptible to taking a bribe to keep his family safe from a threat than a single man."

Her chest tightened, a dull ache settling in. The fact that these were the kinds of decisions they had to make—choosing between integrity and survival—was a painful reality.

"If I haven't told you recently," she said softly, "I'm happy to be working with you."

He gave her a tired but genuine smile before a sudden crash interrupted them. A crate tumbled from one of the stacks, scattering supplies across the floor. Without a word, Farid rushed off to deal with the workers, leaving Mia standing alone.

She turned just in time to see Devlin and Todd walking in.

Even before she spoke, Devlin was already moving toward her, his sharp eyes scanning her face. "What's the matter?"

For a moment, she just stared at him, surprised by the instant recognition of her emotion. There was a time when all he had to do was look at her to know what she was thinking, to read every shift in her mood without her saying a word. The fact that he could still do it, even after all these years, sent a warm peace through her.

Blowing out a frustrated breath, she finally said, "Food was taken last night."

Devlin's gaze flicked toward Todd. They didn't exchange a single word, but something unspoken passed between them. With a nod, Todd turned on his heel and jogged outside.

Mia arched an eyebrow. "Was it something I said?"

Devlin smiled and shook his head. "We put up several security cameras in each of the food warehouses. We don't have them everywhere or at all angles, but Todd's going to check the footage and see what we can find out."

Her jaw dropped slightly as her gaze shot around the interior of the building. "Why didn't you tell me you had done this?"

He crossed his arms over his chest. "Because you might not have acted normally with your staff."

Her eyes narrowed. "Do you not trust Farid?"

"Mia," he said, his tone even but firm, "other than you, I don't trust anyone here."

She stared at him for a long moment, reading the conviction in his gaze. Finally, she murmured, "That sounds like the voice of experience speaking."

He nodded slowly. "It is. You can't work as long as I did

in the military, for the reservation, or even for LSIMT, and not know what people are capable of."

Mia exhaled, running a hand through her hair as she looked around the warehouse. Outside, life continued as babies cried, children laughed and played, and women gossiped in different languages while men shouted instructions to one another. The world outside this warehouse was full of movement, but inside, the weight of her job, of these stolen rations, pressed down on her shoulders.

"I don't know," she admitted, her voice quiet. "Maybe my predecessor had the right idea."

Devlin frowned. "What do you mean by that?"

"The man who had this job before me didn't use the main distribution warehouse much. There was talk about repurposing it for something else. Instead, he just used his office to direct where the trucks should take the food directly to the villages."

She hesitated, then added, "But then when I took over, there seemed to be a lot of loss and mismanagement. I quickly realized that unless the food came to one distribution center first, there was no way of ensuring each village got exactly what they needed. Trucks would end up bouncing between villages, and it became a logistic mess. I talked to Dr. München, and he gave me free rein to set up the distribution my way. And for a long time, it worked. We weren't losing food."

Devlin gave a knowing nod. "You filled up a hole."

She blinked, slightly taken aback. "I'm sorry?"

He stepped closer, his gaze intent. "Your predecessor was taking kickbacks."

Mia's lips parted, confusion flickering across her face. "What?"

"If there was a loss of food under him, and it stopped when you changed the system, then it means he figured out it was easier for smugglers to steal food when it was being delivered straight to the villages. He was probably getting a cut of it. You came in, saw something that didn't make sense, and changed it. And it worked. You filled the hole."

Understanding dawned, and with it came a heavy sigh. "And now, more holes have popped up."

"All you can do is the best job you know how," Devlin said, his voice steady. "You can't contain or control other people's evil."

She didn't speak for a long moment, simply holding his gaze, her mind racing with the implications of his words. Finally, she whispered, "Again, you're speaking from experience."

A shadow crossed his face. "In my job, we try to protect and investigate what others are doing. We're not always successful. And because crime always exists…" His voice dropped slightly, edged with something darker. "I'll always have a job."

Just then, Devlin's phone vibrated against his thigh. He pulled it from his pocket, his gaze flickering over the screen. Whatever message he read made his expression sharpen, his posture straightening with a new sense of urgency.

Before she could ask, he looked up, his voice decisive. "Let's go. Todd and Cole have some information for us."

Mia nodded, a renewed sense of purpose sparking through her. She turned, catching Farid's attention with a wave, then gestured toward the door. He gave a quick nod in understanding.

"Okay, let's go," she said, already moving.

"Todd took the Jeep, so we'll start walking and hitch a ride with someone," Devlin suggested as they stepped out into the sun.

The dusty road stretched ahead, heat shimmering off the hard-packed ground. Mia moved briskly, but with Devlin's height, his natural stride was nearly twice the length of hers. She had to take almost two steps for every one of his, a fact that used to never bother her because he had always adjusted to her pace. Now, he hadn't. Not at first, anyway.

Then as if realizing, he suddenly slowed. "Jesus, Mia, I'm sorry."

She laughed, shaking her head. "That's okay. Keeping up with you will get my steps in today."

His gaze swept over her, a quick but thorough assessment from her face to her feet and back again. Then he sighed, a quiet exhale that carried more weight than she expected.

Something in his expression made her self-conscious. She tilted her head, her tone light, but her stomach knotted. "What?"

He hesitated, then admitted, "I was going to say that you didn't need more exercise but needed to eat more. But of course, considering where we are and what everyone else has, I knew that would be insensitive."

Mia's hands instinctively smoothed over her waist and hips, as if tracing the loss herself. She knew she had lost weight... more than she probably realized. The long days, the constant stress, the lack of consistent meals had all taken its toll.

But the thought that maybe she no longer looked the same to him, that maybe he didn't see her the way he used to, struck deeper than she wanted to admit. Before she could pull away from the thought, Devlin reached out, his knuckle lifting her chin gently.

He bent close, his breath warm against her skin. "Stop that," he murmured.

Her brows furrowed. "Stop what?"

"Wondering if you're still beautiful to me," he said, his voice low, unwavering. "Because the answer is hell yes."

Mia's heart stuttered, her breath catching. Years and distance hadn't dulled his ability to read her thoughts. He still knew her, still saw her in ways no one else ever had.

A slowing truck broke the moment. Dust kicked up around them as the old flatbed truck ground to a stop. Several refugees reached for her arms, steadying her as Devlin placed his hands at her waist and lifted her effortlessly into the truck bed. A second later, he climbed in behind her with the same ease. They smiled and greeted the others, finding seats among them.

The truck bounced over the uneven terrain on the short ride back to the administrative area. When they arrived, Devlin hopped down first, then reached up instinctively to help her. She took his hand without hesitation.

"Todd and Cole are in the warehouse," Devlin said as they started toward the building. "We can watch the video in your office."

Mia led him up the stairs and through her office door. The air inside was cooler, shaded from the relentless sun. Todd was already seated in her chair, his laptop open on the desk, while Cole stood nearby, arms crossed as he studied the screen.

"Here are the trucks that came in during the night," Todd said without preamble. "Four of them picked up food here and delivered specifically to Sweswe."

Mia moved behind him, peering at the screen as Todd fast-forwarded through hours of footage. The grainy black-and-white images flickered past—trucks pulling in, workers moving supplies, deliveries being made.

They watched as the food was unloaded into the central

warehouse, the workers moving methodically under the dim glow of the floodlights.

Todd sped through the footage, pausing at key moments and rewinding slightly when needed. "Camera angle is good," Cole murmured. "For two trucks, we can see to the back and tell that the trailer has been emptied."

"That tells me we need another camera installed," Devlin said, his tone firm. "That way, we'll be able to see across the entire loading dock and have an angle to capture not only the workers but the full interior of the truck trailers."

"Okay," Todd agreed, already making notes. He clicked ahead. "Here's the truck that delivered at four o'clock this morning."

They all leaned in slightly, watching as another truck pulled in. But this time, the camera's vantage point wasn't enough to give them the full picture. The screen only showed partial visibility—part of the unloading, but not enough to see if anything else was happening beyond the limited frame.

Mia's stomach twisted. It wasn't enough to fully understand what was happening. They were missing something. And whatever it was... it was occurring right in front of them, just out of view.

"Okay, Sadie, I got the whole crew here, including Mia. What have you got for me?" Todd asked, his voice steady as he leaned against the desk.

Mia jerked in surprise, then realized Todd was speaking into his phone, his attention focused on the voice coming through the speaker.

A woman's voice, warm and slightly teasing, crackled through the line. "Hey, guys! I'm losing my beauty sleep trying to keep up with you all on the other side of the world." There was a brief pause before she added, "Mia? I'm Sadie. Nice to sort of meet you."

Mia grinned at the friendly introduction. "Hello to you, too."

"Okay, I've had satellite images on the truck that left Sweswe as it headed north at about five a.m. I kept watching because it didn't stop at any other farms or make any detours. I lost sight of it when it entered the forested area between Queen Elizabeth National Park and Kigezi Game Reserve. The foliage is thick there, growing right up to the water's edge, but I finally picked it up again." Sadie's voice took on a sharper edge. "There was a boat. I didn't get a great visual, but I could tell something was being loaded onto it. I followed its course until it landed on the shores of the Congo about an hour later. After that, I lost the truck's return path, so I have no idea when it left the park area."

"That doesn't matter," Devlin said, his tone grim. "Thanks, Sadie."

Mia exhaled slowly, her mind racing. "That's it, then. That's the proof we needed," she murmured, standing up straighter as the weight of the discovery settled over her.

Her thoughts jumped ahead, already formulating the next steps. "I need to find out from Robert who that driver was... wait, no! I need to talk to Dr. München. Or should I talk to Margarethe first?"

"Whoa, easy there, Mia," Devlin said, placing his hands on her shoulders, his steady presence grounding her. "Don't get ahead of yourself."

She frowned. "What do you mean?"

"It's like in poker," Cole interjected from across the room. "You don't want to show your hand too soon."

Mia wrinkled her nose, and Devlin chuckled.

"Sorry," he said, smirking. "I once tried to teach her how

to play poker. All it took was one look at her face, and I knew exactly what cards were in her hand."

She huffed in annoyance but didn't argue. She was too focused on the problem at hand. "Okay. I take your point that you all are the experts. So tell me... what should I do?"

"Sadie?" Devlin prompted. "What other initial clearance have you been able to give us on some of the other people here?"

"I was just checking out that list," Sadie responded, her voice businesslike now. "Casper has had Frazier and Dalton working on it, too. Dr. München has been in the business for thirty years. There's never been a hint of scandal attached to his name. I haven't found any unusual transactions in his known bank accounts nor any evidence of off-the-books dealings. He's received multiple awards for exemplary camp management."

"So it looks like Mia can talk to him," Todd murmured.

Sadie continued. "Interestingly, Percival Wilson comes from Gloucestershire... the Cotswolds. His father is a Lord and owns a small estate. From everything I can tell, he's clean, too. Of course, our findings aren't definitive."

"Understood," Devlin acknowledged.

"And the American couple—Elizabeth and Mark Carter—who head the Economic Recovery program? They also check out, as far as we can tell. Their money goes straight into their American bank account, with nothing suspicious going in or out for the past several years."

There was a brief muffled exchange on Sadie's end before she returned. "Robert Ellyson also passes our first muster. He has a checking and savings account at a major national bank in Canada, and nothing looks out of place. But of course, you all know that any of these people could be taking cash and not depositing it into their accounts.

From what we can see, though, none of them appear to be receiving any kickbacks."

Mia's shoulders slumped as the weight of it all settled over her. She should have felt relieved that so many people she trusted weren't immediate suspects, but instead, all she felt was... tired. It was a strange violation, digging into their lives like this, even with good reason. Yet the list was still long. Devlin's team wasn't finished.

As though he could sense her unease, Devlin shifted behind her and, without hesitation, wrapped his arms around her. He pulled her back against his chest, resting his chin lightly on the top of her head. The warmth of him surrounded her, holding her together in a way she hadn't realized she needed.

For a long moment, she just let herself breathe. Let the tension ease. And then, she straightened, steeling her spine. "I'm going to speak to Dr. München. I want to get that done before lunch," she announced, turning to look up at Devlin. "After I finish with him, I'd like to speak to Moses."

"I'll go with you."

She hesitated, then shook her head. "No, I can do this myself." She offered a slight smile, because even though she was more than capable of handling things on her own, there was something undeniably steadying about having him offer to be by her side.

"Okay," he agreed, but sounded reluctant. "I'll go speak to Percy."

With his arms still around her, she reveled in the strength he offered. And right now, she wasn't going to turn that down.

21

While Mia went to speak with the head of the camp and Todd and Cole installed additional security cameras, Devlin decided to pay Percy a visit. The man had passed their initial financial investigation, but Devlin wanted a one-on-one with him and had learned long ago that gut instincts were rarely wrong.

Taking a camp Jeep, he drove toward one of the primary schools. The tires kicked up dust as he maneuvered over the rough terrain. As he approached the school, the laughter of children drifted through the air. The scene before him was a rare, bright contrast to the harsh realities of the camp—kids playing on a grassy playground enclosed by a low, concrete wall.

Devlin pulled the Jeep to a stop and stepped out, his eyes immediately drawn to Percy. The man was out in the field, effortlessly kicking a ball to the children, calling out their names with easy familiarity. His lean frame moved as someone accustomed to physical activity, and from the beaming smiles on the children's faces, it was clear they adored him.

A woman appeared at the school's doorway, briskly ringing a handbell. At once, the children scrambled, rushing to line up in neat rows before disappearing into the building. Percy remained behind, walking the field as he collected the scattered balls, gathering them into a net bag.

Devlin took his time approaching, watching the way Percy moved—casual, at ease, but aware. There was no nervous energy, no stiffness that might indicate someone with something to hide. He wasn't sure if that made him more or less suspicious.

Bending down, Devlin scooped up several stray balls and carried them over, dropping them into Percy's outstretched net.

"What an unexpected surprise." Percy flashed a broad smile. But the flicker of curiosity in his eyes was sharp and assessing as he stared back at Devlin.

Devlin trusted his instincts. Percy hid behind quips and one-liners, and Devlin wanted to know what was behind the mask. "Can I ask what the draw is? What brought you to Uganda?"

Percy opened his mouth as if to respond but then hesitated, staring off into the distance. Finally, he turned back, expression unreadable. "I was trying to decide whether I wanted to give you a flippant answer or simply flip you off," he said.

Devlin smirked. "What did you decide?"

Percy chuckled, shaking his head. "I have a feeling neither would faze you."

They continued collecting the remaining balls, working in a rhythm of silent understanding. Once the net was full, Percy inclined his head toward a couple of wooden benches beneath a lone tree. Devlin followed, taking a seat on one bench, facing Percy as he set the bag at his feet.

"There's a time for flippancy," Percy said, exhaling, "but I don't feel like this is it. I like Mia. I hate that she's stressed about food being taken from the camp. Smuggling is rampant, but I confess, I probably deal with the least of the problems."

Devlin turned slightly, studying the man. Up close, Percy had the lean build of a runner, dark hair curling slightly at the ends, and deep-set blue eyes that missed nothing.

"Well, since we've both sized each other up," Percy said, smirking, "I suppose we should talk."

Devlin found himself appreciating the man's candor. "I guess we should. What did you mean about you dealing with the least of the problems?"

Percy sighed, rubbing a hand over his jaw. "Regarding things people want to smuggle, children's books are probably the least requested on the black market." He gave a wry smile. "Medicine, food, supplies—yes. But children's readers, picture books, and math textbooks? Not exactly in high demand. If anything from the schools goes missing, it's usually taken by a child or a teacher who wants to share it at home. And those kinds of losses?" He shrugged. "I'm good with."

Devlin nodded, considering. "You have an interesting background for someone here."

"If you want a pat on the back for digging into my background, I'm afraid you won't get one," Percy said dryly. "I'm an open book, Mr. Devlin."

Devlin remained quiet, letting the silence stretch. Finally, Percy sighed, squeezing the back of his neck before continuing.

"I often make fun of my family's title." He adopted an imperious tone. "My father, Lord Percival Wilson."

Devlin arched a brow. "I take it your father's not pleased with your career choice."

"Ding ding, give the man a gold star." Percy's laugh was self-deprecating. "It's a worthless title, but it means something to my parents. I can't really blame my father—he was raised with certain expectations. But it was never something I wanted. As his only son, the title would eventually come to me. But I wanted to teach. My father hated that."

Percy shook his head slowly as his gaze drifted off to the side. "After graduating from Oxford, he insisted that if I had to teach, I should at least do it at an influential school. He nearly had an apoplectic fit when I said I was going to teach refugees." Percy leaned back, draping an arm over the bench. "I moved to London and started teaching refugee children there. Listening to their stories made me realize I could do more. So I left." His smile faded slightly. "I've been at this camp for four years."

Devlin studied him. "Is this what you want? A life in Uganda, eschewing everything you grew up with? Living in basic military quarters in a refugee camp?"

Percy's gaze sharpened. "You seem to find that unusual or even impossible to believe. Yet you believe it of Mia." His expression softened, but his voice remained steady. "You will find, Mr. Devlin, that the beautiful Mia is not the only person with the desire to help."

The words struck something in Devlin. A chord he hadn't expected. It was the same thing he used to tell people when they questioned why he worked on the reservation. He nodded slowly. "No, that's not hard for me to believe at all."

Percy leaned in slightly, waggling his eyebrows. "But you don't have to worry about me being competition for Mia. I have my eye on the delectable Karen." His grin turned mischievous. "I'm breaking her resistance down, and I think she finds me at least as adorable as a puppy." He let out a hearty laugh. "And if I'm lucky enough that she'll fall for me, I'll get to take her home to meet my parents. Can you imagine? Me bringing home an Irish nurse?" He laughed, then shook his head. "But you have your own difficulties trying to bridge the gap between you and Mia."

Devlin smirked. By now, it seemed as though everyone knew his history with Mia.

Percy sobered slightly, but his voice remained sincere. "And before you doubt my intentions, I am truly interested in her. Completely enamored. I don't do things just to piss off my father. I do what I want to do and help people in any way I can." He gestured toward the school. "If I can give these kids an education—something that gives them a shot at more than what they were handed at birth—then my life will have been worthwhile."

Devlin nodded, a newfound respect settling in his chest. He stood, extending his hand. "It's been nice to talk, Percy. Thank you."

"I should be thanking you." Percy shook his hand firmly. "If you can find out what's going on and win back the beautiful Mia, I'll be cheering in your corner."

Devlin gave him a small nod before turning away and walking toward the Jeep with a lighter step. His gut told him Percy wasn't involved in the smuggling.

Glancing at his watch, he noted the time. Mia should be with Dr. München by now. Sliding into the driver's seat, he started the engine, turning the Jeep toward the administrative area. He wanted to meet up with her before they went to speak with Moses.

Mia prided herself on maintaining a professional demeanor, especially in meetings with her superiors. But today, as she sat across from Dr. München in his cluttered office, she struggled to keep still. The need to rise and pace gnawed at her, restless energy buzzing beneath her skin. Instead, she shoved her hands beneath her legs, locking them in place to stop herself from fidgeting.

Across from her, Dr. München removed his glasses and wiped them carefully with a tissue, his movements slow and methodical. He replaced them and peered at her over the rim, his gaze sharp but not unkind.

"I know you're upset, Mia, and I share your displeasure," he said, his voice calm and measured. "What you are telling me only proves what we already know. Thefts are happening with the food supplies here at the camp, and at least some of it is heading over the border into the Congo."

"Yes." She nodded emphatically. "I just don't know what to do about it."

"The investigators from the WFP have already installed some cameras, which is, of course, how you were able to see what happened." He set his hands on the desk, fingers steepled in thought. "I'll contact Robert and find out who the drivers were. If we can ban them from our camp, then perhaps that might slow down the leakage of food away from the refugees."

She nodded again, a sense of relief flickering through her. "That's what I was going to do. I can ask Robert if he will—"

"Let me do it." He interrupted gently. "It should be a directive that comes from the top and not just a request from one section leader to another."

Mia hesitated but saw the wisdom in his words. She believed Robert would listen to her and understand the gravity of the situation once she presented all the information. But if Dr. München took charge of the matter, it would carry more authority. He could ensure the drivers were not just questioned but permanently barred from working in the camp.

"Yes, I see where that would be best," she said, nodding once more. She suddenly became aware of how often she was doing it, her head bobbing like one of the old dashboard toys. But her nervous energy wouldn't settle, crackling through her veins like a live wire.

Taking a deep breath, she forced herself to focus. "Is it possible for us to request Ugandan police presence at the area where the food supplies are being taken to the lake?"

Dr. München sighed, rubbing a hand over his chin. "I have no authority to make such a request outside our camp's borders, but I can certainly inform the Ugandan police. It is a central, unified force across the country, and I have met their commander, the inspector general of police."

As he pushed back from his desk and rose, Mia realized their meeting was over. She quickly stood as well, extending her hand. "Thank you, Dr. München, for your help."

He walked around the desk and clasped her hand firmly before gesturing toward the door. She smiled, offering a polite goodbye before stepping out into the hallway.

Mia moved briskly down the hall, her thoughts already jumping to the next task. She was almost to the lobby when a realization struck her—she should've asked about speaking to Moses.

She hesitated. Would it be overstepping if she brought it up now? Dr. München had taken charge of speaking to Robert, clearly preferring that the chain of command remain intact. Would he also want to handle Moses himself? Indecision warred within her, but finally, she turned back. She wouldn't know unless she asked.

Walking purposely, she retraced her steps to his office and lifted her hand to knock. She paused when she noticed the door was slightly ajar. She hesitated, not wanting to interrupt. But then she heard his voice, low and distinct.

"Yes, that's what I said," Dr. München murmured into the phone. "She's getting close, and I want it taken care of."

Mia froze. Her heart slammed against her ribs, breath catching in her throat.

She couldn't make out the muffled response on the other end. Then came the unmistakable click of the old-fashioned phone mouthpiece settling into its cradle.

She's getting close? Was he talking about her? A chill crawled down her spine.

Mia lowered her hand without making a sound and took a slow step back from the door. Her pulse pounded in her ears, each thud echoing in the silence of the hallway. She barely breathed as she retreated, her movements careful. It wasn't until she reached the far end of the corridor that she turned and hurried toward the exit.

She's getting close... Dr. München's words rattled in her head, over and over, slithering through her thoughts. They could have meant anything. Anyone. But unease slid through her, sharp and insistent, making her question everything she thought she knew.

The moment she stepped outside, the hot Ugandan sun hit her skin, but the warmth did nothing to dispel the chill still gripping her spine.

The low rumble of an approaching vehicle pulled her attention up the lane. A Jeep kicked up a cloud of dust as it rolled toward her, with Devlin behind the wheel. He barely had a chance to slow before she climbed in, her movements quick, almost instinctive. He shot her a sharp look, his brow furrowed.

"Are you okay?"

Mia forced a smile, the kind she had perfected over years of working in crises. Calm. Controlled. Unshakable. She nodded. "Yes. Let's head to the police station and talk to Moses."

Devlin held her gaze. He didn't look convinced but didn't push her to talk.

As he drove, Mia kept her hands clenched in her lap, her mind racing. She should tell him. Shouldn't she? But his words were just words... not an admission of guilt or inside knowledge. Maybe he wasn't even talking about her. Uncertainty twisted in her gut.

The Jeep rumbled over the uneven road, the tires crunching over the dry earth. Then suddenly, Devlin pulled to the side and killed the engine, and her stomach dipped.

He turned toward her, his gaze steady, unreadable. "Let's have it."

She didn't even try to feign ignorance. It was pointless. Devlin had always been able to read her... sometimes before she even understood what she was feeling herself.

Exhaling, she relayed everything about her conversation with Dr. München, his reasoning for speaking with Robert, his agreement to contact the Ugandan police. Then she hesitated before telling him the rest. The moment she had turned back... finding the door open... hearing his words.

"And those were his words exactly?" Devlin asked, his tone calm but edged with something harder.

She nodded. "This is so stupid, Devlin. Those words could be about anything or anybody. Yet I felt a chill run down me as though he was talking about me."

Devlin didn't hesitate. He pulled out his phone and pressed a few buttons before bringing it to his ear.

"Todd? Have Sadie or Casper do a deeper dig into Dr. München. I know his bank and professional background look clean, but we just want to make sure."

He disconnected without another word, slipping the phone back into his pocket. Then he turned to her, his eyes searching. "Okay. You ready to go talk to Moses?"

Mia studied him for a moment. It wasn't just what he had done—it was how he had done it. No hesitation. No dismissing her concerns as paranoia. Just action. It was such a simple thing, but it settled something deep inside her. Her lips curved slightly as she gave a nod. "Yeah, let's go. Together."

Devlin restarted the Jeep, maneuvering it back onto the road. And as they rolled forward, she didn't miss the faintest hint of a smile crossing his face.

22

When Devlin and Mia entered the camp's security building, the air was thick, the only movement coming from a few fans creating a hot breeze. Moses and Enock stood at the center of it, handing out orders to their security personnel, their voices steady but firm. A few of the men nodded sharply before hurrying off, boots thudding against the worn wooden floor.

Enock spotted them first, his keen eyes assessing before he waved them over. "Did you need to speak to Moses?"

"Yes, please. As soon as he's available," Devlin said.

"Absolutely. He's almost finished. If you'd like, I'll take you back to his office."

They fell in step behind him, weaving through the building's narrow hallways until they reached the small, cluttered office Moses occupied when he wasn't out patrolling the camp. The space was functional, filled with maps, reports, and a weathered wooden desk that bore the signs of constant use.

Enock had barely stepped out when he returned with Moses in tow. The security chief greeted them with a broad smile, though a sharpness in his eyes said he already suspected this wasn't just a social visit.

"I would say this is a pleasure, but I have a feeling the two of you have news for me," Moses said, his gaze flicking between them.

Mia looked toward Devlin, her expression unreadable. It wasn't like her to hesitate. She was direct, confident, and unafraid to take charge when needed. But he suspected she was still shaken by what she had overheard in Dr. München's office.

So he took the lead. "Using the security cameras we installed, we identified one of the trucks that left the warehouse in the middle of the night, fully loaded with food. It drove to Sweswe, where it *appeared* to unload everything—but it didn't." His tone was measured, but the weight of what they had uncovered pressed down on the room. "Farid is trying to find out who was in the warehouse last night, but some of the workers switch duties without always reporting the changes to him."

Moses's expression darkened, his jaw tightening. "Do you know which truck? Can we discern the driver?"

"Dr. München plans to speak to Robert and see if we can figure that out," Mia answered. "But Devlin has more to tell you."

Devlin didn't waste time. "I had my people track the vehicle. It headed straight to Lake Edward. Crates were loaded onto boats and taken across to the DRC."

A muscle ticked in Moses's jaw. His hand curled into a fist before he exhaled sharply, shaking his head. "Dammit," he growled. "So we have proof of what we suspected."

"Yes," Devlin confirmed. "Dr. München's plan is for Robert to get the driver's name and at least ban him from entering the camp."

Moses gave a curt nod before turning to Enock. "As soon as we get that name, I want you to circulate it."

Enock nodded in understanding. His gaze flicked toward Mia, and he hesitated before speaking. "We can increase the security forces around the warehouse at night. We already have five villages and the main camp to patrol. That gives us six locations we need to cover more often."

"Is that a problem?" Mia asked, her brows knitting together.

Moses and Enock exchanged a look before turning back to her. "Our forces are stretched thin," Moses admitted, "and we need to prioritize the safety of the refugees."

Mia nodded, her expression thoughtful. "I agree. So many people are simply looking for a better way of life, but there will always be a few who look for trouble."

"We'll look at our schedule and see what we can do," Enock vowed.

Mia crossed her arms, clearly working through an idea in her head. "Farid told me that at night, he keeps the warehouse workers on a rotating shift, sometimes changing the schedule with little notice. He does this to prevent anyone from knowing too far in advance when they'll be working, in case someone's trying to arrange a deal with the truck drivers for a kickback."

Moses raised a brow, nodding in approval. "I haven't employed that tactic, but maybe it's time to do so." He glanced at Enock again, who immediately said, "I can start implementing it."

"That might be a good place to start," Devlin agreed. "Since your men are already stretched thin, it's unlikely we'll get additional security guards for night patrols."

When they shook hands with both men, Devlin was caught off guard when Moses patted Mia on the back.

"What will you do when you leave here?" Moses asked, his gaze warm on her.

Mia's gaze flickered to Devlin before she turned back to Moses. She shrugged but smiled. "I'm not sure. I'm considering several possibilities."

Moses gave a nod of understanding. "Well, I hope you go home and see your family before heading somewhere else."

Enock folded his arms across his chest and smiled warmly at her. "I'm sure your parents have missed you. Family should always come first. No matter what else... it's all about what is best for your family."

Devlin caught the soft flush that crept up Mia's cheeks. She didn't respond right away, but he could see the slight tension in her shoulders. He remained quiet for now but would ask her when they had a chance to focus on them and not the camp.

Their goodbyes were quick but warm, and soon, Devlin and Mia stepped back out into the sunlit camp. He fell into step beside her as they walked toward the Jeep, the conversation lingering in his mind. As they climbed into the seats, he glanced her way.

Devlin pulled the Jeep to a stop in front of the camp's main food warehouse, dust settling in the warm afternoon air. He turned to Mia as she unbuckled her seat belt. "Are you going to stay here the rest of the afternoon?"

"Yes," she said, brushing stray strands of hair from her face. "Farid is making the rounds to all the food distribution centers in each village, and I'll be working on my food contacts. I need to talk to Margarethe to see what I can order." She tilted her head, her perceptive gaze narrowing. "What are you going to do?"

"I'll check in with Todd and Cole about the cameras they

installed. It may take tweaking to get the angles we need. Then we'll talk to Logan to see how long we can stay. It's only been a few days, but I need to find out his thoughts."

Devlin searched her face, looking for a reaction. Instead, she pressed her lips together, her expression unreadable. When she finally spoke, it was with a short, polite nod and an abbreviated smile that didn't quite reach her eyes. "Will I see you later?"

"Are you kidding? Absolutely." His voice softened. "Let me know when you're ready to return to your room, and I'll come get you."

She offered another nod, then moved to get out of the Jeep. Before she could step down, Devlin gently wrapped his fingers around her wrist. She stilled. He saw her glance down at his hand before lifting her gaze, a silent question in her eyes.

He gave the smallest tug, just enough to bring her closer. She leaned toward him, and he caught her lips in a soft, lingering kiss. He felt her smile against his mouth, and when he pulled back, his own spread in response. "My Mia," he whispered.

Her smile widened, warmth flickering in her eyes before she slipped out of the Jeep and disappeared inside the warehouse.

Devlin watched her go, but the contentment in his chest didn't last long. The weight of everything pressing down on them returned quickly—Mia's concern over the thefts, the uncertain timeline of their reunion, and the unanswered question that had been gnawing at him since Moses's parting words. *"What are your plans when you leave here?"* He wondered what part of the world she would travel to next. Would it be dangerous? How long would she be gone?

That was a question Devlin hadn't been prepared for. And one he fully intended to bring up tonight.

Frustration loomed, heavy and unavoidable. It felt like fate had gone to great lengths to bring them back together, only to conspire against them again.

With a deep breath, he turned the Jeep back toward the guest quarters. Inside, he found Todd and Cole in their shared space, both just returning from the latest camera installation. Todd had his laptop open, reviewing the footage, while Cole leaned against the wall, arms crossed.

They ran through the new angles, watching the grainy security feeds. The setup looked solid.

"I've set up the feed to go back to the compound," Todd said, tapping the screen. "I know none of them can sit and watch everything, but maybe whoever has the night shift can check when the trucks come in."

"Sounds like a plan," Devlin acknowledged, rubbing his jaw.

He filled them in on his conversations—Percy's insight, Moses's and Enock's concerns, and, most importantly, Mia's unease after what she had overheard in Dr. München's office.

Cole's brow furrowed. "Do you think he was just warning somebody to be careful and not let the smuggling get out of hand?"

Todd leaned back in his chair, propping his feet up on the bed. "Or he was talking about someone warning Mia."

Devlin exhaled sharply, running a hand down his face. "Or it had nothing to do with Mia. Who the fuck knows? I called Sadie and asked her to have them dig into him a little more. A thirty-year career, heading this camp—he wouldn't risk everything over smuggling." He hesitated. "Then again, maybe he's the perfect person for it because no one would suspect him."

"Might be padding his retirement," Cole muttered.

"Where's Mia now?"

"She's back at her office with others around. The warehouse is its usual hub of activity. I told her to call me when she's ready to head to her room."

Devlin sat on the edge of his bed, clasping his hands together. He inhaled deeply before lifting his head, first meeting Todd's gaze, then Cole's. They waited, giving him space to gather his thoughts.

"I need to talk to Logan," he said finally. "When he sent the three of us here, we didn't know what we'd be walking into. We sure as hell didn't expect to solve everything in a week. But Logan can't afford to keep all three of us here indefinitely."

Todd straightened, dropping his feet from the bed. "Devlin, we'll do whatever we need to do."

"I appreciate that." He exhaled slowly. "I need to make sure Logan understands that Mia and I have reconnected, and I'm not ready to leave here until I know she's safe."

Cole shook his head with a smirk. "You do know Logan doesn't want you to leave until she's safe."

"I know." Devlin sighed. "It's been four days, and we've made good progress. But I think we're close. We're closing in on which leader in the camp is behind the smuggling ring." He sat up straighter, admitting, "And the progress Mia and I have made together is also good."

Todd nodded. "Go ahead. Make the call. We'll back you up all the way."

Devlin dialed LSIMT, requesting a conference call with Logan and the Keepers at the compound. When the line connected, he gave a full rundown—what they had uncovered, the smuggling route, the stolen food, and the gaps they were still working to fill.

When it came to Mia, he didn't hold back. He told them

about the possible threat hanging over her head. About how close she was to uncovering something dangerous.

He wasn't surprised when both Logan and Sisco immediately responded with the same order.

"You don't leave until she's safe," Logan said firmly.

Devlin swallowed the lump in his throat.

"You didn't just find her to lose her again," Logan continued. "You do whatever you need to do to make sure she's protected."

"Appreciate that," Devlin said, his voice rougher than he intended.

"Sadie, Frazier, and I are still running deeper checks on the camp leaders," Casper chimed in. "Moses has a clean record—no flagged financial transactions, nothing outside of his regular salary. But for the Ugandans there, hiding money is easier. Kickbacks would be in cash, handed off to family members or funneled outside traditional banking systems."

Devlin nodded to himself. "I'm going to talk to Robert and Charlie tomorrow. Just like with Percy, I want to look them in the eye and see what my gut tells me." After wrapping up the call, he checked his watch. He had no idea when Mia would call, so for now, he'd stay close.

The three Keepers reviewed the surveillance feeds for the next few hours, studying the camera angles and discussing patterns.

Devlin couldn't explain it, but something in his gut told him they were close. And he never ignored that sixth sense.

23

Mia had always greeted her staff, the refugees, and all the workers with the same warm smile every day. It was second nature, a part of who she was. But now, that effortless kindness had turned into something else—something laced with quiet wariness. She studied faces more intently, searched for fleeting expressions of deceit, tuned into conversations with sharper ears, and filtered every interaction through a lens of suspicion.

She hated it.

The day was winding down, and soon, she'd call Devlin to come pick her up. Eager to finish, she closed out the last of her work, locked her office door, and descended the stairs to the warehouse floor. The scent of dust and grain hung in the air, mingling with the sharp scent of diesel as the last delivery truck finished unloading crates of rice and beans.

Determined to shake off her lingering dark thoughts, she politely greeted the driver with a smile. The drivers, along with her staff, worked tirelessly. She wondered what was allowed in Dr. München's budget for the local drivers and if it was a good salary compared to others in Uganda.

The driver gave a small nod in return, barely meeting her eyes, and turned back to the unloading process. Not wanting to be in the way, she stepped to the side, standing near the back of the truck.

Her mind drifted, already anticipating the moment she'd see Devlin. Just the thought of him sent a gentle warmth to her chest, like the first days of spring after a long, cold winter. It was a comfort she hadn't allowed herself in years. *It's only been a few days... am I crazy?*

Some would call her naive, foolish even, for letting him back into her heart so soon after their reunion. Others would scoff at her willingness to believe his words, to accept his truth without demanding penance. But none of them mattered. None of them understood. Because he was right—no one else knew them. No one else had felt what they'd felt, had lived in the quiet spaces between then and now, in the memories that had shaped them into who they were.

Time had carved them into different people and forced them to grow in separate directions, yet somehow, impossibly, those paths had led them back to each other. And wasn't that something worth trusting? She hadn't forced him to grovel, hadn't needed to see him on his knees to know what was real. It wasn't about retribution—it was about knowing. About trusting. And, more than anything, about wanting. And she wanted him.

As her thoughts roamed, her gaze absently traced over the container truck, seeing rust streaking the metal edges, bolts worn down from years of use, tires balding, their tread nearly nonexistent. The vehicle, like everything here, had seen better days.

Maybe I need a break. Perhaps it is time to go home. See my family... hold my nephew.

The thought settled in her bones, heavy yet hopeful. She craved time to clear her head, to shift her focus to different problems—simpler problems. Time with her family would help, but with that thought came another. *What happens to Devlin and me when the future is so unknown?*

She lowered her gaze to her boots, blocking out the chaotic bustle of the warehouse for a moment. Her parents had adored Devlin, just as his parents had welcomed her with open arms. But after the breakup, especially the cruel way it had ended, her parents had mourned alongside her. They hadn't just lost the relationship of a man they thought would be their son-in-law, but they had lost the faith they had placed in him.

Her mother, always protective, had offered the advice that came with a quiet warning... please be careful.

And Mia was being careful. But just as Devlin had to prove he had changed, prove he regretted his choices and the pain they had caused, their families would have to navigate those same emotions.

A sharp shout echoed from inside the truck container, jolting her from her thoughts. Instinctively, she stepped forward to investigate. Before she could reach the edge of the truck bed, the driver moved swiftly into her path, blocking her.

She tilted her head, offering him another polite smile despite the unease prickling at the back of her neck. "Excuse me."

He bowed his head slightly, murmuring a reply, but there was no warmth behind it. When she stepped to the side to go around him, he adjusted his stance, mirroring her movement with subtle precision.

Mia frowned, surprise flickering through her as

another shout rang out from inside the truck. Then just as suddenly as he had blocked her, the driver dipped into a deep bow, mumbling an apology before stepping aside. Still on alert, she moved past him, scanning the container's interior, but spied nothing untoward.

The crates were emptied and stacked neatly against the walls. If something had happened, there was no sign of it now.

She forced herself to shake off the nagging suspicion. Farid had adjusted the schedule, so no additional deliveries would be made tonight until the workers could be reassigned. There shouldn't be anything unusual. Before she could dwell on it further, a familiar voice called out from the loading dock.

"Hey, gorgeous! Haven't you left yet?"

She turned, her expression immediately relaxing as she spotted Charlie coasting toward her on his bicycle. He braked to a stop, lifting a water bottle and taking a long drink.

It was a common sight—Charlie zipping around the camp, always in motion. He'd even taken a trip to Kenya during one of his breaks, competing in a race that combined running and cycling.

"Hey!" she greeted with a grin.

"When are you finally going to join me?" he asked, flashing his signature wink.

Mia laughed, shaking her head. "Charlie, I'm on my feet all day long. By the time I'm done, I have zero energy to hop on a bike. Or jog. Or play tennis. Or participate in whatever reindeer games you dream up."

He smirked. "I wouldn't care if you had a shiny red nose, Mia Rudolph. You could play in my reindeer games anytime."

He climbed off his bike and leaned it against the

loading dock, resting his hands on his hips as he took in the scene. After a long, exaggerated sigh, he shook his head. "If you were stuck in an office crunching numbers all day like I am, you'd beg for fresh air."

She smirked. "Sounds like you're ready to trade places with me."

He shrugged, nodding. "Maybe. I probably shouldn't complain. I do have a fan in my office while you're out here breathing in truck exhaust."

Her nose crinkled. "You've got that right."

Just then, the truck driver climbed into the cab. He gave a quick wave through the window before rumbling away, heading toward the local market where he would reload supplies for the next day's deliveries.

Mia turned her attention back to the warehouse. The workers were finishing up, sweeping the floors. She waved them off as soon as they were done, watching as they dispersed into the fading daylight. Charlie stepped in to help, and together, they lowered the massive metal doors, securing them with heavy locks.

As they walked back toward his bicycle, Charlie shot her a curious look. "Do you ever think about doing something else?"

She let out a soft laugh. "Almost every day."

He raised an eyebrow. "Yet here you are."

Mia sighed, then smiled. "Because I'll see a child so excited over a piece of fruit, or an expectant mother savoring a meal, knowing she's not just feeding herself, but nourishing her baby too. Those moments... they remind me why I do this."

Charlie didn't answer right away. Instead, he studied her with a quiet intensity she rarely saw in him. After a beat, his voice dropped, his usual teasing replaced by something more serious. "I know everybody thinks I'm just a joke," he said. "But, Mia... you're a really good person. Just... be careful. Not everyone here is who they seem to be."

The low rumble of an approaching Jeep cut through the evening air, breaking the easy rhythm of their conversation. Mia turned instinctively, her gaze settling on the familiar vehicle as it slowed near the warehouse. The moment she spotted Devlin behind the wheel, a smile tugged at her lips, and she lifted a hand in greeting.

Charlie followed her line of sight and let out a dramatic sigh. "And this is my cue to hit the road." He grinned, but his voice had an unmistakable note of mischief. "Damn, I thought I might have you to myself a little longer."

Rolling her eyes, Mia swatted playfully in his direction before waving him off. He didn't linger—just hopped onto his bike, kicked off the ground, and pedaled away, disappearing into the fading light.

Without another glance back, she jogged toward the Jeep, her pulse kicking up for reasons that had nothing to do with exertion. She barely waited for Devlin to put the vehicle in park before climbing inside and turning toward him.

Before he could say a word, she reached out, cupped his face between her hands, and pulled him close, pressing her lips to his.

He stiffened for the briefest second, clearly caught off guard—but then he sank into the kiss, meeting her fervor with equal intensity. His hands slid to her waist, anchoring her in place as their breaths mingled. The scent of him, something warm and familiar, laced with hints of mosquito repellent, wrapped around her, grounding her in the moment.

When they finally broke apart, his lips curved into a

smile, his blue eyes bright with amusement. "I'm not complaining, sweetheart, but what was that for?"

Mia shrugged, still a little breathless. "I don't know. I just wanted to kiss you."

Devlin chuckled as he shifted the Jeep into drive, shooting her a sideways glance before winking. "Then let's get somewhere where we can kiss as much as we want."

The drive back to her quarters was short, the quiet hum of the engine filling the space between them. The night was settling in, the air thick with the distant scent of cooking fires where the refugees prepared their evening meals.

Just as they were nearing her room, Mia broke the silence. "You know, I think Charlie has a lot of sadness."

Devlin let out a scoff, his hands steady on the wheel. "Sadness? Charlie?" He cast her a doubtful glance. "What were the two of you talking about that gave you that idea?"

She sighed, turning slightly in her seat to face him. "As usual, Charlie always tries to hide behind a quip, flirting, or even saying something outrageous. But I think that can be a way of masking something deeper. I think it's his way of coping."

Devlin pulled the Jeep to a stop outside the staff quarters, then shifted in his seat to look at her more fully. His expression was considering. "That's an interesting insight, Mia. I've been talking to some of the staff, and he was already on my list to check in with tomorrow—"

"Don't tell him what I said!" Her eyes widened in alarm.

Devlin laughed, shaking his head. "I won't. Believe me, I'm not sure sadness is the emotion I'll get from him." He reached out, cupping her cheek with one warm hand, his touch gentle as his thumb brushed lightly over her skin.

Then he leaned in, capturing her lips in a slow,

lingering kiss that had nothing to do with urgency and everything to do with savoring the moment.

When he pulled back, his voice dropped into something huskier, something meant just for her. "But enough about him. I want your undivided attention for a while."

Mia let out a laugh, nudging his shoulder. "Sorry, big guy. Feed me first."

His face softened. The amusement was still there, but something deeper flickered in his gaze. His thumb traced one last caress over her cheek before he murmured, "Whatever you want, my Mia."

24

All through dinner, Devlin felt like a caged animal. He made himself converse with the people at the table, exchanged jokes with Cole and Todd, and even managed a conversation with Percy. But his thoughts remained locked on Mia.

No matter how much he tried to focus, his attention kept drifting to her. The way her fingers absently traced patterns on the table, the slight tension in her shoulders, the way she responded to conversation with just a fraction less warmth than usual. She had something on her mind. He could feel it. Apparently, he wasn't the only one.

"Mia, are you okay?" Robert asked, his voice tinged with concern.

Devlin turned his head sharply, his attention snapping to Robert, then to Mia.

She offered a small, tight smile and nodded once. "I'm fine, thanks."

Robert wasn't convinced. "You seem to have something on your mind that's troubling you."

Devlin's jaw tensed, his gaze narrowing slightly. He didn't

like someone else pressing her for answers, not when he had been waiting all night to ask his own questions. Leaning closer to her, his voice dropped. "Are you ready to head back?"

She met his gaze, her lips curving in relief. "Yeah."

Offering a polite smile to those at the table, she stood, and Devlin followed as they stepped outside into the cool evening air. The walk toward her quarters was quiet. Too quiet. The air between them practically crackled with her irritation, though she said nothing.

By the time they reached her room and stepped inside, the tension had thickened.

Mia whirled on him the moment the door shut, planting her hands on her hips as she glared up at him. "You were in a weird mood at dinner. What's going on? If you're rethinking our newfound relationship, I want to know. The last thing I want is another surprise from you."

His head jerked back slightly, her words hitting him like a punch. Of all the things she could have suspected—that wasn't what he expected. His voice came firm, decisive. "No, not that. Not that at all."

Her arms crossed, skepticism clear in her stance. "Then what's going on?"

"You seemed tense."

"I was tense because you had growly vibes coming from you!" she bit out.

There was no smooth way to ease into it, so he just blurted it out. "What are your future plans?"

She blinked, then blinked again, her head tilting slightly as if she hadn't heard him correctly. "I'm sorry?"

He sighed, running a hand down his face. "It's something Moses and Enock were discussing earlier. It's been stuck in my head all day."

Mia frowned, confusion etched into her delicate

features. "Devlin, you have to give me more than that. I don't know what you're talking about."

His shoulders tensed, frustration curling at the edges of his voice. "Your future plans," he repeated. "After here. And when is that, by the way?"

She licked her bottom lip, her gaze thoughtful.

"It's not a trick question, Mia," he said, softening his tone. "We've talked so much about the past that I don't even know what your future looks like." The admission cost him more than he cared to admit. He didn't know if she saw him in that future, and the uncertainty gnawed at him.

Mia turned away, walking to the bed before sinking onto the edge. Her hands clasped together in her lap, her fingers twisting slightly. Devlin glanced at the chair nearby but dismissed it. He didn't want any distance between them. Instead, he moved to her side, settling beside her on the mattress.

"I only have another month at this camp with the WFP," she said quietly.

Devlin's brows lifted slightly, surprised by the short timeline.

"Dr. München has said that if I want to renew, he would love to have me. Margarethe said she would approve anywhere I wanted to go, even staying here if that's what I chose."

Keeping his voice even, he asked, "And what do you want?"

Her gaze dropped to her hands, fingers pressing together. "I haven't seen my parents in almost eighteen months. I want to go back to Kansas and reconnect with my family, at least for a while. The last time I was home was for Toby's wedding. He and his wife just had a baby boy two months ago." A faint, wistful smile touched her lips. "I'm an aunt, and I haven't even met my nephew."

Devlin nodded, processing her words. The thought of her younger brother, who he still pictured as a high school kid, now a husband and father was strange. "That would be good for you. I'm sure your parents would love to have you home."

Silence settled between them, heavy with unspoken thoughts. Clearing his throat, he nudged, "And after your leave time is over?"

Mia hesitated before exhaling deeply and lifting her eyes to him. "I'm tired, Devlin. I've spent the past ten years traveling the world, working in refugee camps. I've been a WASH coordinator, a food security officer, a livelihood coordinator..." She let out a short, humorless laugh. "Margarethe thinks I have a career moving up in the WFP, maybe to a managerial role. But that would still mean constant travel. More time away."

Devlin watched her closely and saw the exhaustion in her eyes, the quiet weight pressing down on her. He reached out, brushing a strand of hair behind her ear, his fingers skimming along the curve of her neck.

"I hate to see you tired," he murmured. "You give a hundred percent every day, Mia. But everyone has a breaking point. I don't want this job to break you."

She nodded, but a small, self-deprecating snort escaped. "I'm proud of what I've done. I care about the people I help —the ones who have fled their homes, escaping war, famine, regimes that want to crush them. Yet it feels wrong to want to go home, where I'm safe, fed, where I can shop in a market without worrying about the water making me sick."

Devlin met her gaze. "Do you know any refugee camp workers who never take a break?"

Her brows drew together as she considered the question, then slowly shook her head. "No. You're right. Everyone does."

A small smile tugged at the corner of his mouth. "Maybe your break will be longer than just a month. Maybe that's what you want—what you need. But you're afraid of letting someone down. Margarethe, Dr. München... the refugees." His voice softened. "But Mia, sometimes life takes us in different directions."

She looked up at him, her eyes searching his. "You did that, didn't you?" Her voice was soft, but he detected a sliver of need as she continued. "A Marine, a SEAL, working on a reservation, now working for a private security company."

He exhaled, nodding encouragingly. "Yeah. That's exactly right."

Reaching for her hand, he gently pried her fingers apart, linking them with his own. His thumb traced slow circles against her skin, and he felt the subtle shift in her posture in the way her body relaxed slightly.

"So," he prompted, squeezing her hand gently, "tell me about some of the jobs you've thought about taking."

She hesitated, her eyes flickering with something unreadable. "Well... if I stay with WFP but want to be based in the US, they have an office in Washington, DC." A pause, then a small grimace. "But I really don't want to live there."

Her voice trailed off as she dropped her gaze again, scanning the room as if looking anywhere but at him.

Devlin watched her, his grip on her hand steady. Something was weighing on her. He could see it in the way her shoulders held tension and her fingers fidgeted against her lap. He had a feeling there was more to say—something she wasn't quite ready to voice.

"Mia, what's going on?" His voice was gentle but firm. "And don't try to tell me there's nothing on your mind."

She exhaled slowly, her fingers tightening around his. "It's just something else I've considered doing, but I don't want you to think it's a new plan."

He narrowed his gaze, giving her hands a reassuring squeeze, not understanding what she was saying. "What do you mean, a new plan?"

Mia hesitated, her expression unreadable. "We've only been in each other's presence for a few days. I don't want you to think I made a big decision just because we reconnected after so many years. It's just that... I know the timing seems suspect. But it's not."

"You're doing a good job of beating around the bush, Mia, but I'm not getting what you're trying to tell me. Come on, honey. You've always been direct."

She inhaled deeply, then grimaced. "Oh hell, let me just show you."

She slipped her hands from his and stood, crossing the room to her desk. Devlin leaned forward, watching as she flipped open her laptop, her fingers moving quickly over the keys. After a moment, she clicked on her email. Twisting slightly to glance at him, she said, "Before you read this, just... take note of the date. It was sent almost four months ago."

Brows furrowed, Devlin stood and stepped behind her. Resting his hands on her shoulders, he leaned down, scanning the open email.

The words blurred for a moment before sharpening into focus. Feeding America – Tribal Communities Initiative. They were offering her a position working to combat food insecurity in tribal areas.

His lungs expelled air in a rush. He barely had time to absorb it before Mia clicked on another message.

"There's another one from three months ago," she murmured, opening a second email. "The name of the organization is a bit antiquated, but their work is good."

This one was from the Food Distribution Program on Indian Reservations, offering her a role in food assistance, distribution, and nutritional education. Devlin's pulse pounded in his ears as he moved around to kneel beside her chair, placing his hands gently over hers. "Why are you afraid of me knowing this?"

Mia didn't answer immediately. Instead, she stared at the screen, her lips slightly parted, as if choosing her words carefully. Finally, she exhaled and spoke, her voice quiet but steady.

"Before we reconnected, I had already come to a place in my life where I realized that I've had incredible worldwide opportunities. Work, life experiences... I've participated in things I probably never would have done if we'd stayed together." Her voice caught slightly, and she winced as if the words caused her pain. "Maybe it's serendipity that we found each other again on the other side of the world. We've even said that maybe it was part of our life plan to spend these years apart, learn, grow, and become who we are now."

He nodded slowly, absorbing her words with caution. He understood what she was saying. But that didn't make it any easier to know that he had been the reason for her pain.

She gestured toward the laptop. "I've been considering these positions for a while. I want to be back in the States. I want to take my knowledge and experience and use it to help people at home. I've been in contact with both organizations and even some tribal health departments as a nutritionist."

Devlin stood and pulled her to her feet, wrapping his

arms securely around her. She wasn't telling him everything. He could feel it. Something still lingered in the space between them, something that made her hesitate. And he hated that he couldn't immediately read her thoughts the way he once could. He had to relearn her, rediscover the parts of her that had changed.

Brushing a strand of hair behind her ear, he murmured, "Something about this is still bothering you, and I can't figure out what it is. So, for our sake—just tell me. What are you afraid of?"

Mia leaned back slightly, her gaze searching his. Then, with quiet hesitation, she finally admitted, "Each of these offers that I've considered includes reservations in Montana."

Devlin's breath hitched, his chest tightening at her words.

"They also include opportunities in other states," she added quickly, "but... I didn't want you to think I was chasing you. Or trying to force my way back into your life. Or taking advantage of this... this... whatever this is between us."

Devlin's grip on her tightened, his expression firm. "Mia, I'd never think that." His voice was rough with emotion. "Because it's not taking advantage of anything. You didn't even need to show me the dates on those emails. I wouldn't care if you'd only started looking last night. But the fact that you considered jobs that could bring you closer to me? That's just another example of serendipity."

She searched his face, uncertainty flickering in her deep brown eyes. "Do you really think so?" she whispered. "Because as much as it pains me to admit... if you hadn't pushed me away back then, I would have always wondered what was out here for me."

Devlin swallowed hard, his hands sliding down her

arms, anchoring her to him. "It kills me to know I caused that pain," he said honestly. "But I had to set you free. And yeah, the way I did it was fucked. I tore us apart in the worst way. And I'll always regret that." He cupped her cheek, his thumb brushing along her skin. "But we've already realized that we needed that time apart. We had to grow, to figure out who we were. And now?" His lips curved slightly. "Now, this just proves that our lives are realigning."

Mia's lips twitched, her chin lifting slightly. "What makes you think I want us to be together?"

He grinned, leaning in slowly, his breath fanning across her lips. "Because if you didn't..." His lips brushed hers, the contact sending electric currents through him. "Then you would have stopped me by now."

She didn't. Instead, she melted into him.

Devlin deepened the kiss, pouring every ounce of emotion into it. He held her close, feeling the shape of her, the warmth of her. Everything about Mia was familiar, yet new. She was the past, the present, and—if he had anything to say about it—the future.

When they finally broke apart, he didn't pull away completely. He needed to see her face, to read her expression. And what he saw made his chest tighten.

No words were necessary. The emotion in her eyes said everything.

He kissed her again, slower this time, savoring the feel of her. His hands slid up her back, his fingers memorizing the curve of her spine. When he finally lifted his mouth from hers, he pressed a kiss to her forehead, breathing her in.

"So there's no misunderstanding," he murmured against her skin. "We owe it to ourselves to see what's ahead. We had a past, and it was incredible. And now? Now, we've grown into who we are today. But I don't believe our story is over, Mia. I won't walk away again. I want you to take the job that's best for you. If that means coming back here, going to another camp, or staying in the States—even somewhere close to Montana..." He tightened his hold. "We will make it work. We will work."

She stared up at him, her lips curving slowly into a beaming smile. "I think I'll email them back and find out what positions are in Montana. I won't make any promises—"

"I don't expect any," he rushed to say.

She nodded slowly, still holding his gaze. "But I have no particular desire to go to a specific place. Arizona and New Mexico are beautiful, but I'd rather visit and not live there. Same for the South. I considered Kansas, simply because that's close to my parents. But the offers in the north, near Canada, were of interest to me even before we met again."

Devlin felt like he was waking from a long dream—a dream where he had been searching for light, always reaching but never quite touching it.

She leaned her head back once more, and whispered, "Can you stay tonight?"

Now, holding Mia in his arms, he grinned. "Oh, yeah." He lowered his head to kiss her again. He had found the light. And he wasn't letting go.

25

Mia was so lost in the kiss that she didn't care if she never came up for air, or food, or sleep. Every need her body required could be found in his arms. She would breathe his air, feast upon his mouth, and rest with her body sated by him.

Her hands slid beneath the hem of his shirt, fingers splaying over his warm skin as she tugged it free from his waistband and pushed it upward. The fabric bunched against his arms, and she let out a small, impatient sound.

Devlin stilled, his mouth hovering over hers, his breath warm against her lips. Then with an easy shift, he reached behind his neck, grasped his shirt, and pulled it over his head in one fluid motion. The discarded fabric hit the floor at their feet, forgotten the moment her hands explored the hard planes of his chest.

He was a big man—not sculpted like an airbrushed model's photograph but powerfully carved from years of discipline and hard work. There was strength in his frame, a steadiness in the way he held himself, a quiet confidence that made her knees weak. His body bore the marks of his life. She spied the small scar on his chin from the dirt bike accident he had when he was still in high school. And now, the raised scar on his upper chest from the enemy fire he'd nearly died from. She placed a light kiss on the puckered skin, wanting to memorize the place where she now knew had changed his life.

She gazed at the tattoos etched over muscle, stories inked into his skin. Her fingers traced over the new designs, lingering on the lighthouse that stretched across his shoulder, the symbol mirroring the one on the necklace he had given her. The sight sent a wave of emotion crashing through her.

His fingers worked the buttons of her shirt with deliberate slowness, and she clung to his arms, breath catching as the fabric parted. When his fingertip skimmed along the lace of her bra, following the curve of her breasts, she shivered in anticipation. Her arms dropped, letting him slide the shirt from her shoulders, the material slipping down her arms to join his on the floor.

His hands spanned her waist, his touch reverent, but his restraint seemed to flee. With a deft flick, he unsnapped her bra, baring her to him. His gaze raked over her, darkened with something primal, something possessive. His hands followed his eyes, cupping her breasts, thumbs brushing over taut peaks, drawing a gasp from her parted lips.

She wanted to close her eyes, to drown in the sensation of his touch, but she refused to look away. Not after ten years. Not when she had spent so long dreaming of this moment, aching for it. She needed to see him—needed to memorize every flicker of emotion across his face, every shift in his expression that told her this was real.

His chest rose on a sharp inhale, his pupils wide, his nostrils flaring as if he were struggling to control himself.

His voice was raw. "You are the most beautiful woman I've ever known."

For a fleeting second, a shadow of doubt crept in—memories of the years apart, the women who might have touched him and whispered his name in the dark. But as the thought surfaced, his expression hardened as though he had read her mind.

"There's no one else in this room besides us, Mia. No one from my past. No one from yours. Everything we are starts right now."

Her breath hitched. She nodded, the weight of his words sinking into her soul, grounding her at this moment. *Everything we are starts right now.*

Her fingers trembled as she reached for his belt, fumbling with the buckle. His hands covered hers, steady and patient, as he freed the leather strap and let it fall. She undid the button, dragged the zipper down, and felt his arousal press against her fingers through the fabric. A spark of satisfaction curled low in her belly. She started to push his pants down, but he caught her hands, stilling her.

"This would work if I was barefoot, sweetheart," he murmured, a teasing glint in his eyes. "But if we're going to do what I hope we are on that small bed over there, I need to get my boots off first. Otherwise, I'm going to be tripping with my pants around my ankles and my ass hanging out while I bend you over your desk."

A surprised laugh bubbled out of her, unexpected but welcome. The tension cracked, and she shook her head, grinning. "If that's a threat, it's not working. The idea of you doing that to me is a turn-on. But I take your point. Shoes off... at least for tonight."

His deep chuckle rumbled between them, rich and warm, melting her a little more. As she toed off her shoes, he sat on the edge of the bed, tugging off his boots. The moment he was free of them, there was no hesitation.

Pants. Gone. Underwear. Gone.

And then it was just them, skin against skin, standing in the dim light of her small room, nothing between them but the years they refused to let define them.

She hesitated for the first time. Not out of shyness but out of overwhelming emotion. Jim Devlin—her first love, the man she had never stopped loving—was in front of her, offering everything. A piece of himself she thought had been lost forever.

Her throat tightened, her eyes burning as tears welled, unbidden.

He stepped closer, his knuckles brushing her cheek, gentle despite the callouses. "What's wrong, my Mia?"

She swallowed, shaking her head slowly. "It's as though everything I wanted but never admitted how much I needed stands before me."

A rough sound escaped him, something close to a groan. "I feel the same way. Almost as though you're a mirage, and if I blink, you'll disappear." He framed her face in his hands, his thumbs tracing over her cheekbones with aching tenderness. "Everything I thought was lost is now found. I'm waking up from a long fucking dream and realizing that what's in my arms is the only thing I ever want to wake up to."

Emotion surged, tightening her chest. She clutched his face, bringing their mouths together in a slow, searching kiss. The touch of lips was tentative at first as if making sure this was real. But then the dam broke, and everything they had held back for a decade—the longing, the ache, and the love was poured into the kiss, consuming them both.

He lifted her, and she wrapped her legs around his waist, their bodies pressed together, heat merging. Laying her gently on the bed, he let his weight settle over her, grounding them both. Her legs stayed locked around his back, heels digging into his skin as if she feared he'd vanish.

He knew he wouldn't last long. Slipping a hand between them, he found her ready, slick with need. Her body arched beneath him, pleading without words.

"Take me now, Jim. Make me yours once again. I'm ready. I don't want to waste another minute." Her voice was breathless and urgent. "All the other fun stuff we can do later. Right now, I just want you."

With her plea, all rational thought left him. He lined himself at her entrance, feeling the heat of her body welcoming him home. In one firm thrust, he was buried deep inside her, filling every empty space as if he had never left.

She gasped, back arching, breasts pressing against him, and he bit back a groan. Afraid he might lose control too soon, he bent his head, capturing a taut nipple in his mouth, teasing and tugging until she writhed beneath him, breath coming in desperate pants.

"I should've taken care of you first," he rasped, barely able to form words.

"You are taking care of me," she gasped. "I feel every inch of you inside me. Your body on mine, your kisses... I feel—" A sharp cry ripped from her throat as her nails sank into his shoulders, her body clenching around him, shattering as he drove her over the edge.

He swallowed her cries with his mouth, desperate to be as close to her as possible. As she trembled beneath him, he thrust harder, faster, until the bed rattled beneath them.

His release barreled into him like a freight train. He

buried himself as deep as he could, a deep groan escaping his lips as pleasure crashed through him, leaving him breathless and undone.

One thought eclipsed everything else—he loved Mia Duff. He always had. He always would.

Still joined, he slowed his movements, savoring every last moment, every lingering connection. He laced their fingers together, pressing her hands into the mattress, and when he looked down, she was staring up at him, love shining in her eyes.

Call it providence, serendipity, luck, fate, the stars aligning—whatever it was, they had been given a second chance. And he wasn't going to waste a single minute. Not ever again.

26

Mia woke and instantly knew everything was different. The early dawn cast soft streaks of light through the edges of the curtain, just as it had every morning since she arrived in Uganda. The distant sounds of people stirring, voices carrying through the morning air, were familiar.

But the solid, warm presence of a very large man curled around her, his naked body wrapped around hers in a protective embrace—that was new. Different. Yet not unfamiliar.

Memories from long ago flickered through her mind, weaving seamlessly into the present. The mosquito net was still bunched on the side beside the wall. She grinned… she was surprised it hadn't gotten yanked down during the night. Her bed was small, but somehow, they'd made it work. As though the dam had broken, they'd made love, then fucked hard. They discovered each other's bodies, noting the changes and remembering what neither had forgotten. And when they fell asleep, his large body had curled around her as their legs tangled. It was more than being protected. It was more than having great sex. It was like coming home.

She stretched in a slow, languid motion and felt a deep ache in long untouched places. A smile curved her lips. Oh yeah. They had definitely made the small space work.

She hadn't made love in almost ten years. There had been lovers for both of them, but she had always known, even with Robert, that it wasn't forever. Devlin had admitted as much himself—no relationship of his had lasted beyond a weekend.

Turning carefully, she twisted in the bed without waking him, shifting so she could face him. His features were both familiar and changed—the lines at the corners of his eyes and a few strands of gray mixed in with his black hair. She stared at the lighthouse tattoo inked onto his skin before gazing at the scar on his chest. Strange... if it hadn't been for that scar, or rather the bullet that caused it, he wouldn't have left the service when he did. And he might not have been available when Logan wanted him to join his security company. And he wouldn't have reunited with her...

Stop! If her mind continued down this path, she would go crazy. *Life happens, and we take it as it comes. Make the most of the good and deal with the bad.*

She smiled as she stared. He was sleeping peacefully while her mind raced in all directions. Her gaze continued to roam over him. He was neither the same nor completely different. And she loved him.

She was risking her heart, trusting him not to break it again. But wasn't that what love was? A chance. A step into the unknown. Trust and peace and want and desire and need all rolled into one.

His eyes blinked open, hazy with sleep, just as his arms

tightened around her. A slow smile spread across his face. "Morning, babe," he rumbled, his voice rough with sleep.

She felt the vibration of it in his chest, straight through to hers. "Good morning."

As his gaze focused on her, she caught the flicker of uncertainty that passed through his expression. "Do you have any regrets, my Mia?"

She lifted a hand, trailing her fingers through his beard, and slowly shook her head. "No regrets."

Relief filled his face, the tension easing from his body.

"What about you, big guy?" she murmured.

He answered with a kiss, deep and consuming as his tongue swept over hers, drawing her back into the heat of the night before. She melted against him, sighing into his mouth.

When he finally pulled back, he grinned. "Does that seem like I have any regrets?"

She laughed softly, still stroking his cheek.

"What's on your agenda for the day?"

"Well, since I don't get paid to stay in bed with you… though I'd gladly make that my new career—"

"Hell yeah," he said, swatting her ass playfully.

She rolled her eyes, chuckling. "Anyway, just another day at the office. Watching trucks, taking in food, giving out food, and hoping there's enough to go around by the end of the day. What about you?"

He held her gaze, peering deeply. "First thing on my list —I'm going to talk to Robert."

She frowned, pushing up on her elbow. "About what?"

"I'm doing a little digging. Getting a feel for people."

Her brows furrowed. "Surely you don't think Robert has anything to do with the smuggling." He didn't answer right away, and her stomach twisted. "There's no way."

"I don't trust anybody," he said simply. "Plus, I want to make sure he knows you and I are together."

She gasped, pushing against his shoulder to get a better look at him. "That's not your place—"

"Are you and he together right now?" he asked calmly.

"No! You know that. We dated years ago and just happened to end up here together. We haven't been anything more than friends for the past three years."

"Then it's not a problem. If you were recently breaking up with him, I'd let you handle it, though I'd be right there with you. But as it is, I don't trust him."

"Devlin—"

"Mia, honey, I don't think I'm a Neanderthal. But there are some things men just understand from other men. This is one of them. Do you trust me?"

"Of course, I trust you, but it's just—"

"No. Simple answer. Do you trust me?"

She swallowed, taking a deep breath before slowly nodding. "Yes. I do."

"That's all I need to know, sweetheart."

She held his gaze, searching his expression without speaking for a long moment. Emotions crashed inside her, threatening to steal the newfound joy she'd experienced. Finally, she lifted a brow, giving a pointed look. "Do you understand what it means when I say *I trust you?*"

Now it was his turn to hesitate, his eyes locked on hers. Slowly, he nodded. "Yes. You trusted me once before, and I broke that trust. I'm not that man anymore. No matter what, I promise I will never break your trust again."

Seeing only sincerity in his eyes, she nodded slowly. Her lips curved, but before she could fully smile, his mouth was on hers again, claiming, devouring, reminding her that this was real. They had been given a second chance. And she wasn't going to waste a single moment.

The warehouse was alive with motion. Large semitrucks rumbled in and out, their air brakes hissing as drivers maneuvered them into position. Smaller delivery trucks weaved through the organized commotion, picking up their designated shipments. Stacks of food crates lined the loading docks, workers moving like clockwork to keep everything flowing smoothly. The organized chaos of loading and unloading, the hum of engines, the clang of crates, and the chatter of workers created a steady cacophony that Mia usually found invigorating. Today, she focused on the conversation she had shared with Devlin—the idea of returning to the States and accepting a new job.

In his arms, thoughts of working closer to him felt right. Now, she wondered if she was jumping too soon. She didn't want to doubt him or their second chance, but they had only reunited less than a week ago.

Mia wiped the back of her hand across her forehead, pushing a few strands of hair away from her face. The heat of the morning sun mixed with the physical labor, leaving her damp with sweat.

She frowned, narrowing her eyes at the semi being unloaded in front of her. Something didn't look right. She took a few steps closer, her head tilting slightly. The inside of the container wasn't as deep as the exterior length suggested. A subtle difference, but from the angle she was looking, it was enough to catch her attention. Just like before when she'd noticed a difference.

"Huh, that's weird." She squinted, taking a step back, then forward again, as if a different angle would make sense of what she was seeing.

"You finally hitting that age where your eyes are playing tricks on you? Should I start calling you Grandma Mia?"

She took a deep breath and turned just in time to see Charlie riding by on his bicycle, his wiry frame hunched over the handlebars. He lifted both hands in the air as he continued to pedal, remaining upright as he dodged trucks.

"You're gonna get killed on that thing one day," Mia called out, concern knitting her brow.

Charlie slowed his pace, grinning as he balanced precariously on the pedals. "Nah, I'm too talented!"

Mia laughed, shaking her head. "Are you heading to work or just showing off your two-wheeled deathtrap?"

"Bit of both." Charlie shrugged, kicking a foot to the ground to steady himself. "You staying out of trouble?"

Mia huffed, glancing around at the whirlwind of activity. "I don't have time for trouble."

Charlie chuckled, but his gaze shifted over Mia's shoulder. "What had your attention?"

"The inside of the truck doesn't look as deep as the outside."

Charlie looked over her shoulder and scoffed. "Optical illusion, kiddo! Either that or you do have granny eyes!"

Mia shot him a dry look. "So what am I? A kiddo or a granny?"

"A real beauty!"

She rolled her eyes and waved as Charlie gave a mock salute and pedaled off, disappearing into the mayhem of the warehouse yard. Mia turned back toward the semi, her unease lingering, but there was no time to dwell on it. Work needed to be done.

Thirty minutes later, Mia was in the middle of helping sort another shipment when Enock drove up in a security Jeep. As usual, he offered his ready smile, but it was tinged with concern. "Mia," he called, drawing her attention away from the crates she was inventorying.

She wiped her hands on her cargo pants and looked up. "What's up?"

"One of the food trucks stalled out on the back road. Driver radioed in. I'm gonna head over, but he said he might need you, too, in case some of the food needs to be transferred to another truck before it spoils."

Mia frowned. "What happened?"

Enock shrugged. "Didn't say. Just that he took the backroad toward the village. Figured I'd check it out."

Mia hesitated only a moment before nodding. "Alright, let's go." She turned and waved to Farid, pointing at Enock. Farid hurried over. "I'm going with Enock. He said one of our trucks has broken down. I'll check the food."

"Let me know if you need assistance," Farid said before turning his attention back to the inventory. "If so, I'll get another truck to you."

Thanking Farid, she followed Enock and climbed into his Jeep. Dust kicked up behind them as they left the busy lot and turned onto the narrow, winding backroad. The deeper they went, the quieter everything became. The sounds of the warehouse faded, replaced by the rustling of trees and the occasional chirp of unseen birds. Mia felt the tightness in her shoulders relax.

But as they continued down a different lane, Mia adjusted her seat belt, unease settling in her gut. "Why'd the driver take this way? It's not close to the village."

Enock kept his eyes on the road as he shook his head. "I don't know. New guy? Maybe didn't know the main route was faster? Got lost?"

Mia exhaled, rolling her shoulders. Something didn't sit right. She glanced at Enock, but his expression remained unreadable. They rounded a bend, and up ahead, a truck sat idle on the gravel shoulder. She breathed a sigh of relief at the sight. Then she realized no other trucks were around. "Shouldn't someone from maintenance be here already?"

Enock slowed to a stop, shifting into park, not answering her question. Mia opened her door, stepping onto the uneven ground. The back of the semi was already open, its dark interior filled with crates before her.

"I'll check it out," she said, moving toward the truck. "If the temperature is too high, we'll need to move fast to get the food onto another truck."

Enock nodded. "I'll talk to the driver."

"Call Farid for another truck to come, just in case. And call to remind maintenance we need them."

Mia stepped up to the back of the semi, her boots echoing against the metal ramp as she climbed inside. The air was thick, carrying the scent of produce and packaged goods. She swept her gaze over the cargo, checking for signs of temperature issues.

Then she heard a voice that sounded like Charlie. "No. There's got to be another way!"

Mia froze, her pulse spiking. The voice came from outside, somewhere close. It was definitely his Australian accent. She turned sharply, not understanding what was happening.

Before she could react, something hard struck the side of her head. Pain exploded behind her eyes as she stumbled, the world tilting. Hands grabbed her. A rough, scratchy bag was yanked over her head, plunging her into darkness.

Panic surged. She fought, kicking out, twisting her body, but whoever held her was strong. Arms pinned her own, jerking them behind her back. A rope cinched around her wrists, cutting into her skin.

Charlie's voice was muffled now, but she could still hear him desperately arguing. "You don't have to do this!"

Mia sucked in a breath, trying to center herself. She wasn't going down without a fight.

But as the world around her shifted—footsteps, the sound of the truck door slamming, the vibration of an engine coming to life—realization hit her. This was a setup, and she was right in the middle of it... along with Enock and Charlie and God knows who else. As the truck lurched forward, she lost her balance and fell. This time as her head hit the side of the truck, she crumpled to the floor unconscious.

27

Devlin, Cole, and Todd talked as the three finished breakfast. "Logan said we can all stay three more days, and then Cole and I'll fly back," Todd said. "You stay as long as you're needed."

"She's thinking of coming back to the States."

That pronouncement had both Cole and Todd staring wide-eyed at Devlin before erupting into grins. "Holy shit, man," Todd enthused. "I would say that you move fast, but then this reunion was a decade in the making."

Devlin chuckled ruefully and nodded. "Our breakup was on me and for all the wrong reasons. But, we're looking back, realizing we've spent the time apart growing. Our meeting here wasn't planned. We're not knocking how it happened, just fucking glad it did happen."

"Happy for you, bro." Cole leaned back in his chair. "Who are you talking to today? I'm going to keep reviewing the video feeds from last night."

Todd added, "I'm working with Casper and Sadie on a few more workers. Casper said he found out that Charlie had a minor criminal record in Australia before coming over here. Said his dad bailed him out several times for minor drug offenses, illegal gambling, and public intoxication. Nothing major until he stole some money from an employer. It appears Charlie's dad bailed him out every time but must have threatened him with his last brush with the law. Next thing, Charlie is here working in a refugee camp."

Devlin's eyes narrowed. "Shit. I was going to talk to Robert this morning, and I don't want to wait. But Charlie will be next on my list." He turned and watched Robert walk out of the dining hall. "Think I'll hit that now."

With that, the three men cleared their trays and headed outside. Robert was already out of sight, but Devlin headed straight to the logistic office in the admin building. As soon as he approached, he spied Robert at his desk, firing up his laptop. Robert looked up, and his lips pressed tightly together.

"I'd like to talk to you," Devlin said, stepping inside the office.

Robert inhaled deeply, then waved his hand toward the chair in front of his desk. "Yeah?"

Devlin settled into the chair and, without delay, said, "Mia and I are back together."

Robert looked to the side, his jaw tight, but he said nothing.

Continuing, Devlin said, "I know you two were close. I know you dated. I'm coming here to let you know that as long as there's no interference from you, I have no problem with you. I also want to inform you that Mia wanted to tell you herself."

Robert's gaze jumped back to Devlin.

Pressing on, Devlin said, "She's a good woman with a good heart. She cares about you as a friend and wasn't in favor of me coming here, even though I need to talk to you about some things happening in the camp. I told Mia that men understand things differently and that you'd appreciate me coming, even if you didn't like what I had to say."

Robert held his gaze, then finally scoffed. "I bet she was real happy with that, wasn't she?"

Devlin shook his head, but his lips quirked upward. "Mia is her own person, and I would never interfere with that. And she's also a person who would've preferred telling you about us herself. I'm not here to swing my dick or piss a circle around her. I just wanted you to know and hear it from me. I don't interfere with who she's friends with. I respect her choices and friends. And the fact that she has remained friends with you after you two dated a few years ago tells me that you must be a good man."

At that, Robert's brows lifted in surprise. The two men were quiet for another moment, and then, finally, Robert nodded. "I knew it was over years ago between us. She's an easy woman to fall in love with, but something always stopped her from becoming mine. She never gave me details of her past relationship with the mysterious man who broke her heart, but I knew a part of her would never fully allow herself to give everything to me. When she realized my feelings were deeper, she broke off our relationship, offering friendship only. It hurt like hell, but for a woman like Mia, I would take friendship with her over nothing any day."

Devlin understood exactly what he was saying and nodded in agreement. "Did you come out here because of her?"

Robert hesitated for a moment, then shrugged. "Honestly, yes and no. I was looking to move up, and being the lead logistics and supply chain officer for a huge refugee camp was going to look fucking good on my résumé. We hadn't talked for a few months, but I heard she'd taken a job out here, and that settled it for me. I didn't know if she was still hung up on the guy from her past, but again... just being around her was enough to make anyone happy."

"Fair enough."

A muscle in Robert's jaw tightened, and he held Devlin's gaze. "My question to you is, can you make her happy? From what I understand, you broke her once."

"I'm not going to discuss my past relationship with Mia, but years have passed... a lot of water under the bridge. We're back together now, and I don't plan for it to change. And that, Robert, because you're a friend of hers, is all you need to know."

Robert nodded slowly. "Okay. Well, if you'll excuse me, I have work to do."

"That's the other reason I wanted to come talk to you—"

The sound of running footsteps caused both men to turn toward the door. Farid burst through, his gaze darting between the two men. Panting, he gasped, "Something is not right!"

Before he could say anything else, Devlin's phone buzzed in his pocket. Grabbing it, he answered, "Cole, talk to me."

"Moses is looking for you. I told him you were with Robert, and he's headed your way. Something's up with Enock."

"Get over here now. Farid just came in and said something is happening."

More footsteps sounded, and Moses barreled into the room. With all the commotion, Dr. München followed from his office. "What is happening?"

Leaping to his feet, Devlin growled, "What the fuck is going on? Where's Mia?"

Farid cried, "Mia said a truck broke down, and Enock

came to take her to it. She never called back, and when I checked, Moses didn't know where Enock was."

"There was no call about a truck breaking down," Moses said.

"Where the fuck is Mia?" Devlin roared just as Cole and Todd raced into the small office.

"We don't know," Moses said. "I rallied my men and told them to head out in all directions."

Devlin stood, his eyes wild as complete mental paralysis hit him. The only thing running through his mind was Mia.

"I have access to a helicopter," Moses said as his expression tightened. "We could cover more ground, but my pilot isn't here now—"

"I can fly it," Cole said, jarring Devlin as he jerked his head up and down.

"I'll get our group on it," Todd said, pulling out his phone.

"The truck... she said it looked odd," Farid said, his chest still heaving from his dash from the warehouse.

All eyes turned toward him. "What? What did she say?"

Farid swallowed. "She was talking to Charlie. She said that the inside of the truck wasn't as deep as the outside made it look. He joked with her, and then it wasn't too long after that truck left that Enock came by. Said a truck broke down, and he would look for it. He said she needed to go because the driver was worried about spoiled food. They left. It's been over an hour, and she hasn't called back."

Devlin whirled around to Robert. "Find that truck driver."

Robert leaned forward and tapped on his keyboard. "I... I don't know... which one would it be?"

Todd stepped back into the room. "I have the security

view. The truck Mia was looking at when talking to Charlie is this one." He turned his phone to Robert, who nodded as he continued tapping on his keyboard.

"The driver is a former refugee who got a job with Nyanza Trucking. Ngelema Bwanga. That's the driver's name."

"Congolese," Moses barked, stepping closer. "That name... he is from the DRC."

"We have many Congolese refugees here and are now working in Uganda," Dr. München protested. "We can't suspect a man based on his name."

"No, but we can based on their actions," Devlin growled, heading to the door. "Robert, pull up anything you can from his employer, then work with Farid to see if that truck and driver has worked on the days you've noticed food missing. Moses, show Cole where the helicopter is kept."

"I'm going, too," Moses said. "If one of my men is in danger or in on what has happened, I want to know."

"As long as you don't get in my fucking way," Devlin said, his eyes narrowing on the security officer. "No one gets in my way when it comes to Mia."

Moses barked out the location as he and Cole hurried from the room. "We'll meet you at the bird once Todd gets our people on the satellite and I get our equipment. Five minutes tops."

Ravi and Elizabeth were standing just outside the doorway. As Devlin started past them, Ravi asked, "Has anyone seen Charlie today?"

Devlin whirled around. "Charlie?"

Elizabeth said, "We had a meeting this morning, but he never showed up. I've called around, but no one has seen him."

Farid's eyes were wide. "He left the warehouse area right after he and Mia talked this morning."

"Fuck!" Devlin shouted as the web of people grew who might know something about Mia's disappearance.

Dr. München's conflicted expression left his face as he hastened over to Robert. "You're right, Mr. Devlin. Go find her." Looking down at Robert, he said, "I'll help you and Farid."

Devlin stormed out of the office with Todd, his pulse a drumbeat of fury and fear. Every step felt like he was moving through quicksand, his mind racing ahead to one singular goal—find Mia.

Todd was already on the radio with LSIMT, relaying information and coordinating their search plan. Cole, without hesitation, climbed into Moses's Jeep and sped off down the dusty road toward the waiting helicopter. The urgency of the moment crackled in the air, electrifying every movement.

Devlin and Todd didn't waste a second. They barreled into their guest quarters, where everything they needed was prepped and ready. Without a word, they pulled on their body armor. Weapons were loaded with precision, fueled by adrenaline and determination. Their tactical gear was donned, and after grabbing Cole's equipment and gear, they headed back outside, where the heat was oppressive as the sun cast waves off the baked earth. The vehicle rumbled to life, and Devlin barely waited for Todd to get in before gunning the engine. Dust billowed behind them as they sped toward the helicopter's location, urgency pulsating in every fiber of his being.

Mia was out there. And whoever was responsible was about to learn that there was no force more dangerous than a man willing to burn the world down to get her back.

28

Suffocating darkness pressed against Mia's senses as she drifted into consciousness. The sound of a diesel engine vibrated beneath her, jolting her awareness back as she tried to figure out what had happened. Her shoulders throbbed, but as she tried to move her arms, she found them locked into place behind her.

She became aware of rope digging into her wrists, but the feel of someone else touching her fingers caused her to scream, although the sound was muffled by the canvas bag over her head. She stiffened and struggled to fight, but a voice came low and urgent near her ear.

"Mia. Don't move. I'm trying to get these off."

The bag over her head was yanked away, and she gasped, squinting against the dim light filtering through the slats of the moving truck. Charlie's face hovered close, his expression tight with desperation. Relief surged for a split second before confusion took over.

"Charlie?" Her voice was raw. "They got you, too?"

He hesitated. His hands kept working at her restraints,

but his eyes flicked away from hers, unable to meet her gaze directly. Finally, her hands were free, and she moved her arms, wincing at the prickling pain radiating from her fingers to her shoulders.

Mia's breath came faster, her pulse hammering in her chest. She scrambled to her knees and looked around. They were alone in the back of the truck, crates stacked high against the metal walls, shifting slightly as the vehicle rumbled down an uneven road. But instead of seeing the full container, they were in a much smaller area. "Where are we?" she whispered, afraid of being heard.

Her gaze continued to take in their surroundings... or rather their prison. She recognized the wooden crates with food, but they weren't in the full container of the semi. Her stomach twisted as realization settled in. The back of the truck had a false wall. One that divided the food that was being stolen and smuggled from what was being delivered.

"No," she said softly, shaking her head as her mind connected the pieces. "No. Tell me you're not in on this."

Charlie flinched like she'd struck him. "It's not like that—"

"Not like what?" Her voice pitched higher, her fear melting into fury. "You're part of this? You helped them? Charlie, what the hell is going on?"

He let out a sharp breath, sitting back on his heels, fingers curling into his hair as if he could rip it out. "I didn't have a choice. I... I got in too deep. It was supposed to be just one thing, just moving supplies, but then Enock..."

Mia jerked away from him, her knees scraping against the floor. "Enock? You're working with Enock? He's stealing from the camp? Smuggling food?"

Charlie's face twisted in agony. "I didn't want this! I

swear, Mia, I didn't! I just... I always screw things up. Always." His breathing came out in erratic pants. He looked like he wasn't sure whether to beg for forgiveness or collapse under the weight of his own guilt.

She shifted closer and placed her hands on his knees as he sat on the floor. "Talk to me, Charlie. I know this isn't you... it can't be you. Not the person I've come to know."

"I got into trouble in Australia," he admitted, voice hoarse. "Kept choosing the wrong friends, looking for the easy way to make some money. My dad always bailed me out and then tore me a new one. Finally, he'd had enough. Said I had two choices—join the military or the Peace Corps. I picked the Peace Corps, figured it'd be easy. Did a couple of tours with them and then finally ended up here. I was stuck, hating every second. Just crunching numbers all day long. I didn't come here to be a damn accountant, Mia!"

His voice cracked, and Mia saw the years of frustration brimming in his tired eyes.

"I got into trouble again," he admitted, barely above a whisper. "I was trading food for some alcohol, which I'd sell for a profit. Enock bailed me out. Said I owed him and had to help. And now..." He gestured wildly at the truck, at their surroundings. "Now we're here, and I don't know how the hell to fix this mess."

Mia swallowed hard, her mind racing. Fear still curled in her gut, but beneath it, anger flared hot.

"You don't fix it by kidnapping me," she snapped. "You don't fix it by stealing food meant for starving people!"

Charlie's face contorted, shame and regret battling against desperation. "I didn't know they were going to take you! I swear to God, I didn't. But I knew I had to do something when I realized what was happening."

Mia glared at him, chest rising and falling in quick, shallow breaths. "You'd better start figuring out whose side you're really on. Then do something about it, Charlie. Right fucking now."

"I don't know what to do," he groaned.

Mia stared at the man she once thought attractive, even if she'd never considered dating him. But now, she just saw a kid who had always been bailed out of trouble and had no real idea how to make decisions on his own. "What is going on? What are they doing?"

He grimaced. "The food goes into the trucks, but some of it is hidden behind false panels. After they make deliveries to the warehouse or villages, the drivers take it to drop points, where it gets mixed with other stolen supplies —stuff taken from farms and other deliveries. Then it all goes to Lake Edward, where it's smuggled into the Congo."

Mia's stomach turned. "Why?"

Charlie wiped a shaking hand across his mouth. "Insurgents. Enock said his family was being threatened if he didn't cooperate. And I..." He let out a bitter laugh. "I got roped in because I needed a way out. The money they're paying me is enough to get back to Australia. I can finally go back home and live without my dad controlling my life."

Mia's hands curled into fists. "Oh, grow up, Charlie. You think you're the only one who's had a rough time? You think stealing from people who need it is your ticket to freedom?"

He flinched again, but before he could respond, the truck jolted over a rough patch of road, nearly knocking them both over. Mia steadied herself. "What's going to happen to us?"

"I... I don't know. This was never talked about." His eyes widened. "Shit, they can't let us go, can they? Fuck... they might take us in the boats as well."

All the air rushed from her lungs. They would be killed... or worse. She'd be abused... so would Charlie. Death would be a blessing compared to what would happen. *Surely, Enock wouldn't let that happen!* Her chest spasmed as thick air threatened to choke her. If he had no choice... if it came down to her life or his family... *oh God!*

She frantically tried to think of a way to escape. "We've got to get out of here." Scanning the interior, she noticed a thin streak of light in the top corner of the truck.

She stood, weaving on her legs but now glad for the stacked crates. She needed them for support but also to climb. "Help me up," she ordered.

Charlie hesitated, but at her glare, he stood, holding her thighs as she climbed onto a pile of crates, reaching toward the weak spot. "It's rusty here." Pressing against the metal, she felt rust give way beneath her fingers as it showered her with red dust. She squinted as the rust powder flew into her face. She shoved harder, the metal barely giving way.

"Let me," Charlie said, tugging her downward. She traded places with him, and he was soon pulling the edge of the metal downward.

"You're doing it," she cried. "Keep going. We don't need too much space to crawl out."

He looked down, his brows lowered. "Crawl out? Where?"

"On to the top of the truck," she said.

"Why?"

"Jesus, Charlie, just do it. Staying here will certainly lead to our death or worse at their hands if we get taken to Congo."

His face blanched at that, but he turned upward and continued pulling at the metal until it groaned as it peeled away. She climbed up beside him, filling her lungs with the fresh air rushing in.

"Come on! Help me," she hissed, sticking her head through the hole. The truck was on a road similar to the one they'd taken with Jonan through the national park. She placed her arms onto the top, but the metal that had been pulled down caught her pants. Shimmying back down, she said, "We need more room."

Together, they pushed on the triangle of hanging metal as she warned him to beware of the ragged edge. With it out of the way, she repeated her movements and was able to brace her arms on the top of the truck and wiggled her way through the opening with Charlie pushing on her ass and then calves from below. Charlie followed, scrambling up after her.

She emerged onto the top of the truck's container bed, lying flat for fear of falling off. Scooting to the side just enough for Charlie to follow her to the top, she had no plan. She just knew she needed to get them away from the truck and certain death at the hands of the smugglers.

Still lying flat, she lifted her head to look at their surroundings. She had no idea how much time had passed.

The landscape spread out around them—vast, open, and wild. Rolling golden savanna stretched beneath a blue sky, with white clouds dotting the horizon. Clusters of acacia trees dotted the expanse, their twisted branches silhouetted against the background. In the distance, forest trees grew thicker, and she knew they weren't far from the water.

The truck rumbled forward, kicking up dust as it barreled along a narrow dirt road cutting through the wilderness. She didn't care that the air was thick with the heat from the sun bearing down on them. Just being out of the truck prison felt like freedom was at hand.

"What do we do now?" Charlie asked as he snaked along the top to rest near her.

Mia crouched low, gripping the metal for balance. "We need to get to the back end!" She thought he was going to ask why, and she wasn't sure she could contain her frustration if he did. "We need to get far away from the driver and Enock if he's in the cab."

Charlie nodded, his eyes wide. Together, they edged along the container's top, staying in the middle for fear of being seen by someone in the front of the truck or by the side-view mirrors. Something caught the light, causing a flash of silver, and she realized her lighthouse necklace had fallen from her neckline. Tracer! *Oh God... Devlin can find me.* She pushed it back down her shirt, shoving the charm underneath her bra strap.

She almost told Charlie about it to give him hope, then stopped herself from speaking. She could no longer trust him. If he thought the information might buy him freedom, he'd be tempted to give her up.

Glancing to the side, she breathed a sigh of relief that he wasn't looking at her but was working his way toward the back, too. The truck was now near the woods, and she wanted to get away before they came to a stop at the water. At the back edge, she looked down and then immediately felt woozy at the height and the motion of the land beneath the truck. Sucking in a deep breath through her nose, she cleared her mind. With no choice, she opened her eyes again and focused on the back door. There was a handle halfway down and then the metal platform that extended about three feet from the truck's rear.

"If we can get down there, we can drop the rest of the way," she said.

"Then what?" Charlie cried, panic in his eyes.

"I don't know. We run away. Try to get somewhere they can't find us."

He nodded. "Devlin will come for you, right? He'll come?"

"Yes. He'll come." She was filled with the knowledge that he would come no matter the time or distance. If she could hide from the smugglers, Devlin would find her. The truck started to slow to make a sharp curve in the road, and she knew it was now or never. "Come on," she encouraged.

She turned around and let her legs drop over the side as her feet floundered around for the handle.

Charlie grasped her arms. "I've got you. Keep going down, and I'll hold you."

She hated to put her trust in him but had no choice. She slid a little more over the edge, and true to his word, he held her until her feet landed on the handle. Now she grasped the bar at the top corner, praying that anyone in the passenger seat wouldn't see her from their mirror. Shimmying down a little more, her feet hit the bottom platform.

Mia barely had time to suck in a breath before her feet slipped off the truck's back door. The metal was slick with dust and grime, and gravity took over fast. She braced for impact—then hit the ground hard, knees buckling, palms scraping against loose gravel. Before she had a chance to look up to see where he was, Charlie landed beside her with a grunt, rolling instinctively to absorb the fall.

For one precious second, they just lay there, panting, stunned. The truck rumbled forward a few more feet, then hissed as the driver slowed for the narrow bend in the road. The nearby jungle canopy above left streaks of sunlight filtering through the green. She realized how close they were to the water.

Charlie reached for her hand, his grip tight. "Come on," he breathed, already moving.

Mia forced her legs to work, shoving down the pain radiating from her knees. They took off, sprinting toward the trees—

"Stop." The hard command cut through the air.

29

Mia skidded to a halt and turned slowly with Charlie at her side.

Enock stood at the back of the truck, feet planted wide, arm steady as he leveled a pistol at them. He must have been riding inside the cargo hold, hearing them when they had climbed down from the back of the truck. His broad frame was lit by the sunlight, sweat gleaming on his dark skin. His expression was pained, but his intent was clear.

"Balakeli mabe, Mia," Enock cursed.

Mia flicked a glance at the jungle to their side, her heart pounding so hard it drowned out all other sounds. The truck's engine idled a few feet away, its exhaust curling into the humid air. The driver was still inside, unconcerned, probably thinking this was just another routine problem to clean up.

Charlie shifted beside her, his breathing heavy, his fists clenched.

Enock's dark eyes burned with something close to regret. He looked at Mia, his fingers tightening around the gun. "You weren't supposed to be part of this." His voice was rough, nearly breaking. "I never wanted it to come to this."

Mia swallowed hard. "Then let us go."

Enock shook his head. "I can't."

Charlie took a step forward, his hands still raised. He was afraid—Mia could feel it in the way he moved, the way his breath hitched—but for the first time, he wasn't running as he placed his body slightly in front of hers.

"Enock, this isn't who you are," she said.

"You have no idea who I am... who I've had to become," he bit back.

"Then we can fix this," she begged. "We can... can... I don't know, but there has to be some other way."

Charlie spoke in a low voice that was as shaky as hers. "You think you're trapped, Enock, but you're not. You still have a choice."

Enock scoffed, but there was no real heat behind it. "Like you? Like you had a choice? You did this just to go back to your homeland with money in your pocket so you could act superior to your father? You don't know what you're talking about." His face twisted in a sneer aimed at Charlie. "Me..." he yelled, his free hand slamming into his chest. "Me... I have no homeland. My father was killed. My mother and sister were raped before having their throats slit. I was forced to fight alongside the ones who did this. Then I make it over the border in a boat with the clothes on my back. I've spent ten years in this country working and learning. I got married. I have children. So when they came for me to help, they threatened my family. You? You did this for money. I did this to save my family. Don't talk to me about choice!"

Mia stared at the hatred pouring from Enock's eyes as he stared at Charlie. The air felt so thick it was hard to suck in oxygen. Spots formed before her eyes, but terrified of passing out, she forced her lungs to expand.

She finally opened her mouth and gasped, "I know you don't want to kill us."

Enock flinched. Before he could respond, the truck's driver leaned out the window, voice sharp. "Enock! Hurry up! We need to get them to the boat."

Mia's stomach turned to ice at the mention of the boat.

Enock's jaw clenched. He didn't turn around. "Just leave them."

The driver snorted as he climbed down from the truck cab. "No. They're worth something over there. The pretty girl will bring a pretty price." He laughed. "So will the pretty boy."

Mia's breath caught, and she heard Charlie whimper.

Enock hesitated as he looked back toward them. The driver narrowed his eyes at Enock, but the damage was done. Mia saw Enock shift his shoulders, and his grip on the gun faltered as his arm lowered slightly.

Charlie must have seen it too, because he inhaled sharply, then turned to Mia. His voice was urgent, desperate. "Run."

Mia's eyes widened. "No—"

He pushed her, yelling, "Run, Mia!"

A gunshot shattered the air. She felt rather than saw Charlie stagger next to her. For a heartbeat, he just stood there, his expression frozen in shock before his legs gave out beneath him. He collapsed onto the dirt, his breath a shuddered gasp. Blood bloomed across his chest.

Mia screamed as she dropped to her knees on the ground next to him. She glanced over her shoulder, the idea that she was next flashing through her mind. The truck driver still had his gun raised, but he wasn't smiling.

His expression seemed almost blank, as though he had expected compliance, not this mess.

Enock didn't hesitate. He swung his gun up and fired. The driver barely had time to react before the bullet struck him in the forehead. He slumped by the truck wheel, his body jerking once before going still. Birds squawked as they flew from the trees, taking wing to escape the loud noises.

Enock's chest heaved, his expression carved in stone. Slowly, he turned back to Mia, and she held his gaze for a few seconds. Terror filled every fiber of her body, knowing she was next. Death would be better than being taken by the smugglers to be sold along with the stolen food. Devlin's face filled her mind, and tears threatened to choke her. He would find her body lying near Charlie's. Suddenly, everything she felt for him that she'd suppressed for ten years hit her as fat tears rolled down her cheeks. Still crying, she lifted her chin as she stared at Enock.

His face fell, and a sob left his chest. He exhaled shakily, then lifted the gun to his own head.

Mia barely had time to whisper, "No—" before he pulled the trigger. His body crumpled, falling lifeless near the back of the truck.

Mia couldn't breathe. *Fuck! Fuck!*

The sound of a gurgle brought her attention back to Charlie. He was gasping for air. Her hands landed on his shirt, ripping the fabric and then pressing it against the wound as if she could hold back the flow of blood.

"No, no, no," she sobbed, dropping her chin to her chest as she tried to think of what she could do to save him. "Please, Charlie, hang on. Please, hang on." His blood was seeping into the earth, warm and thick between her fingers. "Charlie, please," she cried. "You saved me. Now you hang on."

"Mi…a," he whispered.

"Yes, yes," she gasped, leaning closer to him.

"Tell… tell my… father that… I… I finally… did something good…" His chest stopped moving, and his eyes closed as his last breath left his body.

Kneeling in the dry grass at the edge of the jungle, she bent over his body and sobbed. "I'll tell him… I'll tell him."

Her hands were bloody, but she swiped her tears and nose with the blouse material at her shoulders. She wondered if she could wait for Devlin to find her there, but the notion flew from her thoughts as she heard the pounding of boot steps rapidly coming closer from the direction of the water just over the ridge. Her stomach lurched at the thought of more smugglers, and she knew she couldn't stay there.

Mia forced herself to release Charlie. Her entire body trembled as she stumbled to her feet. Her legs reacted before her brain fully caught up as she raced toward the trees. The humid air clung to her skin, her breath sharp in her throat. Behind her, shouting voices tangled with the cries of more birds taking flight.

She didn't know what the men were yelling, but the understanding was clear. They wanted her, dead or alive. A shot cracked through the air, and bark from a tree next to her exploded. A sharp sting burned through her shoulder, and she gasped, stumbling forward. Her knees hit the earth, but instinct shoved her back to her feet. The pain barely registered over the pounding of her heart.

She didn't know much about guns, but she guessed the bullet had struck the tree, and then caught her in the spray of debris. Or maybe it had grazed her. Either way, warm blood now slicked down her arm, and the wound throbbed with every movement.

But she couldn't stop now. She wove between the trees,

pushing through thick underbrush, her breath coming in ragged gulps. Her feet slipped in mud, toes catching on roots and rocks, but she forced herself forward. Hopelessly turned around, she had no idea which way to go.

The jungle was dense only near the lake, its tangled web of trees offering her cover. But beyond the lake, the terrain would open into sweeping grasslands dotted with occasional trees. There, she'd be exposed, vulnerable. If the smugglers didn't catch her, something else would.

She remembered the obligatory orientation class she'd had to attend when she'd first arrived in Uganda. She swallowed hard at the reminder of what roamed their lands. Lions. Herds of elephants. Rhinos. Even venomous snakes slithering unseen until too late.

When Jonan had taken them on the trip, she'd admired them from the safety of a vehicle, in awe of their beauty and power. But on foot alone, while bleeding, was not how she wanted to experience anything in the wild.

The sun baked the air. Sweat mixed with blood, making her shirt cling to her skin. She fought to keep her breathing steady.

Devlin would come for her. He had to. He said he could find her. Her hand flew to the necklace around her neck. The tracer. He had given it to her and told her he'd find her if she needed him to. It seemed like a lovely gift, but its meaning was overkill. Or so she'd thought at the time.

Devlin, please. Please be looking. She had no idea how long since she'd been taken or if anyone realized she was missing. When Charlie had untied her in the truck, she'd reached for her phone, but it was no longer in her pockets. It must have fallen when they'd grabbed her.

The idea of Charlie had tears burning her eyes, but she couldn't afford them. She came to a stop, listening for any evidence of the smugglers still following her. All she heard was the breeze rustling the leaves and the cries of birds. In the distance, she thought she recognized a hyena. Her arm hurt, but she forced herself to think. The jungle was her best bet. It gave her cover and kept her out of sight. If she stayed close to the lake, she might find a village.

Behind her, she heard movement—men crashing through the undergrowth, their voices sharp, angry. But just as she was about to panic, the sounds were distinctly getting farther away. Not willing to settle for the idea that they were giving up just yet, she pressed on deeper into the tangled wilderness.

The pain in her shoulder worsened with each step, but she gritted her teeth, focusing on the path ahead. *He'll come for me.... I just know it.*

30

The roar of the helicopter's twin rotors thundered through the air as they lifted off the ground, sending a storm of dust spiraling into the sky. Devlin tightened his grip on the steel framework beside the open door, watching the landscape blur beneath them as Cole pushed the aircraft to its limits. The old Army model had seen better days, but it was solid and hopefully reliable.

Cole had assured him he could fly it, but seeing the helicopter in action eased a knot of tension in Devlin's gut. They needed speed. They needed power. And if it came down to it, they needed the ability to shoot from the air. The side doors had been locked open for just that reason, giving Todd and Moses the necessary range if they had to fire.

The wind whipped through the cabin, and the sheer force of their acceleration pressed Devlin back against the seat. At this speed, they had a chance to get to Mia before it was too late.

Devlin adjusted the headset over his ears, the built-in

radio crackling to life. Sadie's voice came through, sharp and controlled despite the tension in the situation.

"Mia is traveling on a road just entering Queen Elizabeth National Park. Casper is coordinating the satellite view. She's with a semi. The same one from the warehouse."

Devlin's grip tightened around the rifle strapped to his chest. He exchanged a look with Moses, who sat beside him, his own weapon secured and ready.

"The security officers checked—there's no record of a broken-down truck anywhere in the area," Moses said.

A slow, simmering fury curled in Devlin's gut. He focused on the landscape blurring beneath them, the vast stretches of greenery and winding dirt roads. If she was still moving, there was a good chance she was still alive. He closed his eyes for a moment and pulled her image into the front of his mind. Slowly nodding, he knew she was alive… he felt it deep within.

Logan's voice cut in over the radio. "I'm in contact with the Ugandan police. They're giving Moses and LSI clearance to engage. Do what you need to do to stop the smugglers."

Devlin let out a slow breath. That meant no red tape. No bureaucratic interference. Just action.

Moses nodded, his expression grim. "This… situation. Enock. How did I not see it?"

"He didn't want you to see it. People are good at hiding when they're desperate."

Moses grimaced, but then another transmission came through. Moses listened intently before turning to Devlin. "Charlie is still missing. And there's no sign of Enock. They must be with her."

"They found the Jeep that Enock and Mia took," Todd

added, his voice clipped. "Charlie's bike was abandoned nearby."

Devlin swore under his breath. He hadn't trusted Charlie from the start, but the situation spiraled faster than anticipated.

Moses added to the voices as his officers reported to him: "A cell phone was found on the ground."

Devlin's gut dipped but before he could process what all that meant for Mia, Sadie's voice returned. "I found something on Charlie. A British bank account. Charlie opened it last year when he was on leave in England. It's not linked to his paycheck. There's over twenty grand sitting in it."

"Twenty thousand?" Devlin's fingers curled around the radio. "That's not normal savings. That's payoff money." Fury burned hot in his chest.

Silence filled the cabin for a moment, each in planning mode or lost in their own thoughts. Devlin inhaled deeply, forcing himself to stay focused. He didn't give a fuck any longer about Enock or Charlie. He just wanted Mia. He turned to Todd. "If we don't get to her before they reach the water, we have to be ready for a water rescue."

Moses turned to him and spoke up. "That's risky. The lakes and rivers here aren't safe. The water is full of hippos, crocs, bacteria, and parasites. You go in, you're taking your life in your hands."

"Then we get to her before it comes to that," Devlin's unrelenting voice growled.

"Good plan," Cole muttered from the cockpit. "I'd rather not fish you out of hippo-infested water."

The helicopter surged forward, the wind whipping past the open door as they closed the distance. His pulse was drumming as his mind became a whirlwind of calculated tactics and worst-case scenarios.

Then Sadie's voice cut through again. "You're getting closer."

Devlin exhaled, gripping his weapon tighter. They were coming for her. And nothing—no man, no beast, no damn river or fucking hippo was going to stop them.

The rhythmic thump of the helicopter blades reverberated through Devlin's chest as he gripped the strap above his head, his eyes locked on the dense jungle below on one side and the tan grassland of the savanna on the other. Sweat trickled down his temple, but he ignored it, his focus sharp as he listened to Sadie's voice crackle through the headset.

"Truck's stopped—near the water, but not at it," she reported, her tone controlled but laced with urgency. "Mia's tracer is moving. She's leaving the area."

Devlin's gut clenched. "Taken?"

"No way to know. But she's heading along the jungle edge, running parallel to the water, not toward the lake."

A slow exhale left his lips. That could mean she'd gotten the jump on her captors and was fleeing.

"The truck is moving again," Sadie radioed. "She's not with it. You're almost where it had stopped. Where the road splits."

"Cole, fly over the road," he ordered, scanning the terrain as the chopper banked sharply.

Below, they spied two bodies sprawled on the dirt, one in a uniform like Enock's. The other man was dark-skinned, and there was no sign of Charlie or Mia.

"Must be the driver," Moses surmised, his gaze on the bodies below.

"Coming around again," Cole called as he adjusted their position.

The second pass revealed Charlie's body farther away,

crumpled on the ground. Blood pooled beneath him. No movement. But no Mia either.

Moses leaned forward, his voice steady but tight. "We go. Now."

Cole didn't argue. He dipped the helicopter lower, skimming the tree line as the truck came into view. It was parked haphazardly near the shore of the lake, its back doors flung open. Through the windshield, Devlin caught a glimpse of men moving, unloading crates of food onto a waiting boat.

Moses grabbed the radio. "Ugandan police, confirm position."

A voice answered in Luganda. Moses nodded, then turned to Devlin. "They're on their way."

"We don't wait." Devlin's jaw flexed. "Todd, we take out the boat."

Cole didn't hesitate as the bird swung around. The chopper's side door was already open, so Todd crouched beside a mounted weapon and took aim. A controlled burst of gunfire shattered the relative stillness. The boat rocked violently as bullets punched holes through its hull. Water began rushing in.

The men on shore scattered, some diving for cover, others shouting in confusion. A few fired wild shots toward the sky, but they had no chance of hitting their airborne threat.

"Sadie?" Devlin pressed.

"She's still moving—southwest. You won't see her for the trees, but she's there."

"Cole, get us as close as you can. We go in on foot."

The helicopter descended, the turbulence kicking up dust and loose foliage as Cole found the best clearing possible. It wasn't perfect, with trees and thick undergrowth forcing them to land just short of the ideal spot, but it would have to do.

As soon as the skids touched down, Devlin and Moses were out, weapons up, scanning the jungle's edge. The heat wrapped around them immediately, thick and smothering, but Devlin barely noticed. His blood pounded with adrenaline, his senses fine-tuned.

Todd stayed behind, gripping his rifle as he crouched near the open door. As soon as they were clear, Cole would lift off and circle to provide aerial support. If Mia emerged anywhere visible, Todd would see her. If predators came near, he could take them out from the air.

Moses touched Devlin's arm, nodding toward the jungle. "This way."

They moved swiftly, slipping into the shadows of the trees. The thick foliage swallowed them instantly, dampening the roar of the helicopter as it lifted back into the air. Now, all that remained was the rustle of leaves, the distant calls of birds, and the pounding of their own footsteps as they searched for Mia.

Devlin clenched his jaw, forcing himself to stay focused. She was close. She had to be. And no matter what it took, he was getting her out of there alive.

31

Mia didn't know which was worse—moving west, closer to the water, where she might stumble into a python, a leopard, or, God forbid, a hippo. Her mind clung to the words from her orientation: More people are killed in Uganda by hippos than by any other animal.

Her breath came fast and sharp, almost painful, as she scanned the jungle around her. She couldn't tell if she should watch the ground for snakes or the trees above her for something with claws. Her pulse pounded at the base of her throat. Pythons weren't just on the ground—they coiled in branches, waiting. *Shit!*

She tried to tell herself the jungle wasn't as dense as she'd feared, that she could still see ahead, but it didn't stop the walls of panic from closing in around her. Every sound, every rustling leaf, and every distant cry sent another spike of fear through her.

Moving toward the light, she came to the edge of the jungle. The savanna ahead was open, stretching wide beneath the colors of the blue sky and brilliant sun scorching the dry grasses. It was beautiful, but it left her exposed. If she could see across the landscape, so could anyone looking for her. Maybe it would be easier for Devlin to find her out there.

What if the smugglers were still out there? That thought stilled her feet.

A shriek split the air. Hyenas. Her stomach clenched as she glanced down at her hands, still covered with blood. Charlie's blood. And her own as it dripped down her shoulder. She had no idea how strong the scent carried, but she knew enough about predators to realize she was a walking target.

Her left boot felt tight with swelling, and the ache in her ankle and knee grew worse with every step. She must've twisted it when she jumped from the truck. And her shoulder pain radiated in sharp bursts down her arm.

She didn't see the tree root ahead. Her foot caught, and she crashed forward, hands scraping against rough dirt. Her breath left her in a hard rush, and she couldn't move for a moment. *Mia, get up.* She had to keep going.

Blinking away the tears streaking her cheeks, she forced herself onto her knees, her fingers digging into the ground as she listened. If danger was near, she had to hear it first. That was when the sound reached her. A deep, rhythmic, whooping noise.

Her chin jerked up, pulse stuttering. A vehicle? Another truck? Had they found her? Terror clawed through her, and she grabbed a tree trunk, pressing her body against the bark as she strained to listen.

The noise grew louder, reverberating through the ground. Pressing her lips together, she tried to hear over her galloping heartbeat. It didn't sound like a truck engine. *A helicopter?*

Hope surged, but fear still coiled inside. It could be Devlin. It could be the police. It could be smugglers. She wasn't about to run out into the open without knowing for sure.

The jungle thinned to her left, and the savanna was so close. She crept toward the tree line, staying within the shadows and peering out. A military-style helicopter hovered in the distance, and the side panel door opened. It was too far for her to see who was on board.

The sound of boot steps pounding against the dry earth met her ears. She crouched lower, heart hammering against her ribs, watching as two figures moved fast, closing in. Sweat dripped into her eyes, making it difficult to see clearly.

"Mia!"

Her head snapped around, and everything inside her locked into place. *Devlin!* He was in full tactical gear, weapon out, his gaze scanning the area.

She tried to run. Tried to get to him. But the moment she pushed off the ground, her leg buckled, sending her sprawling into the dirt. A sob tore from her throat, frustration and relief tangling into something raw and uncontrollable.

"Mia!"

She barely had time to lift her head before Devlin appeared, dropping to his knees and scooping her into his arms. She collapsed against him, gripping the front of his vest with shaking hands, her breath coming in gasps. His arms were strong and solid, holding her tightly.

"I got you," he murmured, voice rough, barely above a whisper. "You're safe now, baby. I got you."

Tears burned behind her eyes as she pressed her face against his shoulder.

Moses called out for Cole, but Mia barely registered it. All she knew was the heat of Devlin's body and how his arms tightened around her like he'd never let her go.

He lifted her effortlessly, his arms locking around her as he ran toward the helicopter. The landscape blurred past her as the sound of the rotors grew deafening, the wind whipping, flattening the tall grasses. Mia buried her face against Devlin's chest, her fingers clutching at his vest as he moved with fierce determination, his grip unyielding.

The moment they neared the chopper, hands reached for her, trying to pull her away. Panic seized her. She cried out, her body tensing as she fought against the sudden separation.

"It's okay, Mia. I've got you."

The firm voice was familiar. She forced her eyes open just enough to see Todd's face, his hands steady as he guided her into the massive helicopter. She barely had time to register anything before Devlin was also inside, yanking her into his arms again.

The doors slammed shut with a metallic clang, and the chopper jolted, the floor vibrating beneath her as they lifted off. Mia turned sharply, her stomach twisting, her heart hammering. "No—no, we have to get Charlie!" she cried, clutching at Devlin. "We can't leave his body!"

Devlin's gaze locked onto hers, unwavering, but she saw the flicker of pain there. "Mia—"

She shook her head, desperate, pleading. "He saved me, Devlin. He saved me. We can't leave him!"

For a moment, the noise of the rotor blades was the only sound between them. Then with a tight nod, Devlin jerked his chin toward Cole. "Get him."

A sob broke free from Mia's throat, her fingers curling into Devlin's vest as she collapsed against him. Her body shook, the sheer weight of everything pressing down on her.

He settled onto the seat, his arms still wrapped tightly around her. His body was like a shield, grounding her when everything inside felt like it was unraveling. Then pain. She gasped as Devlin's hand ripped at the fabric of her shirt, baring her injured shoulder. She bit back a cry, her fingers digging into his arm.

"What the hell happened?" His voice was rough, edged with a barely restrained fury.

She swallowed hard, her throat tight, her pulse erratic. "The shot hit the tree first," she murmured. "Then... I don't know. It got me."

Devlin's jaw flexed, his hands working swiftly and efficiently as he pressed gauze to the wound. Todd rummaged through a med pack, handing Devlin what he needed. Mia exhaled shakily when the bandage was secured, her head pressing against Devlin's chest.

She barely registered the chopper dipping lower, the world tilting beneath them as they descended. When they landed, Moses and Todd moved quickly, retrieving Charlie's body and wrapping it carefully. There was a heavy silence as they carried him inside, placing him toward the back.

Mia swallowed against the thick knot in her throat, her gaze following them. Moses returned moments later with another body—Enock. Her stomach twisted. A sudden wave of exhaustion crashed over her, dragging her under. She curled into Devlin, her body giving out.

His arms tightened around her, his lips brushing the top of her head. "You're safe," he murmured. "I've got you, Mia. I'm not letting go."

And for the first time in what felt like forever, she let herself believe it.

32

Devlin sat on the edge of the cot in the camp's hospital, one boot planted firmly on the worn wooden floor and the other leg cocked at the knee beside Mia. Even this close to her, everything inside him felt unmoored. His hands, steady from years of experience, trembled as he accepted the warm, damp cloth Ritah handed him. He gently wiped the blood from Mia's shaking hands, careful to avoid the scrapes and bruises marring her skin.

Doc Elaine worked methodically on Mia's shoulder, the sharp tang of antiseptic overpowering the other scents. The sting of the numbing agent had made her flinch, and even now, her jaw was tight as the doctor began stitching the ragged wound. Across from them, Karen crouched beside the cot, carefully wrapping Mia's swollen ankle with practiced ease. The portable X-ray machine had been wheeled out moments before. The doctor who carefully viewed the film declared that her ankle wasn't fractured. But it appeared that she had not only sprained her ankle but also her knee.

Mia lay back against the thin pillow, swathed in a pale

green hospital gown. The sight of her in something clean should have brought Devlin a sense of relief, but he couldn't shake the image of her as she'd stumbled from the jungle, her body bruised, bloodied, and barely able to stand. His heart had been hammering in his chest ever since, an erratic beat he couldn't seem to settle.

The room, small to begin with, was now filled with people. The partitions that usually offered some semblance of privacy had been shoved aside, making space for the crowd that had gathered. Todd and Cole stood by the door like sentries, their arms crossed, unreadable expressions locked in place. Karen remained at Mia's side, her hands gentle but efficient as she worked. Robert, Ravi, Percy, Elizabeth, Farid, and Ritah had all pushed their way in, their faces drawn with concern. Even Dr. München and Moses stood at the foot of the bed, waiting to hear every word Mia had to say.

Devlin didn't care about their questions. He didn't care about the answers. He only cared that she was here in his arms. She was breathing, warm, alive. Everything else, including the men who had taken her and the danger she'd faced, only stoked the fire of rage inside him. He forced himself to swallow it down, knowing she needed him.

A throat cleared, and Devlin looked up, his gaze locking onto Todd's. His friend gave a slight, almost imperceptible nod toward Mia. Following his cue, Devlin turned his head and found her staring at him, her dark eyes filled with something he couldn't quite name. She still knew him well enough to read his mind and could see the storm raging beneath the surface. He forced his lips into something resembling a smile, though he knew it was more a grimace than anything else, and tightened his arm around her waist.

When Doc Elaine finished with her shoulder, Mia

began to talk. Her voice, hoarse and raw, barely rose above the quiet hum of the generator outside. Haltingly, she recounted what had happened, each word carving deeper into Devlin's chest. When she spoke of being struck and then hooded, his jaw clenched so hard he felt the sharp pressure radiate up his temples. When she described Charlie cutting her loose, his grip on her tightened involuntarily, his heart warring with the knowledge that he had sacrificed himself to help her, yet being part of the food smuggling ring was the reason she had been kidnapped.

The room had grown eerily silent, the only sound the slow, measured inhales and exhales of those listening. Devlin's gaze flicked to Todd and Cole, catching the flickers of respect in their eyes as Mia detailed how she and Charlie had climbed onto the truck's roof, inching their way toward freedom. Shock and awe registered on the faces of the others—Ravi, Robert, even the usually unflappable Moses—as they absorbed the sheer bravery and brilliance of her actions.

But when she spoke of Enock and how he had hesitated and then turned on his captors in the end, her voice wavered. The tears came silently at first, then in slow, unchecked drips down her cheeks as she told them how Charlie and Enock had died. By now, others cried softly as they listened to her tale and absorbed Charlie's duplicity.

"How could we not have known?" Robert whispered. "I've spent time with him... ever since I came to this camp. He was one of the first friends I made."

The tightness in Devlin's chest became unbearable. He watched, helpless, as Mia unraveled, her body trembling under the weight of grief. His fingers interlocked with hers, grounding him even as his own emotions threatened to spiral. Around them, the air thickened with the heaviness of loss. Not just of their friend but also of the loss of their idea of who he was. Karen's hands stilled on Mia's ankle. Elizabeth pressed a hand to her mouth, her eyes glistening. Percy reached for Karen, holding her tightly as her shoulders stiffened with unspoken emotion.

Moses exhaled, slow and measured, his face a mask of sorrow. Even Todd looked away, ever the composed one, his jaw flexing as if trying to hold something back.

Devlin swallowed hard. He would carry this memory for the rest of his life—the sight of Mia, broken but unbowed, recounting the horror she had endured. The knowledge that they had come so close to losing her. But he held tight, knowing she had fought her way back.

And Devlin did the only thing he could... he held her closer and let her know, without words, that she wasn't alone.

Three days later, Mia was assisted into the helicopter Moses provided. Once again, Devlin lifted her, and Todd held her until Devlin could climb aboard. He turned and took her crutches from Cole before settling her into her seat. Moses's pilot sat at the controls, waiting until they were all strapped into the seats. The rhythmic thrum of the rotors filled the humid air as they prepared for departure. They would meet Jonan about an hour from Entebbe, where he would drive them to the airport.

After a long talk with Dr. München and a conference call with Margarethe, Mia finally admitted what they and Devlin had been telling her for the past two days. It was time for her to leave. With her injuries, she wouldn't be able to do her job easily for the last month of her tour at the camp. So she had agreed to take her medical leave and return to the States with Devlin. He would see her safely to

Kansas before heading back to Montana while she figured out her next steps.

She had confessed to Dr. München that she had suspected him when she'd overheard a partial phone conversation. "When you said she was getting too close and you wanted it taken care of, I was afraid you were talking about me."

"Oh, no, no... not you, Mia," he'd exclaimed. "We were expecting a new doctor to be assigned to the camp, but I hadn't received her paperwork yet. I know I spoke sharply to the WHO assistant on the phone, but I wanted everything in order so she could begin practicing medicine as soon as she arrived."

Mia had felt foolish, but Dr. München had assured her that she was right to suspect everyone under the circumstances.

The previous night had been a blur of farewells. The dining hall had been alive with music and conversation, a celebration held in her honor. The men and women of the camp, her family in every way that mattered, had come together to see her off. Devlin had insisted she sit for most of it, and considering she could only move with crutches, she hadn't argued.

The women—Elizabeth, Ritah, Karen, Doreen, and Prossy—had gifted her a beautiful Ugandan kanga skirt, an embroidered blouse, and vibrant jewelry with beads and geometric patterns. She'd smiled at the sight of Percy standing beside Karen, his arm around her, a quiet sign of how much had changed in their time together.

Farid had grasped her hands, his voice unusually soft. "Al-dhahab la yalma' illa fi al-zalam.... Gold shines brighter in the dark. Mia, it has been an honor working with you. You have been a shine in the darkness. Your kindness, your strength, everything about you... you have made a difference here. We are better because of you."

She'd clutched his hands as tears filled her eyes. "I am better for having known you."

Robert had sat with her while Devlin had quietly stepped away to speak with Moses and Ravi. "I'm glad you're going home," Robert said, taking her hand in his.

She lifted a brow, and he chuckled. "What I mean is that you deserve it. But I hope we can still be friends."

She reached over and squeezed his hand. "We will always be good friends, Robert."

He looked at Devlin before saying, "He's a good man, Mia. But I'm sure you don't need me to tell you."

She smiled. "No, but it's nice to hear other people say so."

He stood, bent to kiss her cheek, and moved away just as Devlin reclaimed his seat beside her. She turned toward him, warmth filling her gaze. "Thank you. For everything."

"I'm the one who thanks you, my Mia. You gave me a second chance. Not many people in life get that. And I promise I'll do everything I can to make sure you never regret offering that to me."

She leaned into him, resting against the solid warmth of his frame. He wrapped an arm around her, holding her close.

Now, as the helicopter lifted off the ground, the vibrations shuddered through her tired body. Devlin's arm remained firm around her, offering silent support. Below them, the camp grew smaller, its familiar low-slung buildings blending into the vast expanse of land.

Beyond the admin section of the camp, the refugee villages stretched out, a tapestry of resilience and hope. The sight of them sent a lump to her throat. She had spent so many months here, giving so much of herself. Had she changed lives? She hoped so. She knew, without a doubt, they had changed hers.

As they soared higher, the Ugandan landscape unfolded beneath them—lush greenery and the golden stretch of savanna meeting the sky at the horizon. She committed it all to memory, knowing she might never return but never wanting to forget.

Later, as she settled into her seat on the airplane with Devlin beside her, a deep sense of exhaustion settled over her. But her heart was full. She turned to him, lacing her fingers with his. He glanced at her, his blue eyes filled with something quiet and unspoken.

She exhaled softly. "I'll miss it."

He nodded, squeezing her hand. "I know."

She rested her head against his shoulder, letting the hum of the engine lull her into much-needed rest. Whatever came next, she wasn't facing it alone.

33

TWO MONTHS LATER

Mia adjusted the strap of her bag as she stepped out of her small but cozy office on the Blackfeet Reservation. The crisp Montana afternoon wrapped around her, the scent of pine and earth filling her lungs. She'd quickly come to love this place—the vastness of the plains stretching toward the mountains, the way the early sun bathed the land in a golden glow. It was different from anywhere she'd been before, but in a way that settled something inside her.

She slid into her SUV and started the engine, anxious to end the workweek. She'd spent the past month as a nutritionist for the reservation, consulting with families, setting up programs for better food accessibility, and working alongside the local clinic to ensure expectant mothers received proper nutritional guidance. It was a shift from her overseas work, but no less important. Here, she wasn't in war-torn regions, but she was still making a difference and helping people in a way that mattered.

She pulled onto the road, driving toward town. The radio played softly, but her thoughts drifted to the first month she was back in the States. She'd spent the weeks in

Kansas, where she'd caught up with her family. Seeing her baby nephew for the first time had been an experience she'd never forget. Holding him, feeling his tiny fingers grasp hers, had reminded her how much she'd missed over the years. Devlin had come with her for the first week, staying nearby with his family. His parents had welcomed her with open arms, their enthusiasm a sharp contrast to the quiet wariness of her own family. But the tension her family had presented around Devlin had eased by the time she left. He wasn't the same person he'd been a decade ago, and neither was she.

When she'd accepted the new job, she sublet an apartment near the reservation, refusing to accept Devlin's invitation to move in with him. She just wanted to have a chance to get used to one new thing at a time. And maybe she was still protecting her heart.

Pulling into the parking lot of the local diner, she smiled at the familiar sight of Devlin's truck parked out front. She grabbed her bag and stepped inside, the scent of beer, french fries, and hamburgers greeting her. The diner was bustling with laughter and conversation, blending with the servers darting about.

She spotted Devlin quickly. He stood near a table where a few Native elders sat, his easy smile and deep voice carrying over the chatter. He clasped hands with an older man, nodding respectfully. These were people he'd once worked alongside before his job with Logan had taken him elsewhere.

"Didn't think I'd see you back here, son," one of the men said, his weathered face breaking into a grin.

Devlin chuckled. "Didn't think I'd be back either, but you know how it goes. You find reasons to come home."

Mia's chest warmed at that. Devlin turned, spotting her, and his smile softened. He reached for her as she approached, his hand sliding naturally around her waist. It was a simple touch, but one that she craved.

They made their way to a large table where familiar faces had already gathered. Sisco and Lenore sat with their daughter, Evie, who was busy telling anyone within earshot about a dog at the barn who was going to have puppies. Landon and Noel laughed at Sisco's doting look while Lenore vowed no more pets could come into the home. Logan and Vivian were busy keeping their baby entertained. The other Keepers were there, including Mary and Bert.

Mia sat beside Devlin, reaching for the pitcher of beer in the center of the table. "It's nice to see everyone in one place."

"Rare occurrence," Logan commented, bouncing his baby on his knee. "I think the stars had to align just right for it to happen."

Sisco smirked. "Or maybe we all just got tired of chasing bad guys for a day."

"That too," Devlin agreed, lifting his glass in a silent toast.

The conversation flowed easily, touching everything from work to families to absurd stories from the field. Mia laughed more than she had in a long time, slipping into the group's rhythm. She felt at ease with them now, even if their world differed.

She noticed the gentle expression crossing Bert's face every time Mary spoke, and she wondered if there was a budding romance.

A few of the single men talked about their evening plans of hitting the local bar.

"Tourists are in town," Cory said with a gleam in his eye. He turned to Todd and added, "Be my wingman."

"You've got to be kidding," Timothy said. "Todd would

be the worst wingman. Hell, he'd get the woman before you would every time!"

Almost everyone laughed, but Mia saw the way Sadie pursed her lips. Sadie and Todd, sitting across from each other, weren't exactly exuding harmony. As the others joked about the value of Todd being a wingman, Sadie tapped her fingers against her coffee cup.

Todd lifted his gaze to Sadie, and Mia could have sworn she spied longing in his eyes.

The tension was palpable, and Mia leaned over to whisper in Devlin's ear. "Are they together? Or used to be?"

"Nah," Devlin chuckled. "I'm pretty sure they'd never go there."

Mia smirked. "Famous last words." She leaned back in her chair, watching as the conversation carried on, a swirl of warmth, friendship, and the occasional bickering. This was Devlin's world, and it had become hers too. Different from the life she'd once imagined, but good. Steady. Home.

And for the first time in a long time, she felt like she was exactly where she was meant to be.

Two Months Later

Devlin pulled into his driveway just as the porch light flicked on, casting a warm glow over the front of the house. He cut the engine and sat for a moment, letting the sight settle into his bones. Inside, behind that welcoming light, was Mia. She was here. She had moved in with him, and every time he looked at the house, he knew it truly was a home.

For years, he thought he'd never have a woman he

loved sharing his life. Now, he knew it was a gift he would never take lightly again.

Stepping inside, he was hit with the scent of something warm and familiar, spices blending in the air. And then he saw her—standing in the kitchen, barefoot, a wooden spoon in one hand and a knowing smile on her face.

She turned toward him, and in the next instant, he had her in his arms. She kissed him, long and deep, the kind that could turn into something much more. But she pulled back, laughing softly as she pressed a hand against his chest.

"Let's eat first," she said, amusement dancing in her eyes. "It's my night to cook, and I made something special."

He groaned but relented, letting her lead him to the table. The meal was perfect—kikalayi pork with vegetables. She had occasionally added Ugandan cuisine to their meals, saying it reminded her of the good times and friends still there. They ate while catching up, and their conversation was easy and warm. She told him about an email from Farid—he'd just been made the lead food security officer. And another from Karen, who was now dating Percy. They'd decided to extend their tour in Uganda for another year.

He told her about an upcoming mission—just security planning, nothing dangerous. He'd be gone for a couple of days.

She tilted her head, considering him, then smiled. "Then I'll have to give you a private going away party. And, of course, a welcome home one."

His grin was slow and wicked. "I'll hold you to that."

After dinner, they took her wine and his whiskey to the back deck. The sky had turned into a watercolor of deep purples and oranges, and the sun was dipping below the horizon. She curled into his lap, her legs draped over the arm of the chair and her head tucked beneath his chin.

Silence stretched between them, the kind that spoke of contentment rather than distance. Then she shifted slightly and looked up at him. "Can I ask you something?"

He glanced down, amusement flickering in his gaze. "Mia, we've known each other for twenty years. You can ask me anything."

She studied him for a moment before asking, "What did you think of me when you first saw me?"

His brows furrowed slightly, and then his lips quirked in a smirk. "When I first saw you? I couldn't believe you marched down to the field, wrapped a chain around the goalpost and yourself, and locked it in place."

She laughed softly. "That's what you saw me do. But what did you think?"

His expression softened, and something deep and unwavering settled in his eyes. "At first, I wondered if you were nuts. But then, when I saw you stand up to the two officers and the principal, I thought you were the most fascinating person I'd ever met."

Her smile was slow, but before she could respond, he continued. "But I'm not finished."

She tilted her head, waiting.

"I knew, at that moment, that I would do anything in the world to protect you. I fell down on that once, but I will never let that happen again. I would scorch the earth to keep you safe from now until the day we die."

Her smile spread slowly and radiantly until it beamed. As she tucked her head back under his chin, he exhaled deeply, his arms tightening around her.

This was it. The life he had fought for, the love he had never truly let go of. And now, finally, he had everything he had ever wanted in his arms.

. . .

You don't want to miss the next LSIMT books - there are two ready for you to pre-order!!
A new Keeper (Tyler) will show up in my LSIMT/ Long Road Home book,
Home for Justice

and for Todd and Sadie's exciting story,
Todd

Pre-order them both now!!

ALSO BY MARYANN JORDAN

Don't miss other Maryann Jordan books!

Baytown Boys (small town, military romantic suspense)
Coming Home
Just One More Chance
Clues of the Heart
Finding Peace
Picking Up the Pieces
Sunset Flames
Waiting for Sunrise
Hear My Heart
Guarding Your Heart
Sweet Rose
Our Time
Count On Me
Shielding You
To Love Someone
Sea Glass Hearts
Protecting Her Heart
Sunset Kiss

Baytown Heroes - A Baytown Boys subseries
A Hero's Chance
Finding a Hero
A Hero for Her
Needing A Hero

Hopeful Hero

Always a Hero

In the Arms of Hero

Holding Out for a Hero

Heart of a a Hero

Hidden Hero

More Than a Hero

For all of Miss Ethel's boys:

Heroes at Heart (Military Romance)

Zander

Rafe

Cael

Jaxon

Jayden

Asher

Zeke

Cas

Lighthouse Security Investigations

Mace

Rank

Walker

Drew

Blake

Tate

Levi

Clay

Cobb

Bray

Josh

Knox

Lighthouse Security Investigations West Coast

Carson

Leo

Rick

Hop

Dolby

Bennett

Poole

Adam

Jeb

Chris's story: Home Port (an LSI West Coast crossover novel)

Ian's story: Thinking of Home (LSIWC crossover novel)

Oliver's story: Time for Home (LSIWC crossover novel)

Lighthouse Security Investigations Montana

Logan

Sisco

Landon

Devlin

Todd

Hope City (romantic suspense series co-developed with Kris Michaels

Brock book 1

Sean book 2

Carter book 3

Brody book 4

Kyle book 5

Ryker book 6

Rory book 7

Killian book 8

Torin book 9

Blayze book 10

Griffin book 11

Saints Protection & Investigations

(an elite group, assigned to the cases no one else wants…or can solve)

Serial Love

Healing Love

Revealing Love

Seeing Love

Honor Love

Sacrifice Love

Protecting Love

Remember Love

Discover Love

Surviving Love

Celebrating Love

Searching Love

Follow the exciting spin-off series:

Alvarez Security (military romantic suspense)

Gabe

Tony

Vinny

Jobe

SEALs

SEAL Together (Silver SEAL)

Undercover Groom (Hot SEAL)

Also for a Hope City Crossover Novel / Hot SEAL...

A Forever Dad

Long Road Home
Military Romantic Suspense

Home to Stay (a Lighthouse Security Investigation crossover novel)

Home Port (an LSI West Coast crossover novel)

Thinking of Home (LSIWC crossover novel)

Time for Home (LSIWC crossover novel)

Letters From Home (military romance)

Class of Love

Freedom of Love

Bond of Love

The Love's Series (detectives)

Love's Taming

Love's Tempting

Love's Trusting

The Fairfield Series (small town detectives)

Emma's Home

Laurie's Time

Carol's Image

Fireworks Over Fairfield

Please take the time to leave a review of this book. Feel free to contact me, especially if you enjoyed my book. I love to hear from readers!

Facebook

Email

Website

Made in the USA
Columbia, SC
02 July 2025